Also by Susan M. Nelson

Zoo Girl
Winner - Midwest Book Awards for Fiction Romance

A Dead Woman's Mirror
Finalist - Midwest Book Awards for Fiction Romance

In Search of Emily

Readers' praise for Susan's novels

. . . one woman's story of longing and discovery.

"It was a page-turner . . ."

"I loved this book."

". . . an AMAZING book . . ."

"Great rainy day read."

"Reading *In Search of Emily* was filled with pleasures . . ."

"Marvelous . . . I didn't want to put it down."

"Excellent book."

"I just loved the book . . . I couldn't put it down."

"It's a good read."

Whirlwind

Whirlwind

Susan M. Nelson

Copyright © 2013 Steven R. Nelson

All rights reserved. No part of this book may be reproduced in any form without the written permission of the author and the publisher, except for brief quotes by a reviewer.

This novel is a work of fiction. The depiction of characters & events are fictitious. Any similarity or resemblance to events or persons, living or dead, is coincidental.

Cataloging in Publication data
Nelson, Susan M., 1948-2011
Whirlwind / Susan M. Nelson.
p. cm.
ISBN 978-0-9841250-3-6
Romantic suspense novels. gsafd
PS3564.E4762 W55 2013
Fic

Book design by RocketDog Books
Published by RocketDog Books
Cover art by Claire Butchkoski
Cover graphics by Zelda Productions
Susan photo by Steven R. Nelson

Printed in the United States of America

To Cleo Amelia.
May your life be wholly embraced
with joy, wonder, and love.

Acknowledgements

I am profoundly grateful for the companionship, support, and love I have received these past few years. The publishing of *Whirlwind* is a testament to all the kindnesses I have been afforded.

My warmest thanks to Claire, Elisabeth, and Lissa, for their editorial guidance. And to Bill, Claire, Deb, and Peter for their artistic and technical assistance.

Steven

Introduction

Dear Reader,

Thank you for your interest in *Whirlwind*. Susan M. Nelson, my late wife, best friend, and companion of thirty-three years is the author.

This is her fourth published novel. There are eight additional works including a three-part fairy tale, in various stages of completion, that I hope to publish as well.

Thank you again so very much,

Steven

Whirlwind

Whirlwind

PROLOGUE
St. Paul, Minnesota

Guinevere ran as if her life depended on her velocity, because it did. She needed to get as far from her house as she could, as fast as she could manage. And she needed to stay in the shadows while she fled. The police weren't on her trail yet, but they would be. Or worse, the killers would. Without really dwelling on it, that was what scared her into running. In retrospect, she should have taken her chances with the police, but she was too unhinged. She stopped for a brief moment to catch her breath and to give the sharp pain in her side time to lessen. Each breath was a trial of pain. Guinevere was in such a state of shock, it was nearly impossible to absorb what she had seen. It couldn't possibly have happened, but it had. Just moments before, she and Charles had been arguing while cooking supper so she'd left to give them both time to cool off. When she had returned to her house, the door was wide open and there was blood everywhere. The beige carpet and walls that wrapped around her new sofa were drenched in it. Breathless, Guin saw her stepson, Peter, sprawled on the sofa with a butcher knife sticking out of his chest. Spurts and splatters of his blood were flung on the wall like some modern painting, extending to the ceiling above his still warm body. It was her butcher knife, the one she had been using before she left to walk to the market to buy onions. My God, the child was only ten! She entered the room and, hearing raised voices from upstairs, slipped into the kitchen at the back of the house where she found the remainder of her new family.

Samuel, who was six, was face down in a puddle of blood. He also had been stabbed, more than once—or perhaps shot—Guin didn't know, and in her state of mind it didn't matter. He was dead. His little body, still warm to her touch, held no pulse. Cathy, who was three, had been strangled as she sat in her highchair. The dishtowel was still around her neck. She had also been hit over the head with a golfing trophy, which lay next to the chair. There was blood and bits of blonde hair on the tip. Her husband of five months, Charles, had been both stabbed and hit over the head with another golfing trophy which was lying next to him. When Guin checked his pulse, his eyelids fluttered. Breathing shallowly, Guin stared down at her husband. "The children?" he whispered. She shook her head unbelieving, her vision blurred by tears.

"Who, Charles? Why?"

"Run, Guin! Run away from here!"

One last gasp for air and he slipped away, slumping in her arms. Guinevere gently lay him back down and did as he said. She grabbed her coat on the way out. As she left the house, she heard a male voice calling out to his companions.

"Isn't there supposed to be a wife now?"

"Yeah, find her." But they wouldn't find her. She was already gone.

Whirlwind

CHAPTER ONE
St. Paul, Minnesota

    The doctor came into the waiting room, pulling off his gloves and tugging a pile of hospital forms from under his arm. He was struggling not to spill them onto the shining linoleum floor as he approached Axel. Detective Axel Finley had been sitting on the formed plastic chair for so long, his rear end was stuck to the seat. He awkwardly removed his body from the ugly piece of furniture.
    "Hello Mr. Finley, I am Dr. Jacobs, I am the cardiologist currently assigned to care for Mrs. Finley."
    Axel stuck out his hand and they shook.
    "She's stable for the moment, sir. Good that you reacted so quickly. Since your wife is a Type 1 diabetic, the symptoms for heart failure aren't so cut and dried; most Type 1 diabetics don't realize the problem until ... well, we need your permission to insert a pacemaker," he announced matter-of-factly. He held out the forms to Axel.
    "A pacemaker! She needs a pacemaker?"
    "Right now, no, but later, I can't say, but we would like the forms signed just in case. Things could move pretty fast, depending on how this goes, and I may not have the time to locate you."

"But you are sure it is her heart?"

The doctor suddenly flashed a brief smile. It was unexpected under the circumstances. Axel almost smiled back.

"Yes, I'm sure about that. However, Mrs. Finley called me an idiot when I told her. She insisted it was the flu and she wanted you to tell me off. Or arrest me on the spot!" Another brief smile. "Then, she had another episode, and now she realizes ... she's a fighter, that one."

"Can I see her? Tell her I'm here?"

"Just for a minute. Follow me." But Axel was already halfway through the door.

"Sally," he whispered to her, not wanting to wake her up but needing to say her name. He could barely recognize the woman. Her curly, brown-red hair was plastered to her forehead with sweat and who knew what else. It had been roughly brushed up over the crown of her head just to get it out of the way. Axel gently smoothed it back. She felt cold to his touch. A breathing tube had been slid down her throat and her breath rattled, or perhaps it was simply the sound the machine made. There were what seemed like a dozen machines hooked up to her; some hummed, some chirped, others sent out alarming beeps. Some sent fluids and drugs directly into her veins, others were applied to various parts of her skin. It seemed they were pouring fluids into her blood stream as the flow was steady and rapid. Her face looked pudgy and the skin appeared to be stretched over the puffiness. Her normally rosy cheeks were pale white, her blue eyes closed. Just then the blood pressure cuff began to tighten. He watched the readings. 50 over 40. My God! How low could it possibly go before it was ...?

"Sir?" Someone touched his elbow. "I need to speak with you." Axel was led from the ER cubical.

"Is she going to be all right?"

"We don't know yet. This is extremely serious, though. I won't tell you that it isn't."

Whirlwind

"What are her chances?"

"I don't know."

"Tell me, doctor!" Axel was in no mood for guessing.

"Not good. There seems to be substantial damage to the right side of her heart, damage we cannot repair. It all depends on how she does, and if her heart can repair itself over time. Sometimes, it can. But other times, it's not possible. Her chances, right now, are not excellent. We are adding fluids to make it easier for her heart to pump, with less resistance. We must wait and monitor, test, and wait some more." The doctor was patient. He produced another form for Axel. "We need to give her a blood transfusion."

She's lost a lot of blood? Axel thought. He was having trouble taking all of this in. He hadn't really gotten past the possibility that it might be the flu. But he signed the form anyway.

"You should go home and get some rest. She won't be aware that you're here. The drugs that shield her from discomfort also take away from her current grasp of things."

Axel went back to his chair. He was not about to abandon his wife.

After another hour or so, Sally was moved from the ER to the Intensive Coronary Care Unit on the hospital's fourth floor. Axel was directed to the ICCU waiting area.

Another hour passed in another chair not designed for him. The hard, formed plastic was for individuals smaller than he or people who would not be using it for long. Axel was a large man. Not overweight, but comfortably middle-aged with the sort of softness that comes with a good and full life. Sally said he was adorable. Axel smiled briefly. Adorable. She made him sound like a little girl in ringlets or a kitten. But, as long as she liked looking at him, what else mattered? His hair was thin on top—hell, who was he kidding, it was non-existent on the top—but the sides were grey, wiry curls that Sally liked to twirl around her fingers when Axel let it grow too long. How he longed to feel her fingers on him now.

Finally, a nurse came to get him. She escorted Axel to Sally's room where he saw a more comfortable chair next to Sally's bed. He smiled his thanks and pulled it as close to her as he could. He took her hand that wasn't attached to anything in his, and just held on. His eyes moved from her face to the monitors and IV pumps, then back to her face again.

The events that got Sally and Axel to this moment in their lives had been a night from the depths of hell. Axel had been awakened by his wife, moaning and twisting in her sleep. He had assumed it was a low blood sugar episode, and all he needed to do was get her some juice and coax her to drink it. But when Sally began to vomit and shake and her breathing became labored, rapid, and shallow, Axel became alarmed.

"Sally? What do you need?"

"Call the ER. Ask them about this new flu I've heard is going around. Maybe you need to take me in."

But it wasn't the flu, not like any flu that the nurse in the ER knew about. When Axel told the woman his Sally was a diabetic, she sent an ambulance.

A portable x-ray unit was wheeled into the room. Axel was asked to leave the room for a little while. When he returned the chair was about as far from the bed as it possibly could be. He pulled it even closer to the bed so that he could whisper to her. He wanted to be sure Sally was aware that he was right there with her. In fact, Axel sat there for over a week, watching and waiting. The pacemaker was never inserted. At first, Axel thought that was good news until the doctor told him that the damage had already been done and the pacemaker wouldn't help. It would take more waiting to see what Sally's body did, if anything. The hospital staff tried to prepare him for the worst possible outcome. Axel listened attentively, asked the appropriately timed questions, and he acknowledged their dire words of ongoing events. But in the marrow of his being, Axel refused to admit she might die. He absolutely refused. Even when he was told she had only about a 10 percent chance to come out of this, he told himself they just didn't know his Sally.

Axel rested his head on the edge of the bed, intending it for only a moment, but he slept. Sally reached out her hand and clasped his, waking him.

"Sweetheart?" he mumbled and looked at her. She pointed as best she could at the breathing tube.

"I know you can't talk. Do you think you can write?"

When she nodded, he held a tablet and pencil for her, but she struggled. It was like her fingers and her brain were not connected. What few letters she managed were illegible.

"Do you know what happened to you? Where you are?" he asked. She gave him a blank look.

"I think she understands what is said to her, but she obviously cannot respond. Some of the drugs she's been given cause her perceptions to be altered, also. She most likely isn't sure of any details," a nurse said to Axel as she checked Sally's vital signs. Sally rocked her head in a back and forth way trying to indicate "no."

"You do know?" the nurse asked her. Sally nodded. But Axel could see that even that was difficult. Something was injected into the IV and Sally's eyes slowly closed once more.

For hours, Axel sat next to his wife, reading to her, talking to her, and rubbing lotion into her hands. At one point he got angry with a group of healthcare workers who boldly stood at the foot of her bed discussing how badly things were going and how small her chances were. Axel motioned them from the room, then confronted and lectured them severely.

"Look here. She is able to both hear you and understand what you're saying. How unprofessional this is, in front of her. You should be reported and ashamed of yourselves! This is my wife, you are so cavalierly dooming."

"She's in and out of a coma, induced by the drugs. She understands nothing," one particularly irritating doctor told Axel in superior tones of self-importance.

"And you're positive about that?" Axel demanded.

"Well …

"Just do not do it again. Now, get out of here." The doctors were far more careful after that. Several of the nurses smiled at Axel in understanding and agreement.

The following morning, Axel turned his cell phone back on and attempted to call his office. The phone, however, vibrated in his hand before he was able to complete the call.

"Axel? Detective?"

"Yep."

"Can you come in for a bit?" Louise, his secretary, asked tentatively, knowing what he'd been going through.

"Maybe later. I don't want to leave her like this." Axel said and hung up before any argument could ensue.

When Sally began to come around, nurses and doctors spent more time in the room with them. Since the throat tube restricted Sally's talking, she wrote notes on a tablet. *Water. I want water*, she wrote. She pleaded for it. *I'll do anything, I'll be so good. Just give me water. Only a little.* At least that was the group guess at what was written.

"Not until the tube comes out, dear," said the nurse of the day. Sally had been sick enough to get her own personal nurse each day, someone always available. But there was to be no water.

Later that night, Sally pulled the tube from her throat herself. Someone had forgotten to check the restraints on her wrists to prevent such a thing. The nurse and doctor were appalled, but Sally smiled sweetly and pretended that she hadn't understood what she had done. They gave her a cup full of ice chips to suck on, but threatened to put the tube back in.

    As the hours passed, Axel went to the gift shop on the main level to search out something to read to Sally. He had never read to her before, but he'd run out of things to say to an unresponsive woman and the available magazines did not interest either of them. *Jacob, the Baker* caught his eye and he bought it. Axel read and read. When he stopped briefly, Sally moved about restlessly. He knew she was listening and when he finished one book, he picked up another, knowing that this would please her.

    She hadn't been sleeping, and now pneumonia had set in. Her breathing was worsening once again and the doctor wanted to reinsert the tube. Sally actually cried until her nurse suggested they give some breathing therapy a try. Sally didn't like being bothered by the respiratory therapist, but she gave it her best just so that she could get the ice chips. Everyone, especially Axel, could see that she was exhausted. A morphine drip was added to her meds regimen to help her get some serious rest.

    "Sweetheart? I need to go to the cafe for something to eat. I won't be gone long."

    Axel couldn't be positive, but he thought she might have nodded.

    After a cheeseburger and fries, he stopped back. Sally was out of the room. Axel panicked until a nurse came and reassured him that she was only gone for a test. It was going to take a long while she told him and he wasn't allowed in the treatment room while the test was running. Something about inserting a heart catheter, a camera of sorts, up through an artery in her leg and into her heart. He nearly fainted when they explained it to him. The test would take hours and last into the early evening.

Axel took the time to go shopping for a few clothes: long sleeve T-shirts—underwear, another pair of jeans, and surely some socks. He supposed he could have gone home to get his own clothes, but it felt like that would keep him away from her for too long. Maybe he just didn't want to face the dog.

"The dog! Oh Shit!" Axel reached for his cell phone. "Sorry, Miss," he shyly said to the store clerk. He called Louise in a panic. Sally would never forgive him if something happened to her baby her small, black and tan dachshund.

"Axel ... Axel ... take a breath." Louise said with calm and patience. "Robie is staying with me. You know he and I are buds. He is and will be ... just fine. Axel ... you need to concentrate on helping Sally get better."

"Louise, I owe you big."

"Axel—you, Sally, and I have been friends far too long for any of us to owe the other."

Whirlwind

CHAPTER TWO
St. Paul, Minnesota

Guinevere was terrified with the kind of fear she couldn't even imagine, but she was also too afraid to seek help or to go to the police. They would think she murdered her family and arrest her. Charles had a lot of family money, and didn't the police always suspect a new spouse if there was money involved? Guin knew her sister-in-law would see to it. But, she didn't take time to figure it out. She just ran.

Lynn Stone-Franklin, Charles's sister, had been telling anyone who would listen, that Guin was a conniving bitch who was only after the family money. So, there would be no help from her. Besides, Lynn Stone-Franklin's husband was a lecher who always gave Guin the creeps. Her only hope was to leave town before the murders were discovered, then plan what to do. When she was safely far away, only then would she consider contacting the police. Right now, she just couldn't plan anything. The way her family lost their lives was so far beyond her comprehension, she could not take it all in.

Her first stop was the ATM where she withdrew nearly all of her own money. Next, she went to the bank branch to empty her savings account. Twelve thousand, seven hundred and fifty dollars was all she had, but it would have to do. She left all of Charles's money right where it was.

Startled by every little noise, she made her way the two miles to the bus stop and then on to the airport, where she noticed the blood on her hands and sleeves. No wonder the bank teller had eyed her with suspicion. She was probably expecting a threatening note to hand over all the money or else. The woman had undoubtedly phoned the police by now.

Guin had her husband's blood on her. Charles. She gulped back an audible sob. Guin went to a washroom to rinse off what she could, then rolled up her sleeves to hide the stains. Her coat covered most of the mess on her blouse and pantsuit.

With no passport and limited funds, she simply took the first flight out of the Twin Cities. It was to Portland, Oregon, where she knew no one. She bought a large felt hat with a wide brim, stuffed as much of her shoulder length blonde curly hair under it as she could and purposely avoided the security cameras, keeping her glance low. Even though she was quaking in her black leather boots as she entered the gate, Guin walked with a confident stride that told the staff she knew where she was going. She even managed to smile at everyone when she got her boarding pass.

"Luggage, madam?" the airline agent asked politely. Guinevere had a moment of panic and then recovered smoothly.

"No, I've been here just for the day, and am already flying home ... a business meeting," she answered, very relieved she was still dressed in a suit for work, and not her usual jeans and sweater. Guinevere hadn't changed her driver's license yet, so it was easy to buy a boarding pass with it and in her maiden name, Igraine G. Fairchild. Her mother had been a great fan of the King Arthur legends and

Whirlwind

named all her children and various pets accordingly, with names of the era, Cei, (pronounced Kay), Merlin, Lance, and the pets, Pendragon, Pellinore, and Nemue. *My God, what was the woman thinking.* Guinevere often wondered. The entire family loved the legends of the mythical king, though, and the stories were told and retold every night in the Fairchild home. Stories of knights and quests and magic, bravery, love, and treachery were the fuel of her childhood.

Once in the plane, Guin began to breathe easier. She was safe for now, but what the hell had happened to her family? She was too stunned and numb to cry. She kept asking herself the same questions repeatedly, like a mantra. *Who would want my family dead? Why kill the small children?* As the plane began to taxi toward the runway, she pushed herself deeply into her seat and closed her eyes. They flew open immediately as the pictures of her family came into focus once more. Guin was shivering in shock, trembling so hard her teeth were chattering.

The airplane raced down the runway for take-off. Guinevere could think of nothing but the images of her dead family: the sight of the small bodies of her stepchildren, and Charles's last words: "Run Guin, run away from here."

Guinevere had met Charles at the Saint Paul Hotel in the downtown area, where they both were attending a convention. It was love at first sight; a whirlwind romance ensued. Just like a "neat meet" scene from a Hollywood movie. They noticed each other from across a room packed with convention participants and each simply gravitated toward the other. After they shook hands with introductions, they were goners. The first night they shared a dinner at a little Italian place across the street from the hotel. He ordered shrimp scampi with lots of garlic butter and she had the lasagna stuffed with crab. They switched plates and drank from the same wine glass over the glow of romantic candles. The second day they skipped the convention meetings in the afternoon and spent the time at the Science Museum of Minnesota, only a couple of blocks from the hotel, collecting information about dinosaurs and plastic models of the creatures for the his kids. Charles surprised her with a garnet necklace from the museum gift shop. That evening they had a steak dinner at the hotel where they were so lost in each other they failed to notice the famous people: Garrison Keillor surrounded by his usual gob of adoring fans and the governor of the state with his work-a-day entourage in tow. Later, they went to the Ordway Theater just across a small city park from the hotel. They saw "Rent" and loved it. Walking back to the hotel through the tiny romantic park that was full of couples, they kissed, then kissed again and again. Their kissing grew quite serious and involved. Guinevere had never been kissed so thoroughly and so completely before. Charles and Guin were simply drawn to each other. It was fate. By the third night, Guinevere had stars in her eyes and was sharing Charles's hotel room, number 720. It had a wonderful view of the park, beautifully lit up with tiny lights. Charles was an early riser and there were coffee and scones for her when she finally opened her eyes. It was a living fairy tale. Guinevere was the lost princess saved by her handsome prince.

    The couple had been married within a month of their first meeting. They still had date nights even after they were married. Her new husband (her first marriage, his second) had seemed so perfect for her. They both had careers: he a computer programming engineer for a busy design firm, she a project manager for a millwork company. They shared the household chores and the child care. They took turns driving the kids to school or other activities. Motherhood had always frightened Guinevere, but she found the children so delightful that even when they disagreed on something or fought between themselves, she

Whirlwind

coped beautifully. Charles told her she was made for the job. The children were a constant source of love and companionship; a great reason for getting up on a Saturday morning, something she had been loath to do all of her adult life. Guinevere became more comfortable with the role of mother. She loved the three children with a strength she didn't think possible. As Guin shared her family tradition of the stories of Camelot, she was continually amazed at their imaginations and loved to see their reactions to the feats and adventures of King Arthur. Charles acted like they were hers as well as his own, which made it easier. He had been such a great husband and father. But, Guinevere thought, there must have been more to the man. Why else would this have happened?

    She sighed heavily as she stared out the window, not noticing the beauty of the night sky. Her arms ached to hold sweet little Cathy, her loving blond cherub, and Sammy who just that morning had shyly called her "Mommy". And there was Peter, the dinosaur-loving boy who wanted nothing more than to be a paleontologist when he grew up. He could already spell the word. "I want to dig in the dirt, Mom." Who would want these intelligent, beautiful children dead? So what the hell was happening? Her head was pounding and she felt sick to her stomach. She barely made it to the bathroom before she threw up. Her breathing was shallow and ragged. She washed her face, rinsed out her mouth. Guin was pale and drawn looking in the dim light of the bathroom. The mirror gave her a harsh appearance of someone she didn't know any more.

    "What am I going to do?" she asked herself out loud, twisting her fingers and wedding ring.

    "Are you okay, Miss?" asked the attractive flight attendant. Her name tag read Cynthia and she looked at Guinevere with concern. "Do you need anything? Coffee, tea, a drink? Maybe something to eat?"

"Maybe some red wine?" Guinevere smiled at her and tried to look relaxed.

"Sure, Zinfandel or cabernet?"

"The cabernet would be great."

"Oh my, you have blood on your suit!" Cynthia exclaimed. "Are you hurt?"

Guinevere jumped a little and pulled her coat closed tightly. "I had a nose bleed. I almost always do during takeoff," she offered lamely.

"Oh, lots of people do. I have just the thing. I'll get that for you, along with your wine." And she was gone. She returned with a small stick of something that looked like a clear crayon. Cynthia told her to "Gently rub on the spot until it fades," and lightly patted her shoulder.

Guin thanked Cynthia for her help, and started working on the most visible spots on the front of her coat.

"Don't worry now. The flight will go smoothly," she calmly said, and left to attend to the other passengers. *How kind,* Guin thought. *How normal.* How unaware of who was sitting in this seat, the strange woman who's family had just been brutally murdered only hours before.

Guinevere sipped her wine and dimmed her light. Her thoughts kept returning to the carnage ... she shivered again. It would never fade; the color red would remain as startlingly bright as it had appeared on her family. It was a sight Guin would never erase from her mind or her heart. It would follow her every day, everywhere, forever.

Whirlwind

CHAPTER THREE
St. Paul, Minnesota

When Sally woke up, it took several minutes for her to register where she was. She'd been dreaming that she was in a palatial hall with blonde woodwork and large windows all around her. Oversized green vining plants obscured her vision and kept her from finding her way. She'd been lost, looking for her room and dressed in this flimsy hospital gown. Disney cartoon characters dressed in tall black hats and spats had been talking to her, singing and dancing with fancy canes held high in the air, in row after row across the screen of her vision until they simply disappeared off the edge. It had been both scary and confusing. Now, she realized that only parts of it had been true. She couldn't swallow and she was incredibly thirsty. Axel was sleeping with his head resting on her hand. She stretched her finger and turned her hand to grasp his.

"Sweetheart? Do you need something?" he asked, waking immediately.

"Water. Or ice chips or whatever I can have."

"Ice only, sir," said the nurse who breezed into the room with a smile and a chipper look in Sally's direction." You are doing so well."

"I am?"

"She is?" Axel said at the same time.

"Oh yes, in fact we are moving her out of ICCU this afternoon," her beaming grin grew wider. "I knew she'd make it. Sometimes you can just tell which ones will."

"Excuse me," came a voice from the hallway and a tall well-dressed man came in carrying a white lab coat over his arm. He walked directly to the bed and sat on the edge, ignoring the other two in the room. He clasped Sally's hand and, with a tearful voice continued. "I needed to see one of our success stories this morning. It's been a rough 24 hours."

"I am one of your success stories?" Sally questioned, not even recognizing the man.

"You are indeed. It's wonderful to see you like this." His smile simply beamed. As quickly as the man appeared, he disappeared.

"Who was that?" Sally asked, a bit confused.

"Dr. Jacobs. He was the head cardiologist on the first rotation team of your care.

When Sally was able to keep food down (although it was only lime Jell-O, which she hated) she was moved out of the ICCU. That was a good sign and Axel deemed it was safe to leave her for the afternoon.

"Honey," Sally began. "Ask if you can bring Robie for a short visit. I heard another dog, sounded like a Yorkie, down the hall yesterday."

Axel gave her an odd glance. He'd been sitting there with her and he'd not heard a dog, Yorkie or otherwise.

"Sure, sweetheart. See you later." Axel left the hospital to return to work for the first time in almost three weeks, humming a cheerful melody. His life wasn't over after all.

Whirlwind

Back in his office, Detective Axel R. Finley sat at his oversized cluttered desk, marred by too many rough years of abuse, looking over the notes he had on the cases he'd left when he'd gone missing from the district office. It appeared the majority of them had been solved without his advice and brainpower. Good ... maybe retirement was a possibility. Sergeant Mike Troy had been groomed to perfection, and Axel had no qualms about leaving him in charge. They did things differently, but in the end, the result was the same. Both of them were excellent at their jobs.

Finley noticed a brand new file that Louise had slightly tucked under the desk blotter to keep it firmly in place. It was tagged with a bright red post-it note.

"Axel, this is a priority. Just came in. M.T."

Loose photos, which slipped from the folder when Axel picked it up were disturbing. As with the other cases, this one came with very few notes. Too few. He idly ran his fingers over the grooves of his desk and cigarette burns on the surface of the wood from his years of smoking three packs a day, a lifetime ago. He pondered what was known and what the first officers on the scene had to say.

The hospital smells of Axel's clothes returned his thoughts to Sally. He normally dressed in faded blue jeans with long-sleeve T-shirts under a long-sleeve, button-down-collar shirt with those sleeves rolled up. He did so today as well. With this messy case in front of him now, Axel wished he'd stayed with his wife.

He sighed heavily. Axel was so close to retirement and didn't really want this complication. It wasn't even his jurisdiction, but all the districts called him in on the multiples. The ones that had no obvious motive or suspects. The cases that had low solve rates and were too much trouble for the busy detectives. He read through the case notes again, including the initial report from the first officer to show up after the 911 call. The call had come into the station around noon; the mail carrier had been the one to find the bodies. He was still pretty freaked and was at the county hospital under sedation. Poor guy. He was Axel's age and you'd think he'd never seen blood before. But then, those children ... At least once every twenty minutes the vic's sister had been calling him, leaving messages of nothing but angry rants.

"Let's see," he said out loud, "Lynn Stone-Franklin", or something like that. A president, anyway. No, not a president. Somebody big in American history, though. His mind was too tired to function properly. Mrs. Franklin was sure the new wife had done it. *Guinevere. Pretty name.*

But he seriously doubted that. The crime took someone stronger that a five foot six inch, 120-pound woman. Of course, he guessed at those stats from the wedding photos. Plus, no husband would stand around and watch his wife kill his kids. And the coroner said the husband was the last to be hit. He might even have lived a while. Someone with a great deal of strength must have held him back while someone else took care of his kids. The dark bruises on his upper arms were from big, heavy hands with wide fingers. Damn shame. It had been a beautiful family. Axel hated his job when he had cases like this one. This was the kind of thing that made retirement appealing. Besides, now wasn't the time for a complicated case. He needed to be at his wife's side. He needed to watch over her and speak for her until she was able. Seriously, he knew Sally was now at that point where she could speak for herself, but he just wanted to be there with her.

He looked again at the pictures of the crime scene. The tire prints were quite visible, and wider than either of the family vehicles, which were both still parked in the garage. There were bloody shoe prints from at least two men, and one woman whose tracks went from just inside the front door to outside the rear. The husband, Charles, was in his stocking feet, having kicked off his shoes at the front door.

Whirlwind

The woman's prints could be the wife. Same size anyway. There was DNA all over the house that would need to be tested and sorted out. Where was the wife anyway? Kidnapped? Was she the target? Why wasn't her body found with the rest of the family? Damn, there was so much to do here. Like every case handed over to Axel, he'd dwell on this until it was solved to his satisfaction.

He called the bank. Charles Stone's money was all there, Guinevere's was not. Interesting, but what did it mean? He called David Carpenter, the forensic specialist assigned to the case; he was still at the house.

"Hey David, Finley here. Can you tell if any of the wife's stuff is gone? Empty drawers, hangers, that kind of thing?"

"Already looked. Nothing obvious. Passport and makeup case are here. Her keys are on the floor. Looks like she dropped them when she came in. Her handbag is probably missing, if she used one. Can't find a wallet or driver's license." Axel Finley could hear paper rattling. "There's a grocery bag with onions from that new age market on the floor, too. That's all I've got, Detective."

Axel couldn't help but grin at David. The "new age market" was a member-owned co-op organic food store that had been there for over twenty years. His wife liked to shop there.

"It looks more like the wife was surprised by someone, rather than she did the deed. Looks like maybe she was nabbed." David gave Axel his opinion.

"Yeah, I think so too. But we need to find her. Just stay there in case she shows up, okay?" Next he called the courthouse and had a copy of the marriage license faxed to him. It had the name I. Guinevere Fairchild listed as the new wife, although she took Charles's last name. It shouldn't be terribly hard to track a name like that. Several phone calls later, though, no tickets of any kind had been issued to that name. He jotted down a brief list:

Family?	Doctor, dentist?
Where's she from?	Other residences?
Work?	Other vehicles?
Friends?	Where did she shop, eat, get her hair done?

Check with the neighbors ... did the couple get along? Were the children well-cared for and happy? Did they do things as a family? Has anyone seen anything or any person who didn't belong in the neighborhood? Any new vehicles? Noise? The usual.

That was all he could think of for the moment, but it would surely keep him busy for several hours. Axel had a surprise, though. It took less than one hour to get his answers.

Guinevere Stone, maiden name Fairchild, worked as a project manager at the Grand Avenue Millwork Company in St. Paul. She'd been there less than eight months. Before that, she'd been a student at a technical school in St. Paul, and before that, some fancy women's college out east. No complaints, no close co-workers, did a good job. She had an apartment, which she gave up when she married. There were no other residences, no other vehicles except a bicycle, which was still in the garage. She did her own hair, brought her lunch to work, and went out to eat several different places, different nights of the week, with her family. Detective Axel Finley was frustrated. He felt like this mystery woman needed his help, but she had simply disappeared. Next stop was the crime scene. He drove to the middle class, somewhat trendy neighborhood of Highland Park. Once an upper class neighborhood, then down on its luck, now newly restored homes made it desirable again. This restoration of older neighborhoods was happening all over St. Paul. Lots of trees, lots of kids and bikes, balls and pets. Very pleasant neighborhoods. Axel was happy to see families settling inside the city

Whirlwind

limits once more, rather than spread out in the neverending suburbs that joined the cities of St. Paul and Minneapolis.

Finley pulled on latex gloves as he entered the house. He was met just inside the door by a team of crime scene investigators, his Sergeant and a paramedic who seemed very nervous.

"Detective Finley, can we speak to you before you start in here?"

"Sure, what's the deal here, Sergeant?" Finley was curious, anxious to get a firsthand look at more than the spattered blood he could already see from where he stood, just inside the front door.

The paramedic shifted his feet back and forth before he got his courage up. "There's been a mistake, sir. On the bodies, I mean. Well, in the ambulance, sir."

"For God's sake, man, spit it out!" Axel didn't have the patience for this just now. The bodies had been removed, but the dried and drying blood was a constant reminder of the crime. The chalk outlines of the small bodies made Axel sweat. The smell was strong and rank. This guy was just adding to his misery of the situation.

"Two of the children weren't exactly dead yet, sir." Finley, now rattled, looked to his sergeant for an answer to this.

"It turns out that the baby and the youngest boy were resuscitated in the bus. They are under guard at the Children's Hospital in downtown St. Paul. We didn't alert anyone yet, because it was safer, we thought," said Mike Troy, the all-American good boy cop. Short blond hair, blue eyes, and a ready smile, he was tall and lanky and strong as an ox.

This was good news, but startling.

"Have you seen them?" Axel asked.

"No, sir. Thought you'd want to be there."

Axel stripped off the gloves.

"Let's go," he said. They took the paramedic's unmarked car. When they arrived at the emergency entrance, Finley and Troy went in as the paramedic parked his car. An older nurse with a stubborn tilt to her head took them to the third floor, past two guards, Axel and Mike flashed their gold shields, and they entered the brightly lit room. Several nurses and doctors were bustling around two small bodies on the child-size hospital beds, adjusting tubes, administering injections, and cleaning the blood from the children. The nurse who brought them smiled for the first time and gestured the detectives into the corridor, away from the room entrance. "I'll get the Doctor," she said.

"They're going to be fine." The oldest and smallest of the doctors looked up at Axel. "They were very lucky kids. They had a bright, alert paramedic," the older and very senior doctor said and gestured to the man beside Axel. The paramedic who'd just caught up with the detectives after parking his car. The guy was nervous.

"Davis, here, noticed heartbeats, faint but present. Thready and hard to find under the best of circumstances. However, he did and got them intubated … kept them breathing until we got them here. Then we moved them up to this floor out of emergency, for safety when we heard the story."

Davis beamed with the praise. He was still a rookie, always nervous about missing things. He looked to be in his late twenties and was the leanest man Axel had ever seen. Pencil thin, his Sally would say. *If he turned sideways, you'd probably miss him.*

"Doctors," Finley paused as he looked at the doctors' Photo/I.D. badges. "Dr. Carson, Dr. Lewis," his gaze was moving back and forth between them. He was looking directly into their eyes. "It is **absolutely imperative** that **no one, absolutely no one** says anything about these two

Whirlwind

children. For all intents and purposes they are not here. The bodies of ***all*** family members were taken to the morgue. They did ***not*** survive. Have I made myself ***crystal clear***? Isolate and quarantine them in some fashion, so they are attended to by a very small team of ***extremely discreet*** medical personnel." Axel finished with, "Do we understand one another?"

A very direct "Yes" from Carson.

"Absolutely," from Lewis.

Dr. Carson turned to Dr. Lewis and said, "Kate, please express Detective Finley's urgency to the ER staff. I'm going directly to Jennifer."

"Detective, Jennifer is Jennifer Jackson, the hospital CEO and Administrator," said Dr. Carson.

Finley said, "Thank you, doctors," as he turned to Troy. "Mike, would you please go and have a discussion with the hospital's head of security? Also, get all of the security tapes that show anything of the children. Be sure to initiate an 'Evidence Chain of Possession Form' for him. Don't make him ask. We want his total cooperation. Also, arrange for our people to provide security for the children. Then go and see Dr. Karen Koenig, the Chief Pathologist at the Morgue and tell her about the ***official*** status of the entire Stone family. Tell her I'll owe her some great Twins tickets. Oh, and kindly thank her for her thoughts and good wishes concerning Sally's healing."

Finley walked over to the ever-quiet paramedic. Davis had drifted away from the discussion, figuring the less he knew the better for it he would be. Finley extended his hand to Davis. His lifted to meet Finley's ... they shook. "Thank you, Davis, for saving the children's lives," Finley said with a catch in his voice. "You earned several points with me today, mister. Again, thank you."

Lastly, Finley returned to the room entrance for one last check of the children. He looked at the tiny bodies and a great wave of relief flowed through him. Both children were awake and breathing on their own, the tubes already removed. The baby, Cathy, was happy and playing with a soft cloth doll. She was wearing a hospital gown that was several sizes too large, but was covered in cute little pink, yellow, and blue bunnies. Her hair, blond and curly, and her still babyish chubby body gave her the look of a Valentine's Day cherub. Samuel was remote and scared, silent. He had thick bandages wrapped around his shoulder and upper arm, and around to his back. It looked downright uncomfortable. His light brown curls stuck out in all directions. He was going to be a tall lad and looked like a serious boy. This would be difficult, but Axel thought he would give it a try.

"Hello, are you Samuel?" No response. "My name is Axel. I'm a detective. Do you know what that is?" This time he got a small nod. "I want to find out who hurt your family, Samuel. Can you help me?"

"Maybe." Samuel finally looked at him square in the eyes. "I think so."

"Do you want me to ask you questions, or do you just want to tell me what happened?"

"Three big men with masks on their faces. Blue ones with eyes. One of them ate my candy. First they yelled at daddy and held him tight, then they hurt Cathy. Then they yelled at daddy some more. Then they hurt me," Samuel stopped. "I don't know where Peter is. Where is my daddy?"

Well, Axel thought, *this is not the time to tell you, little man.*

"What kind of eyes?"

"Real ones," he answered and pointed to Axel's own.

"You did just fine, Samuel. Thank you for helping me. Do you know where your mommy is?"

"New mommy went to the store." And that was all he could get. For now, anyway.

Whirlwind

Axel had the paramedic drive him back to the Stone house and his car. He shook the man's hand a second time. "I will say it again, that was a good job, Davis, a very good job. Let's keep this quiet, though. We don't want the killers to know they left witnesses, even such small ones." Davis nodded mutely.

Axel slipped on another pair of latex gloves and went back into the house. The house was comfortable and well built. The architecture was turn-of-the-century Prairie style, a design made famous by Frank Lloyd Wright: lots of brick and dark wood, built-in furniture, and a massive fireplace. He started with the master bedroom, which had been torn apart. Probably by the three intruders, which was the current way his thoughts were moving. Feminine clothes were the only evidence of a woman. She hadn't had time to add her style to the room yet. In her jewelry drawer, which had only a few pieces of value, he found two letters from Savannah Georgia, which were signed from Mom. They were old, though. A more recent letter had a return address and was signed from your loving sister, Cei. *How the heck do you pronounce a name like that?* Those he slipped into an evidence bag. He added a small pile of paycheck stubs and bank receipts. "Nothing else here," he mumbled.

Downstairs, he found a computer covered with dinosaur stickers in bright primary colors. Axel figured it belonged to a child. He'd have to send it to the lab anyway. Idly he turned it on. There was no password needed. He clicked on mail and was greeted by four unread messages. He scrolled down to the first unread email; he wanted to read them in order. No "From" email address on any of them.

"Stone, you are out of time. Be warned." The first one.

"Where are the rest of the schematics? We are done waiting for you. You owe us, damn it!" The second one.

"We WILL kill you!" The third message.

"YOU ARE ALREADY DEAD YOU AND YOUR FAMILY ARE DEAD THOSE DARLING LITTLE KIDS AND YOU'RE NEW WIFE WE WILL GET WHAT WE WANT WE ALWAYS DO." The last and most recent message.

Okay, this was important, if not amateurish. It sounded like a teenager or a not too bright individual. Finley needed to get this computer to the technicians in the lab. It always amazed Finley, the amount of information they could coax out of these little machines. Axel Finley could use a computer, but he was an old-school detective who relied on his eyes and brain more than technology. Finley also knew his days were numbered by the younger, more tech savvy guys in the department, who could use the damn things. Still, his solve rate was the best and usually he had a real feel for his cases. But this one ... just didn't feel right. As usual, there was more than met the eye. He focused once more on the task at hand.

It was pretty obvious for which Stone the emails were intended and odd that they hadn't been opened. Did Stone know these people were coming? Most likely not. Finley was sure Stone had been taken by surprise. His gut thought was that Mr. Charles Stone seemed the most likely target. His history was in the Twin Cities, not hers. Also, the children were his. More leverage there. Had they been killed one at a time to force Charles to give something up? It was time to focus on Charles Stone. Before he got any farther, his cell vibrated rudely in his shirt pocket.

"Detective!" *Oh no, Lynn Stone-Franklin once again.* "What's going on? Have you caught Guinevere yet? I demand that you arrest her right now! My husband has connections, you know. She probably has taken all Charles's money and is on a plane to some island by now." Lynn Stone-Franklin paused for breath.

"Mrs. Franklin, your brother's money is safely in the bank. I'm doing all I can at the moment, but if you keep

Whirlwind

bothering me, nothing will get done." And with that, Axel hung up and turned off his cell. He rarely was brusque with people, but this woman made him both nuts and very angry. It felt like she was trying to talk him into buying something, like encyclopedias. He turned back to his notes.

Charles had worked for many years at Twin City Design and Engineering Company. The firm had a good reputation and had been in operation for at least fifty years, but that was about all Axel knew. Another question came to his mind: What did they design and would someone kill for it?

Mr. Stone had been married before. That wife had died in a car accident on the 694 freeway. Every neighbor he had talked too that afternoon told him this new marriage was a good one, a happy couple.

"Poor Charles needed this new wife and the children just loved her." This was the general agreement among the neighbors. So then, why wasn't the wife dead too? Maybe she was and no one had found her yet. Was Charles the intended victim? Finley's mind kept going back to that one.

It wasn't a simple robbery gone too far. No, Detective Axel Finley was sure that wasn't it. He wondered if the killers had found what they had been looking for. The place certainly had been torn up enough.

As he keyed his wife's hospital number into his cell phone, the forensic team showed up to search through each and every item in the house. Axel didn't need to be there for that; these folks knew what they were doing.

CHAPTER FOUR
Portland, Oregon

When the plane landed, it was 2 AM. Unbelievably, Guinevere was able to get a cab.

"Where to?" the cabby yawned.

"A good hotel? Nice and clean, but not outrageously expensive." Guinevere gave him her best smile. The taxi cab driver was at least sixty and totally uninterested in her, so he probably wouldn't remember her after this.

"I know just the place." They rode for several miles, somewhat out of the busy part of Portland. "What's that water on our left?" Guin asked.

The cabbie replied, "The Columbia River and beyond that is the state of Washington.

"Oh no, this must be really expensive." Guinevere was dismayed.

"Heck no, it belongs to my wife and me and we'll take real good care of you. This is my last fare, so you were on my way home." The driver was proud of his attempt to joke with her, so she smiled again but not without effort.

When she was settled in her small but comfortable room, she let go of the tears. She could not shake the horror of what had become of her life. Her family ... the children

Whirlwind

... all dead! She knew it couldn't possibly be her fault, but the loss was so overwhelming, it took hold of her to her core. She hoped she was having a nightmare, but her exhaustion told her otherwise. It was undeniably real and it had happened to her.

Until her marriage to Charles, Guinevere had always felt she was on the periphery of things. Never quite involved, more like watching life from the sidelines. But Charles and his children changed that completely. For the first time, she felt like she was the center of the household. The heart and hearth of the family. The sensation was wonderfully foreign to her; gone now forever. Guinevere cried for a long while until she fell into a fitful sleep. Her dreams were full of faceless monsters with bloody knives and oversized golfing trophies. After waking abruptly from a third dream with a scream on her lips, she wrapped the blanket around her shoulders and sat at the window in the dark. She had always loved the mysteries of the dark. Not anymore. This new dark would never feel safe again. As the sky lightened with a new day, Guin could see just where she was, and somehow that made her feel less afraid. Guin felt her inner strength reviving.

The motel was situated at the edge of a very small town that was spread out along the rock-and-sand shoreline of the river. It felt as though she were looking at the cover photograph from a huge National Geographic magazine. It was slightly off the main highways and felt rural and uncomplicated. People were bustling about even at this early hour. Many on foot or on bicycles. Guinevere combed her hair with her fingers and straightened her clothes. She had removed the bloody suit jacket and looked presentable enough. She walked down the beach toward the buildings. A café with tables outside on the sand looked inviting, so she sat and ordered coffee and toast.

"Traveling through?" the waitress asked, setting a mug of steaming brew down in front of her.

"On my way home, actually. I'm from Washington. It just got too late to go all the way last night," Guin answered. *Keep it simple*, Guinevere warned herself. Not too much information. Nothing true. Nothing that would invite further questioning.

"Well, you picked a great place to stop. Not too many tourists come this far from the city. We are sort of an undiscovered jewel, if you know what I mean." The girl was young and friendly.

"There's everything you need without the highways and noise. No crowded streets or traffic, either."

Guin finished her breakfast, left money, and walked farther down the beach. She needed some clothes and toiletries. Nothing was open yet except for the café, so she positioned herself directly in the middle of the beach, so she could stand watch for yards on all sides. At this point in time, Guin didn't think she would ever be safe or relaxed again. Every small sound made her nervous and she thought every human being was looking at her with suspicion, or worse, intent to kill.

A soft, warm breeze eased over her from the river. It truly was a gorgeous day; but for Guin it was dark, lonely, a scary hell. She left the beach abruptly when several small children ran past in the sand, squealing in delight, their mother trailing them ... laughing.

The drug store opened first. She bought shampoo, toothpaste, and the other toiletries she thought were necessary. Next was a tiny J. C. Penney store. Left over from the 1950's, Guinevere guessed. The clothes were adequate, though not the height of fashion. She bought jeans, T-shirts, a sweater, New Balance cross-trainers, underwear, and two lightweight dresses, one of which she left on so she wouldn't stand out too much in this beach town. Her work heels didn't look right, even without the pantyhose, so she bought sandals as well. There. She admired herself in the mirror. She looked like a woman from town.

Guinevere left the store and started back to the motel when she passed a newsstand. Her breath caught in her throat and the packages slipped to the sidewalk. On the front page of the newspaper were photographs of her home and thumbnail shots of her family on the front page of USA Today. "Bloody Rampage in Upscale Neighborhood! Wife Sought!" was a general description of Guinevere. *No photo, thank God.* Plus, the police were looking for Guinevere Stone, not Igraine Fairchild. So it was back to the drugstore for hair dye and then to a grocery store for scissors. Too nervous about questions, she didn't want to get everything at the same place.

On the way back to the motel, Guin walked past a ten-year-old Pontiac Grand Am with a "For Sale" sign in the window. It was a faded red and unremarkable. She hated to part with any more money, but in the long run she'd less likely be spotted if she stayed away from bus depots and train stations.

Guin walked up the sidewalk to the house, climbed the three steps to the porch, went to the door, and rang the bell. An elderly man in a wheelchair approached the open door and rolled up to the screen door.

"Ya, what can I do for you little lady?" he asked a bit tersely.

Guin tensed and shot back, "How much you want for that red car?"

"Who's at the door, sweetie?" came the gentle voice of a woman from the next room.

"Twenty-seven hundred dollars, missy," the grump replied. Then he yelled, "Some girl askin' 'bout Daniel's car,"

An elegant wisp of a woman came around the corner and up behind Mr. Grouch.

"Hello dear, I'm Marie. Is this old man bothering you?" she asked.

"Arthur, are you giving this nice young lady your guff?" she asked, with a smile that he couldn't see.

"Dear, our grand nephew, who is in the Army and on his way to Afghanistan, asked us to sell his car for him. He's quite the mechanic and that car will serve you well. Not much to look at, but it runs real good. Did Arthur tell you the price? Twenty-seven hundred dollars. That's firm honey, but worth it." Marie finished her comments.

"That sounds good to me, will you take cash?" said Guinevere.

"Yup," said Arthur.

"Honey, how'd you get here?" asked Marie.

"I walked from downtown. Stayed at the motel last night and decided I'd drive back to Walla Walla. See, my car quit on me just before I left on a flight to see a cousin in Wisconsin, who is dying from cancer. I just returned, flying into Portland last night" explained Guin.

"We have the title, Daniel signed it. You'll have to take it to the courthouse and do all the stuff that needs doin' includin' gettin' new plates," Arthur instructed.

"No problem." Guin hated lying to the couple, but under the circumstances ...

Ten minutes later, she was on her way back to the motel. She paid her bill and told the wife of the cabby that she would leave the key in the room as she hadn't showered yet and wanted to do that before she left.

Guin returned to the room. She scissored her curly light blonde hair short, then dyed it dark reddish-brown. When she looked at herself, she was startled. With this short, slightly uneven, spiky dark hair, she could actually see her prominent cheekbones, full lips, and wide blue eyes. She looked a bit more "perky" than she cared for. But, even Guinevere didn't recognize herself. *Perfect. No one had ever seen this woman before. And they would*

Whirlwind

never see the other one again, She thought. Guinevere Stone had not died with her family, but she needed to make that woman disappear.

Guin had mentioned to several people that she was going home to Washington State, so she drove inland instead. The car's air conditioning was broken, as Marie and Arthur had told her. Unfortunately, the temperatures were unseasonably hot. Deciding to drive at night in the cooler air, she pulled into a motel parking lot, got another room, and slept all day with the aid of a Benadryl tablet.

When Guinevere awoke, she was her usual good natured self for about five seconds ... then she flashed back to her house in the Twin Cities. The shock made her sick. Barely making it to the bathroom, she spent some time in that small, enclosed space, trying to control both her stomach and her nerves. At dusk, quite unsure of herself but aware that she needed to keep moving, she went out to her car and drove.

Night driving had always been relaxing for Guinevere, but not this time. Every car that passed made her worry. When headlights came up behind her and followed for a while, she could hardly breathe. About dawn, she was somewhere in Nevada. She kept going. She just drove. Sometimes she thought she was backtracking, but she didn't care enough to look at a map. She must have driven through mountains, but she couldn't remember them. When she was too tired to drive, she slept. When she noticed her hunger, she ate. She bought gas when the tank was low. When Guinevere reached Salt Lake City, she stopped again to buy gas and food. There was a newspaper on the table in the diner. "**Killer or Killers Still Sought in Homicides of Minnesota Family.**" Fingerprints were lifted, all of which matched family members, except one. It was found on the blade, next to the wooden handle of the butcher knife. Guin knew it was the knife she saw protruding from Peter's chest.

Beautiful, sweet Peter. Guinevere had to clutch herself tightly to keep from screaming. Once she started, there would be no stopping it.

She read that there were also shoe prints outside both the front and rear entrances—three or four sets, the police weren't sure. Black tire marks in the driveway did not belong to the family cars, either.

An interview with a sobbing Lynn Stone-Franklin blamed Charles's wife. "I warned Charles! I said, 'Who could trust a woman named Guinevere?' I mean really! Guinevere! She has delusions of grandeur and wants Charles's money. The children hated her and she was horrible to my poor brother."

To Guinevere, each of Lynn's statements was delivered like a shot from a revolver. She had to laugh through her tears. Lynn sounded insane. But Lynn was always crazy and angry. Her own marriage was fraught with difficulties. She had a sloth for a husband and money problems of her own. They lived way beyond their means and she was constantly borrowing from Charles. Besides, she was the one who hated children. This time, there was a picture of "the wife" but it now looked nothing like Guinevere. The photograph, a wedding shot, made her weepy all over again. She got her food to go and left quickly.

Even driving at night was hot. Guinevere, deep in thought, was unaware of the heat even when the back of her dress stuck to the car's vinyl seat. She drove south until she could no longer keep her eyes open. Visions kept floating over her eyes, blurring the road and traffic to the point of near accidents. Blood, there was lots of blood, and crying small children, and a husband screaming "Run!" The sudden flood of tears blinded her view and forced her to drive into a shallow ditch. It was too real. It was too terrifying. Her face was wet with sobbing. Her lap was soaked and her hands slippery and shaking.

Whirlwind

This constant driving gave her entirely too much time to reflect. Even playing the radio didn't help. She was remembering things she didn't want to think about. Things about Charles and how much he had changed over the past two months. At first he had been so full of life, of joy, of love for her and his kids. But he became reticent to share his thoughts, and he locked himself away in the den or bedroom for hours and hours at a time, leaving her and the children on their own. His whole persona seemed to alter right in front of her eyes. He was short tempered with her and the kids, especially Peter. He had become a nervous person ... extremely edgy at times. When they were first together, he had always been so sure of himself. She had liked that about him. One evening she surprised him, coming up from behind, putting her arms around his neck, and nuzzling his shoulders. He swung around abruptly with fist raised. Who did he think she was?

There also were late night phone calls that he would leave the room to take. Secret meetings often took place in their home with people she hadn't met or even seen before. One time a lawyer stopped by and they were closeted away for an entire evening, but he never told her why. Another time his employer, Sean Connelly, brought an exotic looking woman with him. She was beautiful in an off-balance sort of way. Her eyes had roamed the room and then landed on Guin with disdain that immediately turned to animosity. Sexuality oozed from her perfume and body language. Guin had hoped Sean wasn't having an affair, as she liked his sweet wife.

If she'd ask anything at all about his work, Charles would reply that it was just a routine job. He would toy with the food on his plate and just move it around, never lifting the fork to his mouth, while at the same time admonishing the children for not eating all their meal. Charles wasn't sleeping, at least not in their bed. She'd wake up and wander the house looking for him and find him in the den. Door locked again.

Oh my God! She had just realized something else. They hadn't made love since the honeymoon. In fact, he hadn't touched her at all. This, after he once declared that he'd never get enough of her. But they had been so busy with the newness of it all ... She knew he was working, but was he really? Was there something more sinister going on with her new husband, something terribly secretive, enough to change him so completely? How soon would it have been before he stopped coming home to them at all?

The next time Guin pulled over, she was in Kanab, Utah. She had no memory of how she got there. Nor could Guin say how long she had been on the road or what day it was. Her entire routine was food, gas, sleep, and the road. She was not able to remember which roads she took, nor did she know how to retrace her journey. None of that mattered. She was simply running away from her life. She had even considered turning herself in to the police, but the idea of a long and drawn-out public trial was too much to bear. It might be easier to simply have a sudden and fatal car accident. But, in spite of everything, Guin knew she did not want to die.

The sign at the edge of town told her she was entering Flagstaff, Arizona. Guinevere felt as though she was either a wrung out dishrag or a puddle of sweat, so she found a motel and checked in. She signed in under the name Irena Fairchild. No one would notice unless they really studied her license, but she found that no one cared enough. Guin had never been able to understand such carelessness. She noticed and remembered everything. She laughed ruefully. Everything except the travel of the past several days, that is.

Her motel, The Moonlight Motel, with its garish neon sign depicting the various phases of the moon's cycle, was

Whirlwind

in the center of the downtown area and within walking distance of anything she could need. The city was larger than she expected, but maybe that was better than a smaller one where she would more likely be noticed. The air was so clean and fresh here, drier than in the Twin Cities. She liked it very much.

Seated in a restaurant, she felt comfortable for the first time since the day of the murders. Now it almost seemed like it had happened to someone else, maybe the main character in a novel she had read years before. The numbness of her emotion was probably protecting her. Plus, whenever she felt the darkness creeping into her mind, she pushed it away. She was suddenly aware that she was actually enjoying her meal and didn't feel like she was about to lose it.

The diner was a cozy replica of something from around 1950, all chrome and glass with round, red upholstered stools at the counter. Large windows faced the sidewalk, where there was a constant stream of people passing. Bright and cheerful, it subtly but surely improved her mood.

"Can I get you anything else?" her waitress asked pleasantly.

Without thinking it through, or even hesitating, she responded.

"Yes. I need a job. Do you know of anything?"

"You're joking, right? Didn't you notice the sign in the window?" the waitress grinned.

"We're new and need lots of help." She held out her hand. "Hi, I'm Sherry Brunswick."

"Irena Fairchild. I need an application, please." The lie rolled off her tongue easily. Irena was her mother's name, but she was no longer using it. Guinevere hadn't been a waitress since her high school days, but what the hell. A job was a job. It couldn't be that difficult.

Sherry left, went to the back counter near the register, rummaged in a drawer, and returned with an application, Guin folded it neatly in half and slid it into the side pocket of her purse.

Whirlwind

CHAPTER FIVE
Flagstaff, Arizona

Drinking her morning tea in the motel lobby, that was gleaming with sunshine, Guin looked over the application and realized she would need an address, phone number, and—oh dear!—She needed a social security number. This was not good. As she sat there, a plan began to materialize. She'd already taken a form of her deceased mother's name, why not her social security number as well? She actually could remember the number, as it was similar to her own and Guin was good with numbers. Before she could change her mind, she wrote it in the space provided. She doubted she would have this job for any length of time anyway. Not long enough for anyone to check up on her. There wasn't a space for references, so that was one less lie.

The check-in desk had several local newspapers. She picked up the largest, The Arizona Daily Sun, and turned to the for-rent section. Most of the listings were high-priced town houses or condominiums, tourist time-shares, or newly built homes. Catering to the older retired people from the Midwest, she guessed. What she really wanted was an apartment in an older building and close to the job. Guinevere tucked the newspaper under her arm and went for a walk. After a few blocks, she entered a residential section of town, older than the downtown buildings by far, although the homes were in good shape and sat on large clean yards well back from the street. There were trees and mid-priced cars and kids on bikes in the street. An occasional dog ran across her path, as did boys and girls chasing balls. At the end of the block, she passed a two-story frame house, white with blue trim and with a double-wide yard. It had an "Apartment for Rent" sign at the curb. Several bicycles lay in the sparse grass, and she was nearly bowled over by a lad of six or seven as he came running out of the house.

"You come back here! Joey! Right this minute!" A young Native American woman ran after the boy, who was still going strong.

"Oh! I'm so sorry," she said to Guinevere. "I didn't see you."

Guin smiled. "Your son?"

"My disobedient son." The woman frowned as she watched the small boy disappear around the corner. "Are you here about the apartment?" She looked more closely at Guinevere.

"I guess I am. If the price is right."

She took Guin around back to a remodeled garage or carriage house. It sat apart from the house and at the rear of the large lot. Guin had seen several similar places in old St. Paul and Minneapolis neighborhoods. They were charming places, cozy. This one was no different. There was a front door that opened to a living room and kitchen area, one large room, with a small pantry or storage area. There were bright, woven rugs on the floor and several large windows. No phone. No television. But there were essential pieces of furniture. The way to the second story was a long, narrow stairway with deep steps that took up one whole wall. Kitchen appliances were tucked under the higher steps.

Whirlwind

Upstairs there was a single bedroom and large bathroom. Guinevere loved it immediately.

"How much is the rent?" she asked.

"Four hundred a month, and that includes utilities," the woman answered, as she watched Guinevere for a response. "Is that too much?" she asked, looking at Guin's rumpled and stained clothes.

"Don't you know? Haven't you rented this out before?" Guin asked her.

The young mother shrugged her shoulders. "No, my brother lived here, but he's back out on the reservation now. He didn't like life in town."

"It seems reasonable to me. Shall we try each other out for a while?"

"I'm Maggie. Maggie Oso. The windstorm is my son, Joseph."

"And I'm Irena Fairchild. Happy to meet you."

"I think you'll like it here, most people do. There is a lot to do in Flagstaff, but not so much it gets crazy like it can in Phoenix." Maggie smiled and the two women chatted as they returned to the front of the house. Maggie left Guin at the sidewalk and continued on calling out to her son.

The walk back to The Moonlight Motel was a light hearted one for Guinevere. She had a new life! Guinevere Stone was no longer. She was as dead to the world as her family. In just one day she had a place to live— Maggie said she could move in the next day— and most likely a job.

She slept well in spite of her excitement, woke at nine, and packed up her few belongings, paid her motel bill, and drove toward a mall. On the way, she passed a Goodwill outlet store and stopped there instead. A large grocery store shared the same parking lot. Guin purchased groceries first, then bed linens and towels, along with two more sundresses for work at the well-stocked Goodwill. Many of the women's clothes looked like they were right off the rack of a Twin City boutique, and not south-western at all. Still, the clothes were well-made and relatively inexpensive. Far cheaper than new outfits at the mall.

On her way to the apartment, considering it just a formality, Guin dropped off the job application complete with address: 2193 Sun Canyon Road, Flagstaff, Arizona. Guin entered the diner, walked over to Sherry and handed her the application. Sherry took it, set it on the counter, and excitedly said, "You're hired!"

At her apartment, it took less than thirty minutes to put everything away, make up the bed, and eat lunch. *Now what?* She wondered, not used to having so much free time. Charles plus the kids, the house, and job kept her flying. She had liked that, being busy. She had loved every bit of family life except for the newer version of Charles.

There was a place, Maggie told her, behind the apartment where she could park her car. *Wonderful,* thought Guin. It could not be seen from the road. At the back of the property was a stream and dense foliage, making it very private. It was hard for Guinevere to think of herself being in the midst of a large city when she was in this place. It felt rural and mid-century country. Of course, she couldn't forget that a very modern city was just blocks away. Where there were people and noise and traffic, shopping and entertainment.

A tiny patch of ground had been cleared next to the stream. A wooden table and chair sat there on flat slabs of stone. Maggie's brother must have spent time in this lovely spot as well. Guin sat down and just relaxed. The music the stream made as it flowed slowly by and over the rocky bottom was comforting, hypnotizing almost. There was a dog's chew toy lying at the edge of the stream. She looked up from her musings to see a little brown face watching her.

Whirlwind

"Joey?"

The face disappeared for a moment. Then he was back, closer.

"Hi Joey. My name is Irena."

"I know. My momma told me," he replied. "She said I wasn't to pester you. So I'm not." He cocked his head a little to one side as if contemplating something serious. Sammy had done that, too. "What's pester?"

"Pester is like bothering. But you aren't bothering me."

"Do you like kids? Do you have any kids? Do you have a dog?" His questions came fast and furious as only a child could fire them off. He squatted down in front of her and leaned in a little. She loved the trust kids had at that age; they had no reason to be leery of anyone yet. He had a lively look of interest on his face, bright curious brown eyes, and an open smile.

"I love kids. I don't have any, though, not yet. No pets either."

"That's too bad. You can play with me if you want," he offered this gift with a cheeky grin. "Do you know how to play anything?"

"Joey," Maggie's voice warned. "I told you to leave Irena alone." Maggie came, wiping wet hands on a messy apron.

"Bye!" and Joey was gone in a flash. He was very good at disappearing when his mother wanted him.

"It's fine. He's a sweetheart," Guinevere said. "I really don't mind."

"Good. Because he'll visit you again ... often ... whenever he thinks of it. Anyway, the reason I came back here was there's someone at the front door to see you."

Guin's heart sped up, just when she was beginning to relax a little. No one could possibly have traced her here unless they had been with her the entire way and she'd been alone. She had back-tracked enough to be sure no one had been following.

"It's a woman who says she works with you. Sherry something."

"Thanks. I'll be right there," Guinevere said with relief and slipped into her house for a moment alone. She needed to calm her nerves. Guin had forgotten about the address she'd written on the job application. "I have to do better," she scolded herself. "I can't afford to slip up."

She straightened her clothes and ran her fingers through her very short, dark hair. It felt strange, and it took her by surprise each time she did it. Where were the long light curls her fingers were so used to finding?

"Hi Irena. I'm off today and thought I'd stop by. Cute place. Show me around? When can you start working?" Sherry was a happy person who talked a mile a minute, not unlike Joey. She was vivacious and perky, straightforward and easygoing. The total opposite of Guinevere. It was a little disconcerting, but Guin just knew Sherry was a good person. She led Sherry behind the house to her own place and made them iced tea while Sherry chatted, her blue eyes shining and her cheeks pink with life. She was constantly shoving her medium brown hair back over her shoulders and out of her way. Guin wanted to give her a hair clip, but she didn't have one.

"Irena. It's such a formal name, don't you think? Maybe I could just call you 'Rena'? That suits you. 'Rena.' I like that. Do you?" Sherry finally took a breath and a sip of tea.

From this moment on ... Guinevere thought to herself, *I ... am ...* **Rena** *...* **Rena** *...* **Rena**!

"Yes, I do actually."

"My brother, the cook and owner of the restaurant, said you could come in tomorrow. He actually told me to tell you *Please.*" she grinned in amusement. "Can you do that? We're pretty anxious to have more help. So far it's been just a family thing, but my parents who helped get it going don't really want to work. So we need you. It will be hectic and tiring, but fun, too." My God, but Sherry herself was exhausting.

"Yes, I can come in tomorrow. What should I wear?" Rena smiled at Sherry's excitement over the whole situation.

"Just a nice dress. Like the one you have on. Comfortable shoes, too. I wear tennis shoes or sandals. It gets warm running around. We'll give you a really big apron, huge. I swear, our aprons could cover a Titan. Oh, this will be so great, Rena!"

By the time Sherry left, Rena needed a nap. The trip was still wearing on her and she hadn't been sleeping as much as she needed. She knew what waited as soon as she'd close her eyes. Thankfully, as tired as she was, Rena slept.

When she woke, it was dark and she could hear the distant rumble of thunder. She had heard about the severe storms that came off the mountains, but Rena wasn't prepared for the noise. Storms in the Midwest were mild compared to this! It was truly frightening. The lightning seemed all around, the thunder crashed against the very walls and roof of the building like it was trying to tear it from the foundation. She could hear the rushing water in the creek behind the house, but couldn't see it through the solid curtain of water. She made a sandwich and sat in the dark. There was a sound ... she couldn't quite be certain of. A scratch at the door ... a whine, soft and lonely. Rena opened the door just a crack to listen more closely. A large shadow burst through and into her house. Water flew everywhere soaking Rena. She got the light turned on and saw a very large, very wet dog sitting happily on the hand-woven rug as though it belonged there. Making three circles and then a happy bark, the dog laid down.

"Who might you be?" Rena reached out her hand, which was promptly licked. There was a collar and a name tag: "Chee." There wasn't a phone number, just an address. She was startled, wait a minute. This was the address. The dog must belong to Joey and his mom. Rena was relieved.

"When this rain lets up, I'll take you home, sweetheart." In the meantime, Rena toweled Chee off as best she could, gave the animal a perfunctory look-over, and offered the panting golden dog water and a sandwich of her own as the dog was eyeing what was left of Rena's with hungry eyes.

"I'll bet Joey is worried sick about you," she told the dog and ran her hand over Chee's damp, but sleek coat. She didn't know much about dogs, but she thought this was a Golden Retriever or a Labrador, and not very old. The rain continued unabated and Rena and Chee eventually slept.

When Rena opened her eyes, the dog was pushing her muzzle against Rena's arm to wake her up. When she blinked her eyes, Chee whined and went to the door. Cramped from spending the remainder of the storm curled up on the sofa with a hand stretched down to the dog, Rena rose, and stretched several different ways to ease the stiffness from her body.

"Okay, okay. Let me get you home." The two walked side by side to the house and knocked.

Joey opened the door and squealed. "Mom! It's Uncle Tomas's dog. Come quick!"

"Where in heaven's name did you find her?" Maggie gasped. "We've been looking for her for weeks, ever since we took my brother back to the reservation." She gave Chee a hug as the tail kept wagging. Then her pleased expression dimmed.

"Oh dear," Maggie said. "We won't be able to keep her. Joey is allergic to dogs and my brother has left the reservation again. I don't know where he lives now."

Whirlwind

Rena could see Joey was already having a little trouble breathing, his mother washed his face and hands and sent him to his room. "I'll have to tie her up and call the shelter to come get her."

"Gosh, that's really too bad, she seems like a terrific dog," Rena offered as she turned to go. Chee immediately jumped to her feet and followed her to the door. Chee's liquid brown eyes swept back and forth from Rena to the doorknob and back again. Rena's heart was rapidly melting.

"Why don't I keep her for a while? I think I might like the company. Besides, Tomas might just come back at any time and, wouldn't it be fun to surprise him? If it doesn't work, then we can call the shelter."

"You would do that for us? Thank you so much! I can let her out while you are at your job, but we have to keep her away from Joey, which won't be easy because he loves her to death."

And so it was decided. Rena was now the owner of a beautiful yellow dog, even if it was only to be a temporary situation. No one back home would believe this. Charles and the kids had been asking about a dog and she kept saying no, because she knew who would have to do most of the work—she and Charles—and they had too much on their plates already.

Charles and the kids ... back home. She had forgotten for a minute. There was no "Charles and the kids." Not anymore. Rena let Chee lead her back home.

Sitting in the dark with her new pet, Rena tried to put her life into some kind of perspective. She listed all the things that remained good for her. She didn't come up with much. She had her health, physical anyway, her new home, and this dog who seemed to be hers already. There were her siblings, but they were all too far away, and her married life had been too full to cultivate friendships. She was sad that she had remembered all the negative things about her marriage, but somehow it made losing Charles easier, remembering the negative. Like he hadn't been hers at all, too much of him was secretive and hidden from her. This was not so with the children. Her heart ached for them. She knew that it would always be like this.

Whirlwind

CHAPTER SIX
Flagstaff, Arizona

If the first day at the new job had Rena a bit nervous, she tried not to let it show. She walked in the front door of the Downtown Café with a bright cheerful smile for Sherry, who skipped over to hug her and slipped an oversized apron over Rena's head.

"Hey, Rena! I'm so glad to see you," said Sherry with her usual exuberance. The café had only a counter and maybe twelve tables, but it was bustling and loud. Sherry pointed to the long counter and told Rena to take it and Sherry would do the tables.

"Just until you get used to the place, our customers, and the menu," Sherry told her.

Immediately thrust into the din, Rena found that she enjoyed the work in spite of the confusion. The customers were easy-going and tolerant of the new staff member, more likely to tease than to complain. The menu was typical breakfast with a few southwest tidbits, like huevos rancheros and grits or corn meal pancakes. The clientele was a mixture of White, Indian, Mexican, and a few Asians. A happy, well-fed crowd. They tipped well, too.

Both young women collapsed into chairs when the last of the early guests had departed.

"Whew! You did great!" Sherry hugged Rena again.

"Terrific, for a first day," Sherry's brother, John, added to the compliment.

"You've done this before?" John was tall and slender, with dark brown hair, cut short, and a small beer belly that was cute now but would be unhealthy later in life. He looked more like a well groomed bank president than a gourmet cook. His twinkly smile totally took Rena in. He was warm and comfortable and smelled of exotic spices. Sherry and their parents were his family and there wasn't time, he claimed, for a wife *AND* cooking.

"Not for a while," Rena smiled at him when she answered his inquiry. "Sherry makes it fun and easy."

John patted his sister on the head. "Yeah, she does. The customers love her. One of these days, she'll get swept off her feet and leave me."

"Not likely, brother! It will take more than a sexy smile to win me over."

"We'll see. One of us had better produce grandchildren or our folks will disown us."

"Not me. I've got plans."

Rena took a short walk around the block to unwind before lunch started. Several times Sherry had called to Rena to get her attention, and she hadn't responded right away. **Rena, Rena, Rena** ... *no more Guinevere*, she chastised. It would be safer, anyway. She liked the new name, less pretentious and formal. The soft sound of it pleased her. New name, new life.

Lunch went smoothly. Like breakfast, the menu was limited and folks seemed to know what they wanted. The Downtown Café wasn't open for supper during the week, just the weekends, so by 4 p.m., they were done. Rena slowly walked home with a happy, self-satisfied smile on her lips, and a pocketful of tip money. It probably wasn't

Whirlwind

much, but it made her feel she was taking care of herself, her new self. *This will be okay*, she thought, *it really will*. Chee met her at the door with her leash hanging from her mouth, so a walk was next.

They explored several neighborhoods and met numerous people walking their dogs as well. Much of the area seemed to be made up of families. Extended families with in-laws and grandparents and aunts and uncles. Most everyone was related to everyone else. But there were also "outsiders" like her, and they were well tolerated by the locals. In a city that thrived on tourists, Rena expected people would accept other people into their neighborhoods easily. Chee was well behaved and Rena was proud of her. Tomas must have worked with her. As they neared home, Rena let Chee off lead, and she ran directly to their door and stood there wagging her entire body, waiting for Rena to open the door. Chee ate her kibble that Maggie had supplied along with the leash and a few toys. Rena had leftovers from the café. *Not a bad day,* she thought with a yawn.

But each time she thought of her lost family, Rena pushed the thoughts forcefully from her mind. *Not now*! But late into the night she woke in a heavy sweat with blankets wrapped tightly about her body and a worried dog breathing in her face and licking her cheeks. The remnants of the dream clung to her like thick fog, fragments of children closing their eyes in death and using the last breaths to call her "new mommy."

The remainder of the week and the following month played out in much the same way. Routine was good for Rena at this time. She was relaxing a little more, and not always looking over her shoulders every few minutes. She loved everything about the café and looked forward to work every morning. The menu constantly varied and was always savory and delicious. Rena's taste buds were expanding, as her waist line would if she weren't careful.

One customer, a dark-haired, black eyed, pleasant looking guy, moved from a table where he usually sat to the counter by Rena's second week. Both Sherry and John noticed and teased her about it daily.

"Rena has an admirer already."

In fact, it seemed she did. Friday morning, he brought in a bouquet of daisies and tulips. He handed them to her, blushing. His hair was thick and wavy, not curly, the kind of hair that women liked to run their fingers through. He was tall, well built, but not particularly muscular, just nice looking. Neatly put together. Clothes looked good on his frame like they were custom made for him. His skin was evenly brown from the sun and he appeared to be a happy and contented man moving easily through his life.

"I got these for you," he said. They weren't busy at the café, so Sherry sat them both down, took Rena's apron, and waited on them with her usual flourish.

"Thank you. They are lovely and smell even better." Rena took an appreciative sniff before she smiled at the man.

"My name is Geoffrey Pelleas," he said with a slightly accented voice. Rena choked on her water until tears ran down her cheeks. She stopped when she saw his look of astonishment and terror.

"I am so sorry! It's just that your name, I mean, well …" Rena didn't know what to say to extricate herself from this.

"I know it's odd. The name is British, you see."

"Yes, it certainly is. I expect your long ago ancestor was a member of King Arthur's court," she said with amusement and laughed again. Oh, if he only could be told. "Let me think … King Pelleas, if I remember my Arthurian legends correctly," she added.

"Oh, I doubt that, but my grandparents like to think so. Not many people get the connection." Geoffrey looked at her with a closer inspection.

Whirlwind

"The Arthur legends were very big with my mother. I grew up with them." She held out her hand. "I'm Irena Fairchild and thank you so much for the flowers." They talked for a long while; neither realizing the time was moving so quickly. Geoffrey was an easy man to be with and Rena felt comfortable with him. He was little like her late husband, Charles. Maybe the old Charles, before he got so secretive. She felt a momentary sadness, but refused to let it surface. She said only that she had been divorced back on the East Coast and that she had no children. Geoff said he was also going through a divorce and had three children. He was fighting his ex-wife for custody, but it wasn't looking too encouraging. His wife and children were currently living in England. She'd run home to her parents, who were keeping Geoff from talking to her.

"I don't understand, really. She never wanted the kids until they said they wanted to live with me, that they did not want to live in England with grandparents they'd never even met."

"Perhaps you'll have to learn to share." Rena didn't want to talk about lost children any more.

"I'm not the one unwilling to share," Geoffrey answered with a frown as he thought of his distant family.

"I'm sorry. It's none of my business. I have a tendency to be outspoken when people complain about their family issues, but that's another subject for a distant day."

"What do you do to earn your living?" she asked him to immediately change the way this conversation was heading.

"I own an art gallery in Scottsdale. The Pelleas Creative and Fine Arts Gallery. It sounds prestigious, but it's small. Requires a lot of travel, although that part is rather fun. Meeting the artists and setting up shows and openings and such. I am always amazed at the amount of creativity there is in this world. I'm meeting with a group of Navajo and Zuni artists tomorrow, I sell quite a lot of their jewelry. Tourists, especially people from the Midwest, really like turquoise jewelry. It's always been traditionally beautiful stuff, but these younger artists are adding their own style and it is truly amazing." He pulled some photographs out of his jacket pocket to show her.

"I'm picking up these pieces tomorrow."

"Wow. They're wonderful." Rena flipped through the stack of pictures twice.

"Bloody right! No one else has work like this in their stores. Some of this turquoise isn't even being mined any more. Or, if it is, no one is selling it," Geoffrey was very excited about these acquisitions. Rena liked his enthusiasm.

"What else do you have in the shop?" Rena asked with real interest.

"Paintings, books, baskets, rugs and blankets, clothing and shoes made with deerskin as soft as silk, traditional Navajo blouses and shirts with quillwork designs. My God, I could go on for hours."

So they discussed art and music and literature for a while. It turned out that they had much in common. Both of them liked classical music and concert halls, old movies, picnics, vintage furniture, and comfortable clothes and much more.

"You are not the typical waitress," Geoff told her with no small amount of surprise.

"This isn't a typical café," Rena grinned as Sherry sat down with coffee for all of them. John joined them as well, with chocolate pie.

"Sorry to break this up," John grimaced. "We need to gear up for the dinner crowd."

"It was great to meet you, Geoff. And thanks again for the flowers."

"I'll see you again, Rena." *True words.* She knew it the moment he uttered them.

Whirlwind

CHAPTER SEVEN
St. Paul, Minnesota

Detective Finley called his wife before checking into Charles Stone any further. He called her twice a day, every day, and tried to have lunch with her each day as well. He called more often if she was having a rough day. He'd done it before her heart attack and he certainly wasn't going to stop now. In fact, he had to restrain himself or he'd be dialing her number every few minutes. Sally was still in the hospital, but her medical team said if she did well on her stress test, she'd be able to be released. *Set free,* was how Axel thought about it. She'd be at home with him again, anyway.

Lately she had been having trouble with regulating her blood glucose levels and Axel had found her passed out several times. It scared him more than any case he had ever worked on. She was the bright spot in his life and he didn't know how to live without her. If she didn't answer the phone, Axel or one of his guys would dash over to see her. She didn't always appreciate that, but what was he to do? When she did answer the phone, she would always laugh at him for being a worry wort. This made him happy. Since they never had children, they'd become a very tight couple.

Susan M. Nelson

She wasn't too tall, maybe five feet four inches, and she was chubby, according to her. Curly brown hair that she was continuously tucking behind her ears and that never stayed put. Bright dark blue eyes that missed nothing about him; he swore she read his mind and knew what he was thinking long before he did. When they had first met, he was already immersed in his detective work and had little patience for a relationship. Actually, Axel kept expecting her to refuse him when he eventually did get around to calling her, but she told him she knew there was a good guy in his mind somewhere. Locked up in his "little grey cells." And she'd stuck with him until she found the key. He grinned, remembering.

"I'm sort of scared about the stress test, but my nurse said I shouldn't be. She thinks I'll be fine," said Sally.

"Should I be there? Do you want me to be there?" inquired Axel.

"No, I think that would be worse, worrying about you as well as the test. The techs won't let you be in the same room, anyway. I think all I have to do is walk on a treadmill. Shouldn't be too bad," she told him.

"Okay then. But I'll get there soon. Just in time to hear the good news."

Detective Axel Finley located the Twin City Design and Engineering Company without too much trouble. It was a indistinct brick building, like many along the river. The only windows were on the first floor, which housed some realty firm. The top floor had windows at one time; the bricks were a lighter color where the windows had been bricked up. *Now, why would you do that?* The second floor housed the design company.

Parking was a difficult matter. He finally double parked and stuck his police parking badge in the window. He climbed to the second floor and only got a little winded. The receptionist sat pertly behind her desk, typing away

Whirlwind

busily. Finley had to clear his voice twice before she looked up.

"Yes?" She seemed to be irritated by his presence. Her youth and exotic beauty belied her disdainful and rude manner. She was strikingly beautiful with silky black hair and deep-set black eyes. Axel felt she was from somewhere south of the U.S. border.

"I'd like to see the manager of this company, please."

"Yes, I'm sure you would, but you don't have an appointment." She scanned her book and snapped it closed before he could get a look.

"I don't need one, but I'd be happy to get a warrant."

The receptionist wasn't the least fazed by this. She acted like she was used to a policeman interrupting her day. She turned her back to Axel and picked up her phone, pushed a button, and murmured into the receiver.

"Mr. Sean Connelly will be out as soon as he can."

Finley wandered around the large, airy room checking out the artwork and photos of award- winning architectural designs hanging impressively on the walls. They were obviously from another generation.

"Most of those are my father's," said a voice behind him. Finley turned to a chubby, balding man in his mid-thirties.

"I haven't had the firm long enough to earn and hang mine." He showed Finley a sheepish grin.

He's a fake, Axel knew at once. He intended to watch this guy closely.

"Is there somewhere more private we can talk?" Axel asked.

"Is that really necessary? I'm a busy man."

"Sir. One of your employees has been murdered and I have to ask you a few questions."

"I don't know anything about that!" Mr. Connelly was nervous, but didn't want his secretary to see it. He took Axel by the arm and moved him away from the desk. Axel noticed that he glanced at his closed door twice and quickly looked away as if noticed; Axel would later wonder about it.

"I have a terribly important meeting now, so this will have to wait until later."

Axel took out his notebook and wrote while he spoke; "Mr. Connelly is refusing to cooperate with this investigation."

"Hey! That's not true."

"What would you call it then?" Finley put his notebook back into his pocket.

"Okay, okay. Follow me please." Axel was led to another door across the lobby.

"What was Charles Stone working on?"

"I am not at liberty to discuss that."

"What is the nature of the work this company does?"

Connelly just shook his head. "That either."

"Did Mr. Stone have any close friends working here with him?"

"We are all friends here, so yes. Charles was a valued member of our extensive staff and has worked for us since my father's time. He was one of the original partners."

"I need to see his working area and speak to these friends." Finley knew this would go about as far as the rest of the inquiries.

"That certainly will not be possible," Connelly said as he spun around and left. "Show yourself out, Detective."

Finley shook his head ruefully and thought, *I should have gotten the warrant first.*

Back at his desk, he checked about the laptop computer being investigated at the lab, and was told they had found very little as yet, but that some of the hard drive looked promising. Something was there, at any rate. He donned latex gloves, removed the letters from the evidence bag and read them. Not much. Chit chat about the mother's activities. Using the address, he got a name, Mrs. Irena Fairchild, and a phone number.

"Hello Mrs. Fairchild. I am Detective Axel Finley with the St. Paul Police Department in Minnesota."

"I'm sorry," a soft young female voice interrupted him. "Who did you want?"

"A Mrs. Irena Fairchild?"

"That would be my mother, but she died several years ago. I'm Cei, her daughter."

So Axel told her the story to date, the deaths also, and said they really needed to find Guinevere Stone, for her own safety as well as to question her concerning the deaths.

"Oh my god! This is dreadful! Are you sure it is my sister's family?"

People always asked that question and somehow it always irritated Axel. He found himself biting off a retort: *No, we aren't sure, but we thought we would call just to upset you and ruin your lives for awhile.* But, of course, he didn't say it.

"I'm very sorry, but yes, I'm sure. Have you heard from Guinevere?"

"Not lately. They had been planning a trip to visit soon. All of them."

Axel had the unhappy duty to inform her that it was definitely murder. He truly hated to do that sort of thing on the phone. After waiting out Ms. Fairchild's shock and sobbing, he told her again they really needed to find Guinevere.

"You don't think she did this!" she said with anger now in her voice.

"Not really, no. But until we figure out what did happen, she is in danger herself. We don't know what is going on yet, ma'am. If you hear from her please call me." He repeated his name and his direct phone number. When Finley hung up, he sagged into his chair. This was going to be harder than he thought. It always was. None of the cases were easy and the criminals were getting smarter, wilier, and more creative. *Where was the damn woman?*

Axel was given the warrant, he wanted and it was for the entire business, not just for Charles Stone's desk. Connelly wasn't going to like that.

Finley got half a dozen policemen to accompany him to the firm and they met three more from the Minneapolis Police Department when they arrived. Police from both cities were in evidence. His old friend, Detective Stanley Morse, met him at the door. They once had been partners. Only slightly younger, he was the same kind of detective, no computers for him. Short, neat, muscular and always dressed in blue jeans and flannel shirts no matter what the season, Stanley was a good friend. Morse now worked as a detective for the Special Cases Unit for the Minneapolis Police Department and they rarely saw each other anymore. Finley filled him in on the case.

"Heard about that one, glad it's not mine," Morse chuckled in his gravelly voice, brought on by years of drinking and far too many smokes. He pushed his short, neatly trimmed brown hair off of his forehead and then patted his too large belly. "But we'll give you whatever help we can."

Axel handed the warrant to the receptionist and entered the office space. It consisted of a long hallway with several closed doors on both sides and a waiting area in the center. Most engineering firms Axel had seen had a large communal work space. Not this one. It seemed everyone wanted his or her privacy. Absolutely no one was there. The desks were all cleared as well. No people. No designers and no engineering going on. It was one o'clock in the afternoon. Finley was furious as he went back to the lobby. He hadn't noticed when they came in, but all the artwork and framed photos were gone. There was

Whirlwind

absolutely nothing left but empty furniture and empty walls, and a few scraps of paper on the floor.

"What the hell is…" he stopped. The receptionist was not the same one he had met earlier. This one was very young and scared to death.

"I'm so sorry, sir, but I just started today and Mr. Connelly told me to sit here and wait for you." She was close to tears. "I can't tell you anything, really. I didn't realize there was no one else here, I …"

And he believed her. Finley asked his crew to look into everything they could find about the place and what they did. Mostly he wanted to know who worked here. Morse had his team dust every surface for prints, and they called in a crime scene tech team to search for biological evidence or anything else. This company had been packed up too quickly not to have left something behind. Finley was now very sure Charles had been the targeted victim and that his wife was either already dead or in a lot of trouble.

Susan M. Nelson

CHAPTER EIGHT
St. Paul, Minnesota

Sean Connelly was terrified. He had twisted his jacket pockets into wads of wrinkles and was chewing his nails, something he hadn't done since he was a kid. His boss had issued orders and Sean wasn't able to carry them out completely. Sure, he had cleared the office space as best he could, with no help from that spy of a receptionist. He'd never wanted that witch to be a part of this scheme in the first place, but the boss had insisted. He called her the brains of the operation. Damn this! Thank God most of the rooms had been cleared already. Sean sat in his Jeep Cherokee with dozens of file boxes, manila envelopes, a small box with half a dozen computer external hard drives, and a dozen or so 32-gig flash drives. He gripped his cell phone tightly.

It wouldn't do the police any good even if they did find him. Sean knew practically nothing about the men who were giving him orders, not even their names, false or otherwise. He had accepted their money with no thought of the consequences of his actions. And now he knew he would have to pay. He made plans to move his family out of the area, today. How had this happened to him? He was

Whirlwind

moaning and sweating and near tears. "The old man will kill me! I gotta fix this before ..."

There was a tap on his window and Sean nearly went through the windshield. The bitch receptionist-spy stood there in sunglasses and fur coat. She looked menacingly into his vehicle. Sean rolled down the window about an inch.

"Go to this address." Her sultry foreign voice, which sounded so sexy at first when he met her in Panama, now sounded murderous and sickening. She handed him a typed message, turned on her heel and sauntered away, flipping her long black hair over her shoulder. With hatred in his eyes, he watched her leave and get into a Porsche. The woman had been trouble since the day she walked into his dad's office one week after Panama, and announced she was now working there. Funny, she never got a paycheck ... he knew he should have asked his father for help right then and there, but he didn't want the old man to realize how weak he truly was. He had to prove himself first.

Sean Connelly gasped when he read the slip of paper in his fist. It was his address! His family home ... he spun out of the lot and drove as fast as he dared to his house.

Axel Finley's day wasn't going any better. The crime scene tech had found nothing that didn't belong to Stone or Connelly. The first receptionist hadn't left any prints on her desk or on her phone either, and her computer was gone. Stanley Morse had picked up Connelly's wife and two boys an hour before and had driven them to the homicide squad office in St. Paul, keeping them in protective custody. It seemed to both Finley and his old partner that she knew nothing and was scared out of her wits. She hadn't even known about the murders. Axel brought coffee for her and juice boxes for the boys.

"I want to go home now, please," Mrs. Connelly begged.

"You don't understand why you are here?" Axel was surprised at her request. "The family of a man your husband works with has been murdered. You aren't afraid for your boys? Yourself?"

"That can't have a thing to do with us!" She was shaking and spilled her coffee on her blouse. "Can it? I mean, I never even … his children are dead?" There was a quaver in her voice now.

"Yes ma'am. We brought you here to keep you safe until this gets sorted out." Of course he didn't say that they had so very few clues.

"Where is Sean? Can we see him?" She was pleading with him now.

Where was Connelly, indeed?

Connelly pulled into the driveway of his Minneapolis home with enough speed to hit the garage door before it could fully open. He dashed to the open door and streaked into the house calling loudly for his wife and boys. Frantically, he searched the split-level home. They weren't there. No one was there. Rachel's purse was gone, but nothing else. Lunch sat on the dinette, uneaten. A glass of milk was dripping onto the floor and the television was on, cartoons. Rachel's favorite recipe book lay open on the counter.

Sean turned off the television without thinking about it, and sat on the sofa and held his head in his hands and cried. He was too late. He was too stupid. He was too greedy. His father would be so disappointed in him, again. He had lost his family.

He looked up when he heard the front door close quietly. Two men stood there. No, it was that shorter, heavily muscled man and that horrible raven-haired bitch dressed as a man. Sean was sure it was her. He could tell from the arrogant way she stood there in his house. No one else would have recognized them. They looked like movie

Whirlwind

set secret service men—dark and tall and identical. The one seemed so big. They stared at him, but Sean no longer cared what happened to him. His family was gone, dead like Charles's family, and he had nothing left. He wasn't even surprised when the bullets hit him in the chest and he slumped to the floor. He barely felt them, just the pressure. It was almost a relief.

Finley's cell rattled in his pocket. The text message said neighbors had reported gunfire at the Connelly residence. Shit! He bolted out the door in seconds and jumped into the passenger seat of Stanley Morse's car. Sirens blazing, they sped west into Minneapolis and pulled up behind a Jeep Cherokee that was parked, but still running, in the driveway. All four doors wide open. Several neighbors were standing around idly. *Stupid! They report gunshots and then they stand outside with no protection.* In the house, they found Connelly still breathing, but barely.
"They killed my family," his voice was too weak. Morse shook his head. They couldn't do anything now. Connelly had lost so much blood that his face was white. His freckles stood out like neon red dots.
"No, Sean, we have them. They're fine. We have them in protective custody."
"Not dead?" he whispered.
"Not dead."
"Charles. Not supposed to die either. Not the kids … so sorry …"
"Think now, Sean. Why did all this happen?"
"Computer program. Supposed to be just a new game. These men … that … woman … threats … money … I didn't know…" a final soft exhalation and he was gone.
Just like that. Here one minute, gone the next. It always rocked Finley to his core, this speed at which a person could cease to be.

Back at the station, Mrs. Connelly answered her cell. There was no one there. Soft breathing and then a disconnect.

CHAPTER NINE
Flagstaff, Arizona

Rena was beginning to enjoy her job and new life more than she thought possible. During the short time of her marriage to Charles, she had forgotten what it was like to be an individual. While she loved being part of a family, this was good, too. In the later days of her marriage, Charles had upset her, made her angry, and there were many wounded emotions. Now, there was no one but herself to answer to. If she was upset, it would be of her own making. Rena found it was far easier to live this way.

Her crying jags didn't sneak up on her quite so frequently. Sometimes an entire day would pass without tears. Maybe, because she'd had this family for such a short time, it was easier to forget that they had been a part of her life. Rena couldn't imagine how it would be to lose a family you had loved and known for a lifetime. That was likely a thing one would never recover from. Still, Rena felt a sense of guilt that she could so easily forget her family … that is, almost forget. Charles's face may have faded, but never those of the children.

Rena had been working nearly every day and actually had built up a little extra cash. She'd purchased new clothes and some makeup and was going out more, with either Sherry or Maggie.

She had made a mistake, though. One she hadn't yet realized. Without thinking about it, she used her VISA card for her purchases and signed her name. Rena was becoming too comfortable in her new life and would pay for it in time.

Maggie and Sherry were kindred spirits, like sisters to Rena. women she could talk to and almost tell the whole story. Oh, how she wanted to do just that! But if others knew what had happened to her family, it would be so hard to face them, look into their eyes, knowing that they knew … knowing that they would think about it every time they saw her. No, she would rather forget.

Whenever he was in the area of Flagstaff, Geoffrey ate at the Downtown Café and made it a point to be there to walk Rena home. He usually stayed for dinner of leftover café specialties before driving back to Scottsdale. The past several weeks had been a blur of activity. Geoffrey didn't actually ask Rena to go out on dates; more like the time they spent together seemed to happen naturally, without planning. It was all so easy and uncomplicated. Geoffrey was so kind and amusing. He told her stories that made her laugh, and he joked with her about how mysterious she was. He told her that he found her interesting and a joy to be around. Charles had told her that once ...

It was only 11 a.m. on a Saturday morning and Rena had the afternoon off. She was really happy, even though she knew she had no right to be. Rena had things she'd never had before: friends, a nurturing job, neighbors, and a wonderful companion. *Two companions*, she laughed out loud. What would Geoffrey think, to find out he was rated equally with her dog? So happy was Rena that she was unknowingly skipping in order to get home so she could ruffle Chee's ears as she leaned into her legs and begged for more.

Whirlwind

She loved her job, her apartment, her new friends, and her dog. Even life with Charles hadn't been this good. He had become reticent of late, and moody. He never seemed to sleep and even the simplest things set him off. Like the fight on that last evening. Peter wanted to go to the Science Museum for his birthday, and Charles said they were just there. When Peter started to object, Charles blew up at him. Guinevere sent the children to the other room and yelled at Charles that this was enough! Maybe he should go away for awhile and sort himself out. Her steps slowed and stopped. Something had been really wrong and she hadn't seen it. Not really seen it for what it was anyway.

When Rena arrived home, Geoffrey was sitting on her front step waiting for her. Her heart lifted at the mere sight of him. Chee was curled up next to him, but she took off at a run when she spied Rena. Rena loved the way Chee's entire body wagged when she was happy. It looked like it felt wonderful, like a dolphin spinning over the water before dipping back under again. She bent down to hug the dog and rub her ears. Geoff stood and dusted off the seat of his immaculate trousers.

"Ready to go?"

"Not until I change clothes."

Rena slipped into the house and donned a brand new sundress with Native American designs sewn onto huge pockets. The design was the crippled form of Kokopelli, the flute player. Hopi legend told that he was a trickster, a symbol of happiness, joy and some said, of fertility. Supposedly he had a way with the women. It was loose and airy and made her feel feminine. She also had new sandals. Too bad she had left all of her jewelry behind in Minnesota. Perfume, too. After running a brush through her terribly short hair, she announced she was ready to go. They were driving to see more of Geoff's artists and pick up works for his shop.

"Sorry, baby Chee!"

Rena kissed the dog and closed her into the house. Before the door was closed completely, Chee was on the sofa. Oh well. They took Geoff's large SUV, a Nissan. In Rena's opinion, it was a gas-guzzler of a vehicle and she was very glad it wasn't hers. She caught a glimpse of a few crates already in the back of the SUV. She assumed they contained artwork Geoff had already picked up from his suppliers.

"You've been collecting already!" Rena accused him playfully.

"Well, yeah, it takes you so long to get ready," he teased her right back. "But I saved most of them for you." The couple hadn't kissed yet, but Rena found that she really wanted to. *Maybe today?* They drove for about three hours, through desert lands and past flat mesas, to a town called Shiprock. The pine trees in Arizona were so different from those in Minnesota. These looked forlorn and sparse. Their stripped forms reminded Rena of the malnourished orphans she had seen in television ads for Save the Children.

Funny name for a town, Shiprock, in this neck of the woods, thought Rena. She assumed it had something to do with a rock formation. There certainly were enough of them here. The area was bleak, but beautiful, too. Wonderful colors: golds, siennas, reds, browns, blacks. It was stunning. It was also windy, forming sand into little eddies that kept blowing into her eyes.

They pulled into the parking lot of a diner where several Navajo men and women were waiting. They all entered the diner together and Geoffrey talked business while Rena looked at the art. She was completely amazed. The colors she had so admired were perfectly reproduced in the jewelry, the paintings, and the weavings. The oil paintings were large and expressed many views on the native scenery of the area. Rena thought she would enjoy

Whirlwind

one in her house. The paintings gave her ideas for painting her rooms, new livelier colors rather than the plain white she had now. She would have to talk to Maggie. One piece in particular, a necklace with an oblong silver backing and inlaid stones of turquoise, coral, shell, and onyx, stood out from the others.

"It's Zuni," someone said behind her. She turned to see an older man, stooped and grey, smiling at her. His face so wrinkled and leathered from the sun it was difficult to guess at his age.

"Most people don't know how to do this inlay work properly anymore. It is my son's design." He was so proud. "I taught him when he was very young."

"I think it is the most beautiful thing I have ever seen." Rena turned back to the piece. "Absolutely perfect."

"Yes, it is." The old man knew he had been a good teacher.

"Isn't it difficult to part with such a piece after working it for so long? Hard to sell it to a stranger?" Rena asked as she still looked at the necklace lying on the strip of black velvet cloth.

"I suppose it might be. Depends on who buys it, I guess," he answered her after thinking for a moment.

In fact, everything was perfect and Geoffrey must have agreed, because he took the lot. Handshakes were exchanged and the artwork was crated back up, tied together and placed into the SUV. They had been invited to the old man's home for a meal, and they drove for another hour. These roads were in bad shape and Geoff was glad none of the artwork was ceramic. The late afternoon sun livened up the colors even more, and Rena could hardly pull her eyes away from the view. Supper was tortillas and beans and a meat Rena couldn't identify, but it was delicious and tender and she ate more than her share. It tasted of hickory smoke, a flavor new to Rena. A snack was placed in a paper bag and they were once again on the road.

Rena was too full to stay awake, and she dozed before they were back onto the paved roads.

Geoff slowed and pulled the SUV on to the shoulder of the highway. "Wake up, Rena," Geoffrey said and touched her shoulder gently. "You do not want to miss this." The moon was rising, a huge yellow ball of a moon coming up over a desert hill, the sky sparkling with diamonds and inky deep, soft black. A lone coyote stood at the top of the hill in silhouette, and was soon joined by another. They lifted their noses into the air and sang in unison.

"It's just like a picture!" Rena sighed. "A picture of the southwest at its finest." Geoffrey leaned over and kissed her mouth. He unlocked his seatbelt, slid closer, and kissed her again. She loved the feel of his soft lips, gentle and slow. His kisses were nothing like the rush and urgency of Charles's. Rena sat up and pushed him away.

"I'm sorry," she said. "It's not that I don't want to do this ..." she didn't know what to say. She knew Charles was dead, but she felt strange about kissing someone else just the same. She felt like it was a betrayal, or worse, a letting go of his memory.

"No, I'm sorry, I thought you wanted me to kiss you, and you look so beautiful in the moon light."

"Oh Geoff, I do want you to. I do! Can we try this again?"

"What, now?" He grinned at her.

"Yes, I'm sure I can do better." And she did.

Geoff turned the ignition of the SUV off. Got out and walked around to Rena's door and opened it her.

"Do you want to come in?" she asked him.

"Are you sure?"

"I'm sure I want you to come in, but that's all I'm sure about. Why don't we just see, take it slow." Rena made coffee, decaffeinated or she'd never sleep, while Geoff took Chee out. They ate the bagged snack and drank the coffee,

Whirlwind

then kissed again. Geoffrey settled down on the sofa with a pillow and blanket, and Rena and Chee went up to bed. Sometime during the night, Chee deserted her and when Rena got up she found her sleeping on the sofa with Geoff.

"Did either of you get any sleep?" She laughed at their silly expressions.

"Chee did. She snores," Geoff said in disgust as he pushed the large and still growing dog off his chest and sat up. They stretched in unison and that made Rena laugh again. Rena made breakfast of coffee and muffins with jam. Geoff climbed back into his truck to head for his Scottsdale shop.

"I'll see you later this week?"

Rena nodded and he left. She got ready for a day at the Downtown Café and was sorry she hadn't kissed him good bye. Her dreams of the previous night had still been about her lost family, but they hadn't been bloody and dead. In fact, they had appeared happy in some sunlit world. Charles had smiled at her and waved goodbye. It felt like a blessing, a gift.

Susan M. Nelson

CHAPTER TEN
Flagstaff, Arizona

Maggie had invited the whole crew to her place for a picnic on Sunday afternoon, and John was trying out some new "box lunch" ideas. He said there was no good place to get a takeout picnic lunch and he thought there was a likely market for such a thing, with tourists off to see the sights. Many of the tourist locations offered little in the way of amenities and no food. Most of the tourist attractions, the ancient Indian ruins, petroglyphs, cave paintings and pueblos, were far from the city and John didn't want people to go hungry. There'd been enough of that in the Southwest, he'd said. He referred to his idea as Chaco Canyon Basket Specials.

When Sunday finally arrived, the weather was perfect for a picnic. Rena and Maggie had been getting the place ready, setting up a large table with various chairs. Maggie made her special sun brewed black and green tea with a hint of raspberry. Chee and Joey were playing fetch with a GI Joe doll that was missing his arms.

"The dog doesn't seem to bother Joey's allergies when they're outside," Rena noticed. Maggie looked up and at her son. She watched the play with a smile.

Whirlwind

"No, only in the house and only if Chee licks his face or hand and then he rubs his eyes." Her gaze grew distant. "He looks so much like his father sometime I forget …"

"Forget what, Maggie?"

"That his father is gone. That's all." And she went into the house for dishes. Soon the friends arrived and the sounds of cheering and play filled the afternoon—laughter, food, and scolding Chee when she got to close to Joey while he ate. It was soon discovered that he was tempting her by holding bits of his hamburger under the table. Maggie scolded the both of them and Chee climbed under Rena's chair to hide. This simple gesture of security the dog felt around her brought tears to her eyes. Her mind drifted back to the children; they had needed her too.

John's new picnic ideas were so good that most of the food disappeared. A Mexican flavored potato salad was the all around agreed favorite, but the handheld sandwich burritos were a close second. Soft flour tortillas were filled with an assortment of thinly sliced meat, cream cheese mixed with herbs, and chopped fresh vegetables. A chilled fruit pudding topped off the meal.

They all knew each other, some more intimately than others. It turned out that Maggie and John had once been out on a double date—a blind one, no less. And the others knew each other at least vaguely if not personally. By the end of the afternoon, they were close and companionable, the connections complete. Geoffrey and Joey liked each other immediately and had been playing tackle football without the ball. John and Sherry joined in and Rena and Maggie cheered them on. Chee broke it all up though, when Joey cried out. She thought he was hurt and pushed the adults not so gently aside. Once this was accomplished, she tackled Joey herself. When the boy began rubbing at his eyes, his mother put the kibosh on the sport and sent Joey inside to wash.

Maggie had a croquet set and they played for awhile, but Chee kept absconding with the balls. When the food was devoured and Joey fast asleep with his head in John's lap, Rena brought out the bottles of wine that Geoff bought for the occasion.

The conversation was quiet and philosophical for a while and then turned personal. Maggie told them all about the death of Joey's father in a huge multiple car accident that happened just before the child was born.

"We were so young. Our families didn't want to let us marry, but we were determined. We had been so much in love with the idea of a having a home and family together. We both loved art and music and the idea of combining the Navajo and Mexican traditions. Joseph was an artist and a musician. It was hard when he died, but I had both families to help me, and my brother Tomas was almost like a father to Joey. He lived here until recently. Joey misses him. I told my brother that it was time for him to seek his own destiny and find a life of his choosing," she smiled sadly. "Tomas will be back, he always comes back eventually. But he was here when I needed him the most."

Geoffrey sat with his arm around Rena's shoulders and talked about his family.

"My wife, Phillipa, didn't want children. They were all accidents. She is quite involved in her job at the BBC, and the children spend most of their time with a nanny. They were going to live with me, but Phillipa decided no. The judge agreed and now they are in England with their mother. I speak with them on the telephone, but …" he shrugged.

"I cannot believe how small my life seems without daily time with them. It isn't the same, is it? Children change so fast and I don't get to see that. Pictures … just are not good enough. I want to see and touch their faces with my fingers, hug them and read to them. All the good stuff that comes with being a parent."

Whirlwind

"But there's also the not-so-good stuff, as you put it." Maggie tussled her sleeping son's hair. "Joey has certainly got a mind of his own these days."

Geoffrey laughed. "Yes, well, I miss that, too."

John told them of his lifelong dream of a restaurant with gourmet specialties one couldn't get anywhere else, and how it consumed all his time. How he loved experimenting with the flavors of all cultures and mixing them together to make something completely new to the palate.

"This is the first time I have relaxed since we opened the Downtown Café," he admitted with chagrin.

Maggie lightly slapped his shoulder and chuckled.

"That isn't healthy. All work and no play and all that. We'll have to do something about your life."

She was teasing John and he liked it. "I'm a pretty good cook myself, you know," she added.

"Yes, I do know. Hey, would you like a job?" John thought he liked the idea of spending more time with Maggie and her small son. It surprised him as he wondered about why he'd let her slip out of his life those years ago.

"Maybe."

Maggie patted his hand which was still stroking her son's soft hair.

"Just maybe I would."

She also thought it might be a very good idea, and it surprised her, too, as she wondered about why she hadn't seen him again after their first blind date. She did remember that they had a good time and that they seemed to like each other.

Sherry yawned and stretched.

"We all have to be at work in a few hours. Let's go home." She pulled her brother to his feet and hugged everyone. "Bye all, see you."

Geoffrey led Rena to her house, kissed her lightly good night, and curled up on the sofa. Chee raced up the stairs and Rena heard her flying leap onto the bed. She followed and was still smiling as she dozed off. What an unexpectedly wonderful day.

For the first time in weeks, Rena wasn't bothered by dreams of any kind . . . bloodied children crying out for her in the dark ... Children she couldn't find as she frantically searched the house, finding only their dried blood and her butcher knife. Not even the happier dream of late, of children and dogs frolicking in cool green grass, of Charles waving to her from some far off place.

Geoffrey was already gone when Rena's alarm clock went off at 6 AM. He left a note pinned to his pillow: "Had a terrific time. See you soon. Love, Geoff."

"Love, huh?" Rena said out loud. "Perhaps. Could I be that lucky? Twice?"

Whirlwind

CHAPTER ELEVEN
St. Paul, Minnesota

Lynn Stone-Franklin was well on her way to oblivion by nine in the morning. Vodka with orange juice, vodka in her coffee, vodka with vodka in her glass now, alternating with the bottle when she misplaced her glass. She had to pee, but the bathroom was just too far away. *Hell, who even cared if she did it right here?* Right in Prescott's favorite chair that had cost her plenty. But no, she struggled to her feet and swayed as she moved down the hallway holding onto the bottle and the wall.

She loved this house. She loved her bathroom. She liked balance and insisted that she have it in all things. Even on their plates at dinner, way back when they had dinner together, a spot of all the food groups sat in its defined place and their colors blended so well. Just like the photographs in the magazines that she had copied. Everything had been done to her exact specifications and was so perfectly hers. It was an elegant space full of expensive things that all matched. Like the bronze statue of the Greek, who looked just like her Prescott with his clothes off, that stood in their bedroom with all the other bits of bronze. Or the new set of china that was the same colors as her dining room. Even the toilet paper was the same shade as the towels and the rug. Prescott never noticed how good she was at this sort of thing.

How could this have happened to her? Her anger had been mounting and it was beginning to overtake the fear. So, she was alone again, so what? She'd done that before. But this time there was no Charles to comfort and protect her and to pay her bills. This was the last of the vodka. Soon there would be just the red wine that she hated, and even that wouldn't last the day. *Where the hell did she last leave the car keys?*

Mrs. Rachael Connelly had to be told. Stanley and Axel went into the interview room together. Rachael took one look at their faces and her entire body slumped. Someone had previously brought in two cots and blankets and the young boys were sleeping in one of them.

"Sean is dead, isn't he?" Tears slid down her face. "I know he is. I can feel it. He wasn't an evil man, you know, just lately ..." She was crying now in earnest and her voice dwindled to nothing. Stanley, who was better at this than Axel, held her tightly until she stopped. Her children were stirring and she sat and held them close.

"We can go home, can't we?" asked Rachael.

"Not right now, I'm afraid. I think you are a target, just like the Stone family," said Axel.

"What should I do?" Rachael was out of her element and just as lost as her children. "Where can we be safe? I don't even know what to be afraid of. Or who."

"We'll take care of that for tonight, ma'am, and tomorrow we can all meet with someone who can help. Okay?" Axel was gentle. "Do you think you can answer some questions?" he probed. She nodded. She also reached into her purse and took out a small locked book, like a child's diary.

Whirlwind

"This was Sean's. He had me carry it, so it would never be left anywhere." She handed it to Axel. "But I really don't know anything about the business. When Sean's father ran it, it was a legitimate business, but lately …" Her voice trailed off again. She shook her head to clear it and began again. "Lately, Sean had too much money. I'd ask him about it and he'd say that business was good. But, I'm sure that wasn't the reason for the extra cash. He wasn't working much and he had let most of the staff go. I know this because his secretary called me to ask why. I couldn't tell her. I simply had no idea. Sean would have late night phone calls and he would leave the room to talk." She reached again into her purse. "This is his cell; he forgot to take it this morning. Or rather, he took mine by mistake. Last night it rang, but there was no one there when I answered it." This brief explanation had exhausted her. Axel wanted to get this small family to a hotel, set up a watch, and feed them a warm meal.

Finley contacted the telephone company for the cell phone records. *Damn,* he was frustrated. Most of the calls either went to or from different pay phones; drug stores, the airport, street corners, or out of the country, mostly to some small unheard of town in Mexico; and several to Scottsdale, Arizona, to untraceable cell phones. However, there were six calls to the Franklins' land line. *Interesting, very interesting. So, the Connellys knew the Franklins.*

Forensics finished with the diary in short order as it had been deemed a priority. No prints that couldn't be accounted for, and no other trace evidence of any kind. Axel picked it up and flipped through the pages. It seemed to be in some type of code. Again, he came across the Franklins' phone number. Several pages had times listed next to the initials P. F. Maybe his computer whiz could sort this out. Perhaps it was time for a visit to Mr. and Mrs. P. Franklin.

Axel collected one of his district cops and they headed out. He wasn't expecting trouble but that sister, Lynn Stone-Franklin, made him more than a little nuts. Axel figured he might need someone along just to help him curb his impatience with the woman.

The house was palatial. Three floors at least, and a four-car garage with another unattached and slightly behind the other. It sat on an acre of prime city property, the shore of White Bear Lake to boot, an address known for large and expensive homes. A fancy sailboat with a lower level for sleeping was parked in front of one of the garage doors. It looked new.

The house was multi-layered, with huge windows and massive pillars in the front. A Monsey Lawn Boys truck was parked in the driveway, explaining the formal lawn work and evenly trimmed grass.

Lynn Stone-Franklin, let the detective and officer in. *What, no butler?* She was shorter than he remembered, a stout woman who was still beautiful in a country-club way with a well cared for and expensive look about her. Or, she would have had that look, if she wasn't so drunk.

"Have you picked up that Guinevere yet?" she had fairly shouted at them. "I won't feel safe until you have her in custody!" She definitely looked ragged. Her hair was a nest of snarls, and her clothes were mismatched and stained with sweat and coffee and something red. *Wine,* Axel thought. She was slurring her words now. *Kind of early for this. Maybe she hadn't been sleeping.*

"I don't think you need to worry about your sister-in-law," Axel told her as he steadied her swaying body. "We don't think she was responsible for any of this."

"Of course she did this!" Lynn Stone-Franklin practically spat the words into his face spraying him with wine spittle as she roughly shook his hands off her shoulders. "Who else would?" she asked with complete certainty as she wobbled to a chair and flopped into it with

Whirlwind

no grace at all. A nearly empty glass of the red stuff tipped over on the coffee table, but Mrs. Franklin didn't notice. She flung her arm in a direction of the rest of the room and simply ordered the officers to "sit."

"We would like to speak to your husband, please. Is he here?" Axel wiped his face with his handkerchief.

"Prescott?" she was bewildered. "What for? He doesn't know anything about where Guinevere is." (She didn't say, "You fools!" But it certainly was implied.)

"Ma'am, we aren't here about Guinevere Stone and we need to speak to your husband." Axel was trying to be patient. He had already hung up on her once.

"Well, I don't know where he is." Her large blue, glassy eyes filled with tears that threatened to overflow. She slumped farther in her chair and tightly closed those eyes.

"He isn't here. He wasn't here yesterday either. His clothes are gone and our bank account is empty," she said, her voice barely audible. She reached for her glass, noticed the spill, and picked up the bottle instead. After another swallow or three, she continued, "I think he left me." "We haven't been getting along very well. Guinevere ... well ..."

The bluster was gone. She was really lost and maybe even a little afraid.

"Do you think we can see his office? Does he have an office here in your home?" asked Axel.

She nodded and gestured down a hallway. "Look whereever you want. He's gone."

Axel Finley and the officer looked for several hours, covering the entire house, but found nothing of interest. They did pick up an address book, an appointment calendar, and a hair brush. The latter was to check for prints and DNA. With the way bodies kept turning up, Axel wanted to be prepared. When they left, Lynn Stone-Franklin, was passed out in her chair. Axel covered her with an afghan and left a note listing what he had removed from the house. Both he and the officer signed and dated the slip of paper.

"What do you think, sir?"

"Doesn't look good either way, does it?"

"No sir, not good at all."

Things may have looked bad for Lynn Stone-Franklin, but they were looking up for the Finleys. Sally was coming home. Axel took the entire following day off from the office and arrived at the hospital at exactly eight in the morning.

"Axel! You know it will take them hours and hours to get the paper work ready and get the release signed by the doctors. First, they have to locate them and that is always difficult. And then there's …"

"I don't care how long it takes, I want to be here with you, so knock off the complaining," he teased and then kissed her. "I am so ready to bring you home. Robie has probably forgotten the both of us."

Sally got a wistful look in her eyes. Her glance took in the photo of Robie and herself sitting next to the bed. Axel had brought it to her weeks previously. The plastic frame was covered in fingerprints and maybe a few tears. Sally knew she was far too attached to the dog, but without having any children, she had to act out her maternal instincts some way.

"I can hardly wait to see him," was all she said.

Whirlwind

CHAPTER TWELVE
Flagstaff, Arizona

Sherry and John were bustling about the café when Rena walked in. Scents of cumin and coriander filled the room. They were training another waitress today, Rena remembered. *Great,* she thought, *I would like a little "me" time.* John needed help as well, but no one else had measured up to his standards yet. Rena found herself hoping Maggie would take him up on the job. They all got along tremendously well and it would be fun to watch Maggie and John together. There had definitely been a few sparks there.

John occasionally let Sherry cook, but he watched closely and insisted she follow his recipes exactly. Which, of course, Sherry didn't want to do. Rena and Sherry took the tables and let Constance do the counter. She had been a waitress for years and was quick and much more efficient than Rena at the job. One thing that Rena had already learned from this pro was not to waste any movement; don't just go to the counter for a pickup but carry something back to the kitchen. Or don't just get the requested catsup but also the coffee pot and refill on the way. It was like watching a modern dance. Breakfast and lunch over, Sherry, Constance, and Rena took a short walk just to get a break from the café. Constance was from Phoenix and knew the Pelleas Gallery.

"You just have to go there," she gushed. "It is the most beautiful place. Things you can't imagine. Expensive, though. For those rich tourists, you know." And she winked. "But I suppose it's the tourists that give us our jobs."

They were laughing together and on the way back to the café when, out of the corner of her eye, Rena thought she saw someone watching them. She whirled around and saw a man duck into one of the shops. The color drained from her cheeks. Something was familiar about him, but the man she was thinking of shouldn't be here in Flagstaff. So, if it was Prescott Franklin, why was he here?

"You go on ahead and I'll catch up," Rena said to the girls.

Sherry looked at her with concern. "Are you sure?"

Rena nodded. She walked back toward the shop and pretended to look into the window. Prescott Franklin was inside looking at her. She slowly turned from the window and walked away from the café. He followed.

"Do I know you?" He touched her arm. Rena knew that aftershave intimately and it still turned her stomach sour.

"I doubt it," Rena answered in her best imitation of Geoffrey's voice. "I just moved here from Washington and don't really know many people yet."

"Oh, you're from England?" Prescott smiled. "I guess I was mistaken. The girl I knew is from Minnesota." Rena nodded and brushed past him. She could feel his eyes follow her down the street. Rena walked several blocks out of her way, looking behind at several corners. She also hesitated at shop windows and stared at nothing just to see if he followed. She didn't see him again, though, so she felt

Whirlwind

it was safe to go back to the café. She had her Downtown Café T-shirt on, but never gave it a second thought.

Two days later, on a quiet Wednesday afternoon, she was in the kitchen helping Sherry with the preparations for the following morning while John baked bread. There was Prescott again. This time he was reading the menu at the counter. She held her breath and turned to Sherry in a panic.

"Do you see that man at the counter?" she whispered.

Sherry looked and nodded. "The good looking one?"

"Yes, I suppose he is. I can't let him know I'm here. Please, you go."

Sherry was perplexed, but she went to the dining room and waited on him. Coffee was all he wanted ... coffee and answers. Sherry, not knowing who Guinevere Stone might be, had no answers for him. When he was gone, Sherry went back to Rena for an explanation. By now, John also knew something was up, but Constance, thank God, was oblivious. She stood at the counter filling salt and pepper shakers, humming out loud.

"I need to go home now." Rena said. "But if you come over after work, I'll tell you what I can." Sherry looked thoughtful for a moment then hustled in back. She brought out huge sunglasses, a large straw bag that had "Come to Flagstaff!" printed on it, a scarf and a pillow. By the time she was done, Rena looked like a pregnant tourist. She laughed at her image and waddled out the door. All the way home, she worried. It was her own fault; she was supposed to have moved on by now. But she loved it here. She had friends, a job, and maybe a new love on the horizon. She prayed that she would not have to give it all up.

Safe for the moment, in her house and with her dog, she rid herself of the pregnant tourist charade and collapsed on the sofa. Rena thought she could trust Sherry, John, and Geoffrey with her story. She really wanted to tell someone. She thought about it and realized how little she actually knew. It would be a short and tragic tale. She absently ran her hand over Chee's soft coat as the dog rested with her large head in Rena's lap. "Chee," she said out loud. "What will I do with you?" Chee licked her hand and closed her eyes. There was just too much to give up so soon after finding it. Was she to spend her life loosing those she loved?

When the knock came, Rena was so lost in her thoughts she jumped and startled Chee into barking loudly. It was dark both inside and out. She peeked out the window, but it was only Sherry. And John. And Geoffrey. And Maggie.

Rena opened the door to her worried friends.

"I knew something was wrong," Maggie started. "You always hide yourself away."

"I knew it, too." Sherry added. "You are constantly looking over your shoulders."

"And, you are tense and restless." Geoffrey took her hands. "Plus there are the nightmares."

"Geoff, you've only seen me sleep once. And you weren't even in the room." Rena wondered how he knew about the nightmares and she winced that he did.

"And I didn't have to be in the same room to hear you cry out. Something has you running scared."

"You get no mail, no phone calls, and no visitors." Maggie added.

"And you are entirely too qualified to be a waitress. Plus you aren't particularly good at it." John smiled kindly at her. "But we like you too much to fire you."

"Okay. Here it is." They all sat around the small room and gave Rena their entire attention.

"Several months ago, I was married to a man who had three children. We lived in Minnesota. One day I went to the market, and when I returned home …" Rena gulped and brushed away the tears that were forming. "When I got home, someone had murdered … the children … Charles

Whirlwind

…" She couldn't help but burst into loud, deep sobbing. Geoffrey pulled her into his lap and cradled her like a child. When the sobs lessened enough, she stopped shaking. Looking into the shocked eyes of her friends, she continued.

"Charles, my husband, and I had only been married for a few months and didn't really know each other that well, I suppose, but it seemed good. Now, I don't think I knew him at all" Her eyes met Geoffrey's.

"He was still alive when I got there, but only for a few seconds. He told me to run. I could hear the killers still upstairs, so I did as he said. I ran. Somehow, I ended up here." She shrugged her shoulders and stopped. The room was completely silent. Even Chee sat at attention.

"I read about that in the paper," Maggie said. "The police are looking for you."

"Yes, and I expect the killers are also," Geoffrey added. John nodded.

"The guy at the café?" he asked. "Who is he?"

"He's my not-so-nice brother-in-law." Rena shuddered. "He likes to back me into corners and says inappropriate suggestive things, when no one else is looking, of course. I hate him. He's slimy and sleazy and I don't trust him for a minute. I think he has a condo in Arizona somewhere so that would explain why he's here, I guess. And his wife, Lynn Stone-Franklin, Charles's sister, despises me with a passion. I think she is … was … too involved with her brother, my husband. There was something unnatural about it. She is telling people that I killed her brother. I saw that in the paper, too. I just don't know what to do! I didn't do anything except go to the store. It all happened in the short amount of time that I was out."

John and Geoffrey were communicating quietly. "It's obvious that you can't go to the police if you think you'll just be arrested. At least, not until we know who is after you. Do you have any proof that you didn't do this? Or, I guess you have no idea who did?" John asked her. Rena shook her head.

"All I know for sure is that Charles was working on some secret project with a man named Sean Connelly. Something with computer program design, maybe a game about spying, or museums and ancient artifacts. I'm not really sure because I really wasn't that interested and he never told me enough to get me interested." Sherry jumped as if poked. "Sean Connelly! He was also murdered. The newspapers said there are no leads. I don't know if a connection has been made to your family."

"If this brother-in-law is in town and has already seen you, I think you need to leave for awhile, don't you?" Maggie looked around the room.

"Where could I go?" Rena slid off of Geoffrey's lap and slumped into the sofa. "At least here, I have you guys."

"Come with me to Phoenix. That's easy enough. I have an apartment above the shop. It's very private. Then we can figure out what to do without worrying about this Franklin fellow."

Chee climbed up onto the sofa and again laid her head in Rena's lap.

"Yes Chee, you too," Geoff told her.

So, it was unanimously decided that Rena and Chee would go to Phoenix with Geoffrey for now. Rena looked at Maggie. "Is it okay to take …" Maggie hugged her. "Chee belongs more to you than to my brother now."

"Let's leave now. Tonight." Geoffrey stood. "Pack what you need." Sherry grabbed the "Come to Flagstaff" straw bag and a couple of Safeway bags lying on the counter. She and Maggie went upstairs with Rena to pack her pitifully few things. Geoffrey quietly came up the stairs, tucked the two Safeway bags in his left arm, and took hold of the straw bag handles in his right. He looked at Rena and softly said, "I'll get Chee's food, bowls, and treats too." And he left. The women sat together for a minute on the bed.

"Thank you both so much for believing in me. You really are good friends already." Rena took their hands. "I never want to lose touch, no matter what."

"Hey, if you go to prison for a crime you didn't commit, we'll break you out!" Sherry laughed, but there were tears in her eyes.

"I'll keep this place for you," Maggie said.

Rena noticed how everyone simply assumed she was innocent. However, she was certain that the police would not share the same sentiment.

Geoffrey had Chee and her things in his vehicle. Rena got in the passenger seat. They waved, and drove away. The drive from Flagstaff to Phoenix took at least a week for Rena, who kept looking out the rear window watching for following headlights. Geoff patted her knee often, but it didn't calm her. She was leaving yet another comfortable home, and she was terrified.

CHAPTER THIRTEEN
Scottsdale, Arizona

They arrived at the Pelleas Gallery, and after walking Chee, settled in for the rest of the evening. The night time drive had been lovely, but Rena barely noticed. City lights as they approached Phoenix were the first thing she actually saw. They took her by surprise as Geoff came up over the crest of a hill that overlooked the valley holding the sprawling city. Phoenix looked flat.

The apartment above the gallery was spacious, if a little too modern for Rena's taste. It even had a brand new unused smell to it. Metal and glass furniture and leather chairs were placed artfully in front of a limestone and granite fireplace. Geoff lit the logs and warmed the chilly room. Rena was still a little surprised at how chilly it could get at night in Arizona where it was over 100 degrees during the daylight. They both were being uncharacteristically quiet.

Geoffrey carried Rena's bags into a rear bedroom.

"Rena? Come back here please."

She entered the lovely room. It looked like the room of a young girl, all pink-salmon colored with a golden glow from the lit bedside lamp.

Whirlwind

"Will this do?" Geoff asked, as he laid his hands on her shoulders.

"Your daughter's room?"

"Yes, Sabine. She's eight going on fifteen, which she seems to think is the age she will no longer have to listen to her parents' advice. Or so I've been told." His pleasant face darkened. "God, I miss them."

Rena sat on the bed. "Tell me about them," she invited. "I won't be able to sleep anyway. How about you?"

Rather than answer, Geoff sat next to her and talked. "There are three of them. Sabine is the oldest. Tristan is only four, and Jack is the baby. He looks just like his mother, blonde curls and violet eyes. He is chubby and smart, active and brave . . . he simply watches us all and absorbs everything. Like a sponge." Geoffrey took a deep breath. "They grow up so fast and I haven't seen them for months. Sabine looks like me—tall, dark, inquisitive, as does Tristan. She is the animal lover in the family, always finding some lost creature or another. She will be a veterinarian someday, I'm sure. I swear, she can read their minds. And Tristan will do whatever she tells him to do. It would not surprise me one bit if he becomes her assistant for the rest of his life. Glued at the hip, they are."

Rena took both his hands, with tears staining her own cheeks, she told him about her family. "My three stepchildren, Cathy, age three, Samuel, age six, and Peter, the oldest at ten, were a constant delight and source of wonder to me. I knew them only about six months before they were killed and I miss them more than I can say." They were quiet again.

"And your husband?" Geoff wanted to know more.

"Charles and I fell in love the first time we met. It was a whirlwind romance, probably too much so, in light of how little I knew about him. I don't know what he was into, but it couldn't have been good. I mean, he is dead now, isn't he? I loved him then, but that wasn't enough. Even in our young marriage, I knew something was off. It's really too bad I didn't do something about it before …"

"It's time to get some sleep. I'm just down the hall. He left the room and returned with a heavy quilt which he folded into a bed for Chee and placed it on the floor next to the bed.

"There won't be room for the both of you in that small bed," he said.

Geoff gave Rena a gentle warm hug that Rena totally gave into. They stayed in the embrace until Rena let out a long heavy sigh. He released her, gently kissed her cheek, and wished her a softly spoken "Sleep well."

As he departed, he pulled the door almost closed, leaving it ajar a few inches so he could hear any distressed nighttime sounds Rena may make. He actually did not expect to sleep much.

Rena undressed and climbed under the blankets. Chee turned in more than her usual three circles, then gave up and climbed on the bed after all. Rena didn't expect to sleep, but she did.

Geoffrey greeted her several hours later with a steaming mug of hazelnut coffee and a newspaper.

"It looks like the police are looking for your brother-in-law now, for questioning. A detective Axel Finley is looking for both of you. He has talked to your sister."

"Cei. Oh my God! Do you think the killers would hurt her?"

"Maybe, if they thought she could tell them where you are. We still don't know what they are after, do we?" Geoffrey was very solemn. "I'm going to buy one of those disposable cell phones and make some calls. Will you be okay for a while here on your own?"

Rena nodded mutely. When Geoffrey had gone, Rena had to fight with herself every time she walked by the telephone. She went over her sister's number each time she

Whirlwind

passed the phone, which was every few seconds, as she was pacing furiously. Chee following at her heels.

"Please let Cei be alright." She prayed. "Please please please."

Geoffrey returned with two disposable cell phones, one of which he handed to Rena. "Call your sister," he told her. Rena was already punching in the numbers.

"Cei! It's me. Are you okay?" Her words were rushed and loud to her own ears. She tried to still her rapidly beating heart and slow her voice. Rena didn't want to panic her sister any more than she might already be.

"Guin, thank God. What is going on? A detective called me. I've been so worried about you! Your family … Guinevere, I am so terribly sorry. What can I do for you?"

Rena told her what little she knew.

"I want you to stay somewhere else for a while. Far from the house. Can you do that? But I cannot talk about anything else just now," she added quickly when Cei began to interrupt.

"Yes, I can go to visit …" Cei began.

"No! Don't say it out loud. I think I know where you are headed anyway. Please just go. I'll call again. Go, little sister, go right now." And she disconnected the call. Geoffrey had been on the other cell phone and handed her a slip of paper with a number scrawled over it.

"This is the cell number for Detective Axel Finley. Do you want to call him? Do you want to tell him your brother-in-law is in Flagstaff?" Rena didn't know, so she said nothing.

"You don't have to tell him anything you choose not to, you understand. Maybe he can tell you something, though. Perhaps he knows who you need to fear."

She nodded and made the call.

Susan M. Nelson

CHAPTER FOURTEEN
St. Paul, Minnesota

Axel was yet again poring over his notes on this difficult case that wasn't going anywhere. Sitting next to the double bed that was far too small for both him and Sally, but which they slept in anyway, he also kept a wary eye on his wife. After they'd returned home, she'd been too exhausted to keep her eyes open. Mike Troy had returned Robie to her arms within minutes of their return and the dog was snuggled as close to Sally as possible, with only the tip of his nose visible from under her forearm. Axel took a mental photograph of the pair and tucked it away for safe-keeping.

He was about to go and bother his lab staff about the dinosaur covered computer and the coded diary yet again, when his cell vibrated in his pocket. He looked at the display and saw it was out of his area. First he ignored it, but it rang again. He took the cell with him outside the bedroom and quietly closed the door before he picked up.

"Finley," he barked into the phone, for some reason expecting a salesman and absolutely furious that someone had given out this number. Of course no one at the office would be so careless.

Whirlwind

"Detective Axel Finley?" inquired a soft female voice. "Are you investigating the Charles Stone murder?" This time he heard the voice hesitate over her words.

"Yes. Who is this please?" He had a feeling that he knew who was calling. It sounded like the Cei woman from Savannah.

"Have you heard from your sister?" he asked before he could get an answer.

"I'm confused. What sister? Cei?"

"Isn't Guinevere Stone your sister?"

"This is Guinevere Stone."

Axel stiffened, dropping his notes and knocking over his cold coffee, which rested on the hallway floor just outside the bedroom door. *A really stupid place to put it*, he realized too late. He wished he was in his office and was on his land line, so he could tape this call.

"Mrs. Stone! I've been looking for you. How are you? Where are you?"

"Detective Finley, I can be no help to you. I do not know what is going on. I don't know what else to say to you." Axel now could hear the tears in the words. His heart softened toward this frightened woman.

"Ma'am, I do have some news that will help, so please don't hang up. I know you had nothing to do with these murders, but I do think you need my help. Since we don't know who did this, we don't know where the danger lies. Two men, though, Sean Connelly ..."

"He worked with Charles on some secret computer deal," Guinevere interrupted.

"Yes well, he has been murdered as well. And we think Prescott Frank ..."

"Oh, no! He's here! Do you think he is part of whatever got my husband and children murdered? Detective, please ... I don't know how much more I can stand," Guinevere nearly shouted.

"Please, Miss, we aren't sure about him yet. We do need him for questioning, though."

"He should be questioned. He isn't a good man." Guinevere was very rattled, and Finley wanted to calm her.

"Can you come in for protective custody? he asked. We have taken in the Connellys as well,"

"No, I am not in Minnesota at present." And, although she didn't say this out loud, she probably never would be in Minnesota again. Ever!

"Can I come to you then?"

"No, that will not be possible. Please don't ask me. I have to go now."

"Wait! There's more. News that you are going to want to hear. Two of your children are alive," Axel blurted it faster than he'd anticipated doing, but he was afraid she'd go before he got the chance. That had the desired effect as she didn't disconnect. He could hear her sharp intake of breath over the air static.

"Two? Guinevere's voice was very low, just barely audible.

"The two youngest, Cathy and Samuel. They were able to recover from their injuries and are doing very well. Samuel is shy, but Cathy doesn't seem to remember anything. She keeps asking for new mommy, as does Samuel. Samuel, by the way, told us about the three men with ski masks."

"I never saw them ..." she began. "Sammy and Cathy?"

"Yes, ma'am."

"Please detective, don't give them to Charles's sister, Lynn. She drinks far too much and she doesn't really like chil ..." her voice dropped off to nothing.

Axel could hear ragged breathing, like she was having difficulty with emotions.

Whirlwind

"Mrs. Stone, in your husband's will, the children are to be in your custody. However, if something happens to you, Mrs. Stone-Franklin does take custody of them."

It took a few seconds for that to sink in. "Detective, nothing has happened to me."

"Not yet, no." Axel felt he was losing her.

"I will call you again," Guinevere told Finley. She was gone.

Rena sat with the phone in her hand for several long minutes. Finally, Geoffrey took it from her.

"What did he say?" he inquired after waiting patiently until he felt he'd waited long enough.

"Cathy and Samuel are alive." Her voice was soft with wonder and shock. "But I was sure they were all gone." She looked into Geoffrey's eyes. "I was so sure!"

"Do you think he is lying to you about them?"

"Maybe. No, Detective Finley said the children have been asking for 'new mommy.' That's the name they gave me. 'New mommy.' I believe him."

"What do you want to do, Rena?"

"I don't know what to do!" her voice was rising with her growing panic, now there was so much more at stake.

"He said there likely is a threat from whoever killed the family, and I don't even know anything. Charles's partner has been killed also. And 'He should be questioned … something about Prescott Franklin. Oh no! I said he was here. I gave them a clue.'"

"Not really, as you didn't say where 'here' is," Geoffrey reminded her.

Geoffrey thought all this over as he paced the room. "Did Charles use a computer?"

"Yes, he had one at work and he and the kids shared one at home."

"The same one? There won't be anything on that hard drive, then," Geoffrey mused.

"Well, not necessarily. Charles invented a program that could have parts protected by a password and parts that could be easily accessed by the oldest child. The babies weren't interested yet. So they shared. We were about to get another …"

"Do you know his password?" Geoff was more interested now. Rena shook her head.

"No matter. Let's go to the gallery and talk to my managers about this computer."

He took her hand and they went down the outside steps. The sun was very warm at this early hour and Rena felt the blast. It wasn't, however, enough to warm her. It felt to her that arctic water had replaced the blood in her veins. Geoffrey unlocked the rear door deadbolt and relocked it after they entered. He left the light turned off, led Rena through the back room both by feeling his way and by knowledge of the space, and entered the store proper. The bright light there was dazzling, filling every corner with sunlight. No electric lights were needed here. The natural lights showed the wonderfully beautiful works of art to perfection. Even with all she had on her mind, Rena was awed. She wandered around gently touching everything. She was looking at a mural painted directly on an interior wall, of a mesa over a canyon, river, and a-turn-of-the-last-century Navajo village. The colors were muted and sharp at the same time. Rena felt Geoff behind her as he slipped something around her neck.

"I saw how you admired this piece," he said, as he kissed the nape of her neck. It was at once the most intimate touch Rena had ever experienced. She looked down to see the Zuni necklace from Shiprock, and she relaxed into him as his arms slid around her body and he held her close.

"Geoffrey, I couldn't do this without you. You are a rock and my best friend already."

"More than a friend, I hope."

Whirlwind

"Yes, more than a friend." She turned into his arms and they shared a long gentle hug, the all encompassing kind.

"Well, what have we here?" A chipper, cheerful voice came from the doorway. "Hope I'm not interrupting a private moment. If I am, of course you can just tell me to sod off."

"You are, of course, but let me introduce you." It was obvious to Rena that this was a friend.

"Albert, I would like you to say hello to Rena. Rena, this is Albert Meadows. He and his partner, Winston Hensley, run this place for me. Where is Win anyway?"

"He's getting us some real coffee, not that American swill you have Jennifer make." Albert grimaced. Just then, two more people entered the shop.

"Win and Jennifer, I'm guessing." Rena held out her hand which was firmly grasped, then momentarily held by Win and barely touched by Jennifer. *Oh my,* Rena thought, *she doesn't like to share her boys.*

"I need to get to work on the invoices," Jennifer announced and went into a small office in the corner, behind the mural.

"Sorry for that." Albert gestured toward the office. "She is on a mission on Mondays."

"Jennifer!" Geoffrey called. "Please watch the shop for a bit. We will be back soon." A hand waved at them from the office door.

"You two, come with us and bring your laptops."

Seated around the kitchen table with computers logged on to the store's Wi-Fi, Geoff explained. "Rena's husband was working on a project on a notebook computer, which we do not have on us, but need to see. What can you do?"

Winston flexed his fingers and cracked his knuckles and settled into his machine. Albert chuckled at his serious attitude. "Okay, my gorgeous brainchild, what next?" He patted Win's head like he was a favored pet.

"Name."
"Charles Montgomery Stone."
"City and State."
"St. Paul, Minnesota."
"Company?"
"Twin City Design and Engineering. Co-partner is Sean Connelly. I don't know anyone else, or who their boss was, though," Rena told the team.

"You could try Prescott Franklin, too," Geoffrey added. He looked at Rena who nodded. "Or maybe Lynn Stone-Franklin."

Winston sat back and flexed again. "We need a password here. Any ideas?"

"You are in Charles's laptop already?" Rena was shocked.

"A piece of pie," Winston answered. "It is already on and open."

Albert laughed fondly. "He means it was a piece of cake. He is still having trouble with American slang."

"Password, people!" Winston was fairly dancing in his chair and Rena realized how much he loved this. She gave him names and dates, none of which worked. She thought about it.

"Try King Arthur or some variation," she said. Win raised his eyebrows but tried.

"No. Nothing."

"Maybe Camelot."

A quick shake of Winston's head.

"Try Tingtagle." This got the raised eyebrows of all three men. "It's a long story," Rena shrugged. "Just try it."

They did. "We're in. His computer is still on and running at the moment so somebody is using it. Unless it's one that's always on? But I'm going to want to hear this story."

Whirlwind

Winston grinned. Furious typing went on for about an hour. Both men were wizards at the computer. Geoffrey hooked up a printer but Winston frowned.

"That will take too long and I'm not sure how long we have. Someone else is here. Give me a clean flash drive, at least 64 gig."

Geoffrey rummaged through his many pockets and found a flash drive.

"This isn't good." Winston looked at Rena. "Bloody hell. This program could cause a lot of drama."

"What do you mean?"

"Whoever has this could just about break into any software program anywhere. Are you sure you want this?"

Geoff and Rena exchanged a look. "How about this? You copy what is there and erase it from Charles's machine?" Geoff offered.

"Can copy. Cannot erase without having his computer in front of me." Winston looked frustrated. "But we do need to get rid of this before anyone else sees it, and that will be soon. Someone is trying as we speak. Holy calves! Look at all these lock codes. Museums and art galleries all over the world."

"Holy calves? Do you mean cow?" Rena laughed.

Albert got a huge evil grin on his face. "Move over old chap. This is my area." As the information downloaded to the flash drive, Albert typed quickly. "This is a virus I have been developing. It is a combination of nothing and jibber-jabber. It is only junk and it will replace Charles's words and figures with nonsense." Winston removed the flash drive and Albert hit "enter." "There, finished." The entire project took less than two hours.

"Tell us," Geoffrey said.

"Look at this." Win showed them the computer screen. He had slipped the flash drive into Albert's notebook and opened the program. It was filled with tiny sketches, hieroglyphs, and a short description next to each glyph. "It looks like Charles was working on what he thought was a computer game about government spies and illegal Mayan or Aztec antiquities. The player can break into computer systems in museums and art galleries and private collections to gather up the antiquities. The player has to sort out difficult codes and messages to gain access and unravel complicated clues. Someone else saw it as a real possibility. Probably when Charles figured out what was happening to his "game" he transferred it to his home computer thinking it was safe from prying eyes. It wasn't. But I don't think anyone has it yet."

"And they surely won't get it now." Albert laughed at his genius.

"Not unless they get this flash drive." Geoffrey handed it to Rena, who didn't really want to touch it.

Let's just hold onto it for a little while. Then we can dispose of it. Okay?" suggested Geoff.

"Okay," she agreed. "How do we know Charles wasn't in on it too?"

"Because it looks like he was trying to undo it all, trying to make it into a less realistic game. Hiding what he had accomplished, and turning his information into a fantasy."

She wasn't sure why, but this made her feel better.

"Now, the King Arthur story, if you please." Albert was not going to let it go. "I know everything there is about the mythical king/man. He is my ideal man," he said with pride. "It has been my lifelong quest."

"So did my mother. We were put to bed every night with the stories. There isn't much else to tell. She was Irene, which she thought was ordinary. She married an Arthur, and they named their children Igraine Guinevere, Merlin Mystic, Lance Arthur, and Cei Morgan. Our pets were Pendragon and Pellinore, the dogs; and Nemue, a cat. I am Guinevere." She shrugged.

"I thought you were Rena," Albert said.

Whirlwind

"Yes, well, I'm not."

Geoffrey burst into laughter. He laughed until they all were laughing as well. "And I am a Pelleas! All we need now is a round table, Excalibur, and Camelot. What a world. No wonder you nearly passed out laughing when I introduced myself at the restaurant."

"My mother always said what goes around, comes back at you." Rena wiped tears from her smiling cheeks. Then said, "For now, we'll stick to Rena."

Geoffrey and Rena told their Flagstaff story to Albert and Winston, who listened, spellbound.

"Not a word to anyone gentlemen. I am trusting you two with our lives." He turned to Rena and was startled to see tears running down her face as she watched a young mother with three children in tow entering the shop across the street. She was holding a baby and leading two boys who were gripping her skirt. As Geoff stood watching, an overwhelming wave of protection flowed over him for this woman. It did not take him by surprise, however, as he had felt this way since the first time he'd spoken with her at the cafe. He had detected a fragileness in her.

Susan M. Nelson

CHAPTER FIFTEEN
St. Paul, Minnesota

In the lab at the Headquarters/Central District building, Axel was urging the technician, Bruce Wilcox, to finish. Bruce said he was very close to finding something on Charles Stone's computer. After sorting through all the photo galleries, email, and children's games, he found a coded batch of files, hundreds of sketches, charts, diagrams, and more. There was even an invented alphabet of what appeared to Bruce to consist of Mayan glyphs. under the heading *The Game; Museum Heist.* He was still working on the password, and had run through every family connection he could come up with. Suddenly, right in front of his eyes, the words melted into total nonsense, and the unopened coded files disappeared.

"What the holy hell!" he exclaimed.

"What's the matter?" Alex asked, worried.

"I don't know. The files are changing into this, this nothing. It is something I've never seen before and I can't stop it." The tech showed Axel the screen. A long series of letters, numbers, and symbols filled the monitor in rapid secession down the computer page and kept on going. There didn't seem to be any way to put a halt to the process. Even taking it offline was futile. The virus was already firmly implanted. The entire space of the screen was solid and was scrolling down and filling in as they watched in horror.

"Is it some type of code or something in a computer language?" Axel wanted to know. He didn't really understand any of this, but he was aware that he should learn it. In his opinion, police work was getting way too technical. Crime solving used to be easier; gather the clues and catch the criminal and put them away. Hands-on and instinct, more gut and less technology was the old way. In these newer labs, nearly every bit of information could be gathered online. All one needed was a partial fingerprint.

"You know, I don't think so. It's too solid, no breaks. Someone has just destroyed the files. I can work on it, but I think it's gone." Bruce shook his head. "All of it."

"See what you can do with it, will you?" Finley was at a loss. This entire case was making him doubt his abilities.

Back in his office, he found a message waiting for him from his secretary. Mrs. Guinevere Stone had used her credit card in Flagstaff, Arizona. Axel was really stunned. He thought she was much too careful to make such a mistake. And, if he had this information, the killers probably did as well. A loud knock at his door preceded the entrance of Stanley Morse and Lynn Stone-Franklin. Mrs. Franklin was pale and shaky and sloppily dressed, unlike her public appearances. Her hair was disheveled and she wore no makeup. No, that's not quite right, she had makeup on, but it was days old. She looked a decade older than the last time he'd seen her.

"Mrs. Franklin." He nodded to Morse and they entered his office and sat. "What can I do for you?"

Lynn Stone-Franklin pulled a tattered tissue from her sweater sleeve and wiped at her eyes. Axel's mother used to do that—carry tissue in her sweater sleeves. She would forget it was there until she did the laundry and the clothes would come out covered in lint.

"I heard from my husband," she whispered, her voice ragged from either screaming or sobbing. "He was calling from our condo in Scottsdale. He told me he was in New York City, but I could hear the clock in the background, and I know that clock! I have lain awake many nights waiting for him and listening to that damn clock," her voice rising with each word until she was shouting.

Axel and Stanley gave her a few minutes to compose herself.

"I don't know why he is there, but I'm sure he is. I could hear a woman's voice. He has a *woman* there, too! He said we have no money and he is getting a divorce. We do have money though. My father left me money, but it doesn't seem to be in the bank any more …" Mrs. Franklin's voice trailed off again into a weak whisper. "I don't know what to do."

"Did he say anything else, ma'am?" Morse prodded her.

"He said he was tired and frustrated and couldn't find what he was looking for. Mostly, he wanted to know where that bitch, Guinevere, was. As if I would know that!" She sniffed loudly. "Prescott said he had to find her, that she had something of his. He's going to call me in a couple of days to see if I learned where she is. I'm to be watching the house, but how can I do that with your police all over the property? He will be very angry if I can't tell him anything new."

She looked at the detectives with fire in her red eyes. Axel wondered how she could still be willing to help and take orders from a man who obviously didn't care for her, was divorcing her, and had probably taken her money and security. It seemed to him it was a textbook case of an abused spouse. He thought warmly of his own supportive wife, realizing just how lucky he was. All he felt for this wreck of a woman was pity. He walked away and left her to Stanley.

Whirlwind

So, Prescott did not have whatever had been erased from the hard drive, who did? Mrs. Stone? Or the yet unnamed instigator of this mess? All he could do was wait for her to call again. Looking at his phone, he realized that he hadn't talked to Sally all afternoon. That was unusual, especially since her release from the hospital, and he had a bad feeling. He punched in his home number and listened while it rang a dozen times. Sally didn't say she was going anywhere that day, had she? Finally, the receiver was picked up.

"Sally? Are you there?" No reply.

"Sally!"

"I can't find ... nothing makes ... I need ..." she sounded weak and disoriented. Axel was out the door and racing for his car. He thought about calling 911, but experience told him he could get to Sally before the paramedics could, and he knew exactly what was needed. The Finleys went through this every six months or so. Sally had been a diabetic for fifty years and could no longer tell when her blood glucose level was dangerously low. Often his first clue was Sally not making any sense, as was the case now, or wandering around the house aimlessly. Once, she threw her book across the room in frustration and burst into tears because the novel, which she had been reading for days, suddenly made no sense to her. He kept saying her name into the phone but didn't know what she heard. He turned on his lights and siren and flew down the streets. Less than ten minutes later, he let himself into his home and found his wife in a crumpled heap next to their bed. She was shivering and had pulled the quilt halfway off the bed to cover herself. Their small dachshund, Robie, was whining and pawing at her. Sally's reading glasses were on the floor and twisted with a lens missing. She looked up at him and started to cry. Her short, curly brown hair was plastered to her head with sweat, and her dark blue eyes were jumping around the room.

"I'm so … sorry! I don't know what … I was reading and … I … the floor."

"It's okay, sweetheart." At least she recognized him this time. That wasn't always the case. Axel helped her onto the bed and tightly wrapped her in a heated blanket they kept just for this. When her blood sugar was too low, she couldn't seem to warm up. Sometimes her actual body temperature would drop. Axel got a juice box from the kitchen and forced her to sip. She didn't want it.

"Please, sweetheart, drink this." She tried but it was almost like she had forgotten how to swallow. Axel opened the drawer next to the bed and pulled out a glucagon kit, which was a syringe with a high level of glucose, basically sugar solution. He injected it into his wife's thigh. Within minutes Sally was returning to her normal self, as the glucagon brought her blood sugar level up.

"I did it again, didn't I?" she looked at him, for the first time making eye contact.

"Yes, Sally. But you'll be fine now. Do you want some juice?"

She shook her head.

"Let's check your blood sugar, okay?" Axel was so used to doing this, it took only a few seconds. He pricked her fingertip and put the blood on the strip already in the meter.

"Fifty-seven, that's still too low. Drink this." He pushed the juice box into her hand. This time she drank, now aware of her condition as the fog lifted from her mind. Only now was she able to cooperate with him.

"I think I tried to check this myself." She pointed to the droplets of blood on the quilt. They were flower petals in the pattern, not blood. She was still confused. Axel said nothing.

"I'm so tired," Sally's face sagged and she shivered. This always happened to her after an insulin reaction.

Whirlwind

"You sleep then. I'll check your blood sugar in a half hour or so." Axel kissed his wife lovingly, retucked the heated blanket, turned the heat setting to low, and he left the room. His own heart rate was slowing by now and he was tired also.

This scared him to death each time it happened. So much could go wrong! What if she hit her head? Broke a limb? Fell down the stairs?

Once she left a burner on the gas stove lit. He knew she wasn't at fault, but he hated to leave her alone. Retirement couldn't come fast enough. He wandered into their kitchen and, sure enough, there were small splatters of blood on the counter in front of the microwave. Sally kept her supplies in the drawer just below the microwave and used the counter space to test her glucose level. There was a blood test strip on the counter and two on the floor. Axel cleaned up

everything and shook his head in frustration. *God, how he wished he could do more for her.*

Sally asked him, more than once, why he'd married her and why he didn't just chuck it in and marry a healthier woman. Why he put up with all this nonsense and worry. He'd responded that he loved her and that was that. In actuality, Sally was his life. Without her in it, he would not be able to keep his own life together. He'd be lost, broken, and aimless.

Sally was sound asleep when he next checked on her. The blood sugar was up to 120, so he felt he could return to work. She would sleep for hours now. Maybe even into the night. She spent all of her energy fighting against her body during an insulin reaction. Once her blood sugar had dropped to less than forty, thirty-six he thought it was. He'd almost lost her that time. That was when the paramedics told them about the glucagon kits that they could purchase at any drug store. Now they always had one or two on hand even though the cost was well over a $100 a shot, for basically just sugar water. It had stunned Axel in the beginning, but these days he was just happy to have them.

    Robie was tucked up next to Sally with only his tail sticking out from under the blanket. He growled quietly to let Axel know that he didn't want to be disturbed. Axel gently brushed the still damp hair from Sally's brow, tightened the quilt around her shoulders, growled back at the dog, kissed Sally, and left for the station.

    Lynn Stone-Franklin was firmly planted at his desk when Axel entered his office. He sighed so heavily, she raised her eyebrows at him.

    "I'm sorry to be such a burden to you. If you could just tell me when you will release my brother's home? I want to get it on the market."

    A little soon, isn't it? Axel was thinking.

    "I suppose I could finish over there some time tomorrow or the next day. Soon enough?" Is what he said out loud. She nodded curtly and left. Thank God! Axel had learned that the Stone residence shared by Guinevere and Charles was actually in Charles and Lynn Stone-Franklin's names, not Guinevere's. He guessed there hadn't been time to change that deed yet.

    Lynn Stone-Franklin slowly drove past her brother's home. Twice. She saw no police presence, but the yellow crime scene tape was still all around the property. Who would buy this place? People were always so leery after a murder on a property, especially when three children are involved. She felt no loss, no usual pain; it just made her angry. There were no maternal or familial emotions for those lost children, and only a twinge for her brother. Charles had been her safety net, nothing more. The children had been loud and bothersome and took far too much of her brother's time away from her.

Whirlwind

She parked two blocks away and snuck around the rear yards of the houses until she reached Charles's, in case there were officers watching the house. Her key still unlocked the kitchen door, so she went inside. The place had a closed-up, foul odor, and she almost turned around. The blood was everywhere—dried, but visible even in the dim light. She'd had no idea. Ignoring the chalk lines of the children, she hesitated for a moment at those of her brother. In her own, very cool way, she had loved him. Probably too much. She didn't allow herself to dwell on that as it made her uneasy. She rarely let her mind venture into that territory. She did realize, though, that no other man in her life had ever matched her feelings for Charles.

Now she just needed to sell his house. She didn't even bother to look around, but went straight to the liquor cabinet. Lynn knew exactly where the liquor cabinets were located in every place she'd go. She needed some courage. And that only came from a bottle.

Lynn found a bottle of vodka, struggled to remove the cap, and drank. *Ah, better already.* She took several more swallows and wandered back to the kitchen. Lynn was feeling sorry for herself and her rotten luck with men. She had been good to Prescott, given him total access to her money and body. The money he helped himself to too frequently, her body less and less. She was pretty sure he had someone else. There had been that woman's voice in the background when he called from Arizona. *Damn him anyway!* And she had tried so hard to please him, to give him whatever he wanted. Lynn had even seen him mooning over Guinevere. One man wasn't enough for the bitch!

Lynn Stone-Franklin drank until she felt more relaxed. She didn't really know what she was doing here. She looked around the house with little interest. It was far too bland and tasteless for her. Children's things lay about everywhere and nothing matched. None of the furniture was even remotely like the other pieces, and it almost offended her to see it. There was entirely too much wood, not nearly enough over-stuffed and soft, comfortable furniture here.

Her poor brother. He had deserved so much more. If she had been a more charitable woman, she might have admitted that Guinevere hadn't had time yet, to add her own style … if the woman had any. She set the bottle down and turned to use the tiny bathroom just off the kitchen, when she tripped over her untied shoe laces. *Damn those new running shoes anyway. Yeah, like she ever ran anywhere. Ha!*

"Whoa!" she giggled, and slid to the floor along the cabinets. She rested there, decided it would take too much energy to stand again, and crawled into the bathroom.

"Ouch!" Lifting her hand, she saw a very small cut on her palm.

"What the hell?" She carefully felt the edge of the floor and found the offending object. "Oh my God!" She recognized it as the same style sterling silver medical alert charm she had purchased for Prescott to attach to his wristwatch. It had to be made to order because her husband wouldn't wear the plain metal ones. ***Not** her important man!* He had severe reactions to antibiotics and needed to wear this. But, she realized, he hadn't had it on for several days before he left. *How did it get here?* She looked at it more closely. There was blood on it. Old, dark black-red, dried blood. Who had it belonged to? Her darling Prescott?

Whirlwind

CHAPTER SIXTEEN
Phoenix, Arizona

"What shall we do with this damn flash drive?" Geoffrey asked the group.

"Is it worth anything, do you think?" Albert idly flipped it in the air. "It must be, since it cost lives." He realized what he had said and quickly looked at Rena. "I'm so sorry, love!"

"No, you're right. It must be worth a price to someone, but I just want to destroy it."

"I think maybe you should call that detective fellow. Finley?" Winston looked pensive. "Perhaps this information could get you off the hook and get the killers arrested."

All four of them seemed to agree to that, so Geoff handed her his phone.

"Finley here," he answered before Rena knew what she wanted to say. "Hello? Is anyone there? Sally?" He had a moment of panic.

"Detective Finley, this is Guinevere Stone. I think I found something." She proceeded to tell him about recovering the computer program, while mentioning no names. Nor did she tell him how it had been accomplished. She pretended she had it all along.

"You're the one!" Finley exclaimed. "We were examining Charles's computer when the files disappeared in front of our eyes. So you copied them? What is it? I was afraid whoever did this has what he or she wanted. Ma'am, I can't tell you how relieved I am." Axel literally wiped the sweat from his brow.

At this point, Rena could see no reason to deny anything. "Yes, but I don't want to keep it. All I can say is, it seems Charles thought he was working on one of his computer game ideas and someone else took it seriously and planned to use the software for another purpose altogether. Perhaps to illegally break into files? Maybe museums and galleries? I don't understand most of this. I don't know how this could be used." Rena was tired. More exhausted than she ever remembered being. She felt deflated as she sank into a chair. Geoffrey took the phone from her.

"Detective, this is a friend of Mrs. Stone's. What do you suggest we do?"

"I already told Mrs. Stone, she should come in for protection. We still aren't sure who all is involved. Nor do we understand just how much danger she is in. This would all be so much easier face to face." Then he remembered his words with Lynn Stone-Franklin, and asked for Guinevere again.

"Mrs. Stone, your sister-in-law thinks Mr. Franklin is in Scottsdale. I think he is a threat to you."

"Scottsdale! I saw him in Flagstaff!" With a sharp intake of breath, Rena realized her mistake. Axel did as well, but ignored it for the moment. He made a sudden decision.

"Guinevere? Mrs. Stone? I want to meet you somewhere, anywhere, and get that computer program from you. Next, I'll make it known to the reporters that we have uncovered information that points to a motive for the murders. I want you to go into hiding, if not protective custody, until this is resolved. I know you did not do this thing, and I want you safe. We don't want any more bodies. We need to work together on this. Your children have no one else." Axel tossed in that last bit knowing she wouldn't refuse.

That was quite a speech for Finley, but he believed every word. He was sure of it, and when he was this sure, he was never wrong. It's what made him a good detective. Over his career he'd learned that when he was completely positive about something, no matter if the evidence suggested otherwise, he was usually right. Without even meeting her, Axel knew without a doubt that Mrs. Stone was innocent.

"I will call you," Guinevere told him, and hung up. She looked around at the worried faces. "I just need to think about what to do. Please go about your day."

"Okay, boys." Albert stood and pulled Winston to his feet. "We've a shop to open. Come down if you need us."

"We need a break. Let's unpack the new art. Okay?" Geoff saw that Rena needed a distraction.

It sounded good to Rena, and they descended the steps as well. The crates were piled up at the rear of the shop and Albert was already at them. Rena wandered around the space looking at everything and trying to take it all in. Each piece she looked at was amazing. Some works were bold and daring and very modern. Others were subtle, soft, and pliable. Colors were all over the charts as were textures and design. Rena was most taken by the turquoise and coral jewelry and the hand woven rugs and fabrics. Her fingers kept reaching for the necklace Geoffrey had given her. Was that just today? Once again, time was running together and the days were jumbled and mixed up. Her thoughts turned often to Cathy and Sam. She had no idea how to get to them without exposing herself and Geoffrey. And the children, as well.

People were coming and going, looking, buying, and asking questions. Every so often, an artist would inquire about displaying her or his work. This was a lively shop and Rena was getting into it. She listened closely to Winston, Albert, and Geoff as they explained the pieces and was captivated herself. She thought if she could learn about the artists, pieces, and pricing, she might like to work here. It would be completely different from all of her other jobs. Change was supposed to be good for a person, right?

Jennifer worked in the office most of the morning, left for lunch and didn't come back. Albert and Winston got take-out for all of them from a Chinese restaurant down the block. They sat around the bright space on the now empty packing crates, ate, and chatted. Rena was looking more closely at the building itself. The ceiling was high, over twelve feet in places; the walls, soft shades from the desert, were cut into odd shapes in order to best display the works. She was about to ask about the architect when the conversation took a different turn.

"I've been thinking about the computer program on the flash drive," Winston said, still chewing. "I think you need to get rid of it somehow. Either give it to the detective or destroy it. Perhaps if the detective has it and makes it known that he does, the focus will shift away from you."

"Could you mail or email it?" Albert suggested. "Except, I suppose it could be intercepted if someone were watching the post or hacking the inspector's email." *Or watching you*, he thought, but did not utter it out loud.

"I think she'd have to hand deliver it, in order to be sure the correct person got it," added Winston.

"But, would she then be arrested?" Albert shook his head. "Too much of a risk."

"No," Geoff said. Detective Finley has ruled Rena out as a suspect."

"If I went back to the Twin Cities and gave Finley the flash drive, maybe he'd let me bring back the children. That would be worth the risk." Rena was talking herself into doing just that.

"Call him first. We can listen to the conversation and each of us can gauge his words. It might give us a larger picture of the way things stand. He doesn't seem to believe you are guilty, but he is a policeman who is bound to follow laws and protocol." Geoffrey was worried about Rena making any move that would endanger her. "Please, Rena. At least call him again."

Rena nodded and reached for the cell phone.

Susan M. Nelson

CHAPTER SEVENTEEN
St. Paul, Minnesota

Lynn Stone-Franklin sat in the utter silence that filled her brother's house, looking at the blood covered medical alert tag. She was one 100 percent sure it belonged to her husband, her Prescott. No doubt about it. She finished off the bottle of vodka and started in on the gin. Lynn had never liked the taste of gin, but the vodka was flowing through her blood stream now, and she couldn't really taste it. Her anger was stronger than her dislike of the gin. All she knew was that she wasn't drunk enough yet. Looking around the house, she wondered what it was here that Prescott wanted so badly.

"Prescott! You bastard!" she screamed her frustration to no one. *Who did he think he was, anyway?* She was Lynn Stone, a real catch in her day. Rich and beautiful and accomplished, she had given up a satisfying career in real estate because he wanted her at home. Everyone said he was the lucky one. Lynn knew she had made a mistake in marrying a man so far beneath herself, but she'd loved him, her bastard con-artist husband. The man who'd promised her the world. Not anymore. At least, she sure didn't want to love him. Love and hate could get so entangled, they were virtually the same emotion.

Whirlwind

She was crying now, but she knew what to do. Lynn gathered everything she could find that was even a little bit flammable: nail polish remover, kerosene for the lamp, turpentine, booze, charcoal starter fluid, rubbing alcohol, fluid for the cigarette lighter, and gas for the lawn mower. She then piled up wooden furniture, picture frames, newspaper, paper bags, and everything from her brother's desk, in the center of the living room. This room had a vaulted ceiling that was open all the way to the roof and she could picture the wonderfully cleansing and purifying flames licking at the beams. She was becoming very excited as she took a large swig from the bottle of brandy she was holding now, and then flung the remaining contents onto the pile. Whatever Prescott wanted here, she would destroy. In her drunken angry state, Lynn had completely forgotten that she needed the money the sale of the house would bring. She took the canister of long fireplace matches from the fireplace mantel, lit several, and tossed them onto the pile. With a roar that was symphonic and musical to Lynn, the stack of items erupted into flames. She watched in both horror and delight for a couple of seconds. The flames were roaring out in all directions now, igniting draperies and tapestries that hung on the walls on their way up. It seemed that the flames were racing each other upwards to see which one could reach the high ceiling fastest. It made her smile. The vaulted ceiling acted like a wind tunnel at the center of a tornado, sucking, sucking at her hate, bundling all of it into a twisted thing that became the flames. Up and up, it was a live thing and her avenger, her only friend now that the vodka was gone. All of her hatred for Prescott and Guinevere, her frustration with the direction her life had gone, climbed with the mesmerizing red-orange glow. It was talking to her now, whispering that all would be well. Everyone who had harmed her in any way would be dealt with. The fire gods would see to it personally. She thought just maybe, when the fire was finished, her world might be right once more.

    Lynn turned away from the intense heat intending to flee the scene. However, she swung around too fast and fell into a table. Her head, just above her right eye and ear, slammed into the corner of the oak edge and she slumped to the floor. Her vision blackened around the edges working inward and she thought, *Damn, I've killed myself!* Rather than anger at this turn of events, Lynn Stone-Franklin believed this to be a fitting end to her miserable existence after all. Between the booze, fall, and smoke inhalation she was gone long before the flames reached her.

    Axel, Stanley, Mike Troy, and several others from the station arrived at the inferno about the same time as the fire trucks, ambulances, and gas and electric company vehicles. The alarm hadn't come in until the fire had nearly taken the building and was considering moving on to those on either side. Most people in the neighborhood were still at work or in school. In fact, it had been a school bus driver who had called it in. It was only by chance that he had been in the neighborhood at all, having delivered students home from a sporting event. The kids in this part of town walked to the local schools.

    The flames were both deadly and spectacular. They shot out from the building in all directions and were higher than the tree tops. It was like watching some strange, yet beautiful, fireworks display, the way the flames leapt about and sparks flew off from the tendrils of flame. It seemed that millions of stars sparkled in those flames as well. The birch tree next to the house exploded and sparks were raining on the crowd who then scattered, screaming. The curious onlookers, always too close, as if it would give them fame to see their frightened faces on the eleven o'clock news. Although Axel got angry when crowds gathered for catastrophes, he understood the fascination,

Whirlwind

the horror of these events. He'd probably stand there and gawk as well.

Axel turned back to observe the house. He thought the house was empty, but that would be up to the inspectors and emergency people to determine. It would be many hours, long into the night, before the remnants were cool enough to examine.

Luckily, the firemen confined the fire to just the Stone house. The buildings to either side were somewhat charred and would have smoke and water damage, but they were intact. That was a miracle in itself, since these huge older homes were so close together and very dry tinder.

Axel just stood there, at the edge of the crowd, watching. He thought he saw someone out of the corner of his eye, looking like he was trying not to be noticed, and maybe there was a tall, thin dark-haired woman as well. At any rate, when Axel got over to where they'd been, there was no one.

Stanley Morse ambled over to Axel. "Hey, you got your cell turned off or what?" he asked.

"No, don't think so." But when Axel pulled it out of his pocket, it was indeed off. This was very unusual, since he always wanted to be available for Sally. He turned it back on and checked his messages. Thankfully, nothing from Sally. However, there were four missed calls from Children's Hospital, as well as the same number of calls from Stanley. There were two others from Troy. It was far too noisy here, so he decided to drive to the hospital. *Geez, he hoped the little ones were okay.*

"Hey, Stanley!" he called over the crowd. "I'm going over to the hospital now."

"Thought you would. Later." Stanley lifted a hand as Axel hurried toward his car. He wondered what on earth this could be about and, if there was something the matter with the kids, what would he tell that poor Stone woman? Sally always told him "Don't ask for trouble," and "Don't count your chickens before they hatch." He wasn't sure why he remembered that, but he was sure they applied to this in some wise way or another.

He was greeted by the same nurse he had met before. Her demeanor hadn't improved much. In any case, she took him in to see the kids immediately, albeit grudgingly.

"This is our staff child psychologist, Ms. Elisabeth Reynolds," the nurse introduced the psychologist to Axel, ignoring the reverse platitudes.

Ms. Reynolds was young, maybe thirty, and very serious about her job. Axel could see this at first glance. She smoothed her hands down the sides of her immaculate skirt and picked at invisible lint. Her long, pale hair was pulled back into an attractive ponytail and bounced around her head when she moved. It was mesmerizing to watch it bob. Almost hypnotic. Sally would have poked him in his ribs to remind him not to stare.

Axel stuck out his hand. "Detective Axel Finley." He smiled.

"I called you here because I thought you needed to see and hear this." She shook his hand. Ms. Reynolds held out several pieces of drawing paper with childish sketches on them. The colors were stark black and bright red and one figure wielded a knife and had extremely large blue eyes. Entirely over-sized orbs like a cartoon character. Axel sat next to Samuel who was busy with another drawing. This one had Cathy in her high chair with her mouth wide open and a man, (Charles?), lying on the floor in a pool of red.

"Hi Samuel. Who are you drawing?"

"The bad men," Samuel answered, very serious and shy.

"Uncle Scotty! Uncle Scotty!" Cathy sang in a singsong chant over and over until the psychologist quieted her with a soft touch.

"Who is Uncle Scotty, Samuel?" Axel asked the child although he was fairly sure he knew.

Whirlwind

"This is Uncle Scotty." Samuel picked up a black marker and completely obliterated the man with the blue eyes.

"He is your Uncle Prescott?"

At first, Axel didn't think the boy would answer him. His eyes wandered around the room and settled on those of his sister. Then he nodded as tears formed.

"Yes. He is a bad man now, a really bad man." This was like a movie script, the good uncle who goes over to the dark side. Star Wars whatever. Axel wanted to make absolutely sure.

"Your Uncle Prescott hurt your dad?" Samuel nodded. Cathy did also.

"I not like Uncle Scotty now. He hurted me," the tiny thing said with a lisp.

Ms. Reynolds caught Axel's eye and motioned to the door. They stepped out into the hall leaving the children to their sketching. Finley saw Samuel flip his paper over to the blank side and walk away from the table.

"The children started drawing this morning. They were in separate rooms and drew basically the same thing. Both drawings had the blue-eyed man. Both children said it was Uncle Scotty. Neither of them was coached in any way. Cathy and I were waiting for Samuel to come back from the lab when she drew her picture, and Sam did his while waiting with his nurse."

"Do you think they know what they're talking about?" Axel asked her.

"I'd swear to it in court."

"That's good enough for me, Ms. Reynolds. Thanks."

She nodded and went back to the children where, Axel was sure, she would stay until they were safe or at least out of her care and into that of another.

Wow, this was certainly something; finally, there was a solid clue. Axel and his partner had been suspicious of Prescott and Lynn Stone-Franklin for a while now, but this?

The murders of a brother or brother-in-law, and nephews and tiny niece were beyond Finley's scope. That act would take one cold bastard! He'd have to expand the search for this Prescott Franklin and double the guard on the kids. Time to fly out to Phoenix? Time to talk to Stanley.

He drove by the still smoldering house on his way back to the station hoping to spot Morse. Stanley's car was there as were most of the firemen. A State of Minnesota fire marshal and a coroner were rooting around the ruin.

"The coroner?" Axel said out loud. "What would the coroner be doing here?" Axel hustled over to the men and tapped Stanley on the shoulder.

"My God, man! Where have you been? We got a body in the fire. Coroner says it's a woman. But that's all he can say right now. A woman, though, for sure."

Axel was completely taken by surprise. Had Mrs. Stone come back? Had she set the fire to hide something? Or, had the killers caught up to her as well? Had he been so wrong about her? God, he hoped not. His mind felt like it was doing cart-wheels. Those poor little kids! A body bag—a small one—was carefully carried out of the smoking remains of the house and laid on a stretcher. Axel unzipped the corner to take a quick look, but the damage was far too extensive to make out anything more than the exposed bone of the skull. The coroner snatched back the plastic from him and zipped it back up, glaring at Axel.

"Don't be in such a hurry, man! I'll get the information to you as soon as I know anything. Exactly the way I always do," snapped Will Trelford the coroner.

"It looks like a short woman, don't you think?" Axel felt relief, as he thought Mrs. Stone was fairly tall.

"Can't say for sure, Fire makes a body curl in on itself, pulls the limbs tight. Out of my way now, if you please." Will Trelford pushed past the gaggle of men on the way to his vehicle, finished with his part on the scene. Finley

Whirlwind

wondered who was more possessive of a crime scene, the coroner or the detective.

Susan M. Nelson

CHAPTER EIGHTEEN
Somewhere over the Rockies

Detectives Finley and Morse were trying to get a little sleep on their flight to Phoenix. The flight was uncomfortable and so were the economy seats. Both men were larger than the average flier and there wasn't enough leg room. After an hour of tossing around his weight, Axel sat upright and attacked his notes.

They hadn't left town until they knew the body was that of Lynn Stone-Franklin. She had a crisp, three edged pyramid like indentation in her left temple and smoke in her lungs, so the preliminary cause of death was smoke inhalation. She probably wasn't able to flee the burning house because of the head injury. The coroner speculated the victim had struck the sharp corner of a table or countertop.

She had incendiary residue on her hands and seemed to be holding tight to a tin of fireplace matches.

Who or what caused the head injury was unknown. It was tragic, but Axel was very relieved the body wasn't that of Guinevere Stone. He took the kids' drawings out of his briefcase and added photographs of the Franklin condo in Scottsdale. It was quite large but there was no real place to hide. If Prescott Franklin was in there, he would be found quickly. The search warrant had been obtained over the phone and they would be met at the airport by two of Phoenix's finest men in blue. Axel really didn't think it could be that easy, but he didn't know what else to try. He was fairly sure Guinevere Stone was also in this state. Somewhere between Flagstaff and Phoenix. Hopefully out of sight and safe.

At that very moment, Rena was holding the phone and punching in Detective Finley's number. She had decided to get rid of the flash drive, and he seemed the most unthreatening solution. He sounded like he might just care about the outcome of this drama. Maybe, he even believed her a little. He picked up right away, waving away the anxious flight attendant and showing her his badge.
"Finley."
"Detective, this is Guinevere Stone." Her hands were sweaty and her breathing shallow. She took a deep, calming breath and jumped right in.
"I do not want to keep this flash drive anymore. It's making me nervous."
"Yeah. It's making me nervous, too."
"I don't know how to get it to you."
Detective Finley chose his next words carefully and delivered them in what he hoped was an unthreatening manner. "I am not saying this to scare you, but I am in the air about to land at Sky Harbor Airport in Phoenix. I am not in any way after you, but we have an idea about where we might find Prescott Franklin. Again, maybe I could come to you? Or we could meet someplace neutral?"
Rena wanted to tell him just to come to the gallery, but she still was unsure of his motives. Rena was beginning to *feel* guilty and was suspicious of anyone she was unfamiliar with, whether it made sense or not. She was so damn tired and frightened and sick to death of it all.
"I'll meet you at the airport," she said, and hung up.

"When?" Geoff asked, understanding what was going on.

"Now!" She gathered her bag and the flash drive and slipped on a sweater. "I need you to drive me, but I don't want you to go in with me in case he really wants to arrest me." Geoff nodded, but knew he would go inside anyway.

The drive to the Phoenix airport was tense. Rena tried to relax. She told herself *what will be will be,* which did not help. Geoffrey was also quiet. Every once in a while he'd reach over to touch Rena, but she didn't notice. Her face was set in grim lines and she was trembling.

He was surprised at how strongly he felt about this near stranger already. He wanted to protect her, he wanted to get to know her better, and he wanted her to meet his kids. Hell, he wanted to love her. *Igraine Guinevere,* what a beautiful name. He looked over at her profile in the half light. What a beautiful woman. She had an oval face the color of a peach, slightly rounded cheeks and sculpted cheekbones. She had a well-shaped mouth that he wanted to be kissing. Her short hair looked soft and inviting, even messy and windblown like it was now. She wore no makeup and needed none. Geoffrey thought all women were worth looking at, but especially this one. She was intelligent, loving, and adventurous and he felt like a lucky man in spite of all the danger. He knew no one else like her.

The airport was busy with dozens of flights coming in and leaving. One of them most certainly held Detective Finley. Hundreds of travelers milled about at ticket counters, baggage check, food stands, and coffee kiosks. Many were reading newspapers. All this could be seen through the huge windows across the front of the building. As the car slowed, Rena quickly jumped out at the curb because she knew Geoff would try to follow. He cursed as she slammed the door and ran into the airport.

Whirlwind

"Guinevere! Wait!" The name just rolled off his tongue. He always felt the name Rena didn't suit her, but the use of her given name surprised them both. However, she did not wait for him, didn't even hesitate. By the time he was parked and in the terminal, she was nowhere to be seen. The Arrivals and Departure board listed a flight from Minneapolis that was landing now! He headed to the main lobby of terminal three. He saw Guinevere ahead of him on to the west side of the north concourse. He watched fearfully as a man approached and grab her arm roughly. He ran.

"Here you are, dear sister-in-law! I figured you were still here somewhere. That accent you threw at me couldn't have even fooled a lesser man. We've been waiting for this incoming flight. People shouldn't use cell phones if they want to be secretive. Not with the gadgets they have nowadays." He showed her a small metal box that had a blinking light.

"I knew the detective was coming and that you talked to him. Where is it?" Prescott's voice was as menacing as ever, more evil, maybe, and definitely more demanding. His eyes terrified her and turned her cold. He couldn't focus completely, on her or anything it seemed.

Prescott desperately needed that flash drive. It had been all-consuming for him for days, now, and he was a desperate man. He made a grab for her bag.

"Listen, you bitch! I know you have it because it's no longer on the company's computer hard drive. Charles didn't have it, nor did Sean. It's got to be somewhere."

"Just shoot her, you idiot!" Guinevere noticed the tall slender woman then, with a snub nosed handgun pointed at her head.

"Shoot her and take the bag! We have to go. Now!" Before Prescott could do anything more, the woman fired a shot and all hell broke loose. People scattered and screamed and several fell to the floor, blocking the way that would allow the woman shooter and to get closer to her target. She shot again from where she stood. Suddenly, there was return fire and the hallway lights went out. Somebody yelled "Police! Everybody down!" Guinevere dropped and let go of her bag. Prescott slapped her, grabbed the bag, and threatening whispered, "You'll never be safe!" before he and his partner took off. No one was alert enough to see where, in the darkened hallway. Realizing the shooting was finished, people began to nervously rise and dust themselves off, looking around cautiously.

    Geoffrey reached Rena first and helped her up. Two brawny men in rumpled suits were checking on the crowd and yelling at airport security. Amazingly, no one was more than bruised. It seemed the woman was aiming at the lights with her gun.

    "Mrs. Stone? You alright?" The older man approached her with his hand out. "Detectives Finley and Morse at your service, and just in time, it appears." He took her arm and led her out of the crowded hallway as airport security took over.

    "Sorry, they got away, sir," one of them told Axel. "We're still checking the lots outside, though." Axel shook his head knowing they were long gone, probably by way of one of the dozens of taxis waiting at the curb. The worst of it was that he saw Franklin abscond with the purse. He turned to talk to Mrs. Stone and saw the flash drive in her hand.

    "What …" Axel was surprised.

    "It never was in the bag." Guinevere smiled at him. "Nothing but wadded up newspaper was in the bag." She handed the flash drive over to him and brushed her hands on her skirt, as though they were dirty from handling it.

    "Well, I'm sure they know it by now, so let's move." The four of them left in a hurry and took cover in the security office to plan their next step.

Whirlwind

"I thought you were in Flagstaff," Axel started the conversation as he looked closely at Guinevere Stone for the first time. Her pictures did not do her justice. Then, he thought all women were more beautiful than their photographs. This one, though, was a stunner and made more so by her unawareness of that fact. She was too easy and casual in her movements to be aware of her beauty. Right now she was staring at the detectives in surprise.

"You used your credit card, Miss." Morse showed her the copy of her receipt.

"No, I ..." Guinevere stopped mid-sentence. "Oh no! I did. My God ..." She reached for Geoffrey. "I didn't think! Do you think that's how Prescott ..."

"Yes. I'm sure it is." Axel could see and feel her fear. The man next to her looked stressed as well and protectively wrapped his arm around her shoulders.

"Prescott just said that he knew we had talked. How could he know that?" Guinevere was still clearly rattled.

The detectives looked at each other. "I don't know the answer to that." Axel stated bluntly. "Not yet." But he was wondering about the security of his office and his phone. Just a year before, they had been notified of all the surveillance gadgets one could purchase over the Internet. Everything, it seemed, could be bought. This crime, however, didn't really seem to warrant the use of such expensive equipment. But then, who knew what else was happening?

"Can the two of you get back on the plane with us and fly to the Twin Cities right now? I'm sure you want to see your children and there is a lot to fill you in on." Axel was thinking about the fire and the dead sister-in-law. *Just what more would Franklin do, if he found out about his wife?* "I don't think you should stay here now."

Geoffrey turned to her so he could look into her face. "Go with him. He's right. Franklin and his friend know by now, more than we do. They most likely know about the gallery. I'll follow after I turn things over to Winston and Albert. Okay?"

"Chee?"

"The boys will take very good care of her. I bet she's sleeping with Albert by now." Geoffrey was trying to help her make up her mind to go without pushing. *He's good,* Axel thought, *I could learn something here.*

"Okay then." Guinevere straightened her shoulders, stood up tall and faced the detectives. "Let's do this."

Guinevere sat between Axel, in the aisle seat, and the window. Stanley was in the aisle seat opposite Axel, all in the rear of the passenger cabin. The men were looking closely at everyone who entered. They missed nothing and didn't relax until the plane was in the air. There weren't many people on this "redeye" flight and it was quiet, easy to keep track of everyone.

"Tell me." Guinevere stated plainly, so Axel answered in kind.

"It appears your sister-in-law, Lynn, has burned down your house. It's completely gone. She started the fire and died doing it. There is no sign anyone else was involved. We don't know why, yet, but I suspect it had something to do with her anger at her husband and perhaps at you. We also know for sure that it was Prescott Franklin who committed the murders of your family, although he had help from two others, a man and a woman." He watched her expression go from fear to shock to anger in only a second.

"How do you know this?"

"Your children drew pictures for the hospital psychologist, who specializes in children's PTSD." Axel took them out of his case and handed them to her. "Samuel and Cathy both say this figure is Uncle Scotty." He pointed to the blue-eyed man. "We also have his print on the knife that was used to …" He felt Stanley's eyes on him. "The knife that was used. He was in our computer system several times for theft and fraud. Were you aware of his criminal record?"

Guinevere shook her head and had a disgusted expression on her face. "I didn't like him and stayed away as much as I could." She shuttered. *So many dead ... so difficult to believe.*

"Where are the children?"

"At present, they are under guard at the Children's Hospital in St. Paul. Their injuries are healing rapidly. Both of them will have some minor scarring." Then he added when her face paled, "No one is aware they are alive except for some of the staff at the hospital and some of my men."

"Will I be able to see them?"

"Absolutely. As soon as we land, if you like."

She nodded and sighed. Yawning, she rested her head on the back of the seat and both detectives could feel her body relax as she drifted off.

"Poor woman." Stanley whispered. "And it isn't over yet."

"No, it isn't." Axel turned off their lights and kept watch as the other two napped. Axel's mind was busy and he couldn't rest. He was formulating an idea. He was as certain as he could be that she was innocent of any involvement in this. He'd bet his long career on it. He also knew he'd soon be on the road back to Arizona, to try and track down Prescott Franklin and the woman shooter. Unless, of course the criminals followed them back to Minnesota. There certainly was access to several smaller planes for rent by the hour available at the Phoenix airport.

He wanted to leave Guinevere and her kids with someone he trusted. That would be Sally and Stanley, and his second in command, Mike Troy. His house with its big wooded and fenced-in backyard was a possibility. They'd get the kids, pick up some things of Stanley's, stop at the district office, and head home to talk to Sally about it. Even in her weakened condition, Axel knew Sally would agree. They'd done this kind of thing before and Sally was a sucker for mothers and their children. They had an apartment set up in the basement that was nice and private and couldn't be reached from outside the house. That settled in his mind, he removed his tie and loosened his shirt collar. He finally succumbed to fatigue and fitfully dozed until they landed in Minneapolis. When he woke, he wondered who Chee was.

Whirlwind

CHAPTER NINETEEN
St. Paul, Minnesota

    Axel didn't like flying. He could never rest or sleep like the other passengers seemed able to do. He never wanted a drink even though he thought it might relax him, nor did he want food. Axel was positive that whatever he put into his mouth would come right up again. He was sweaty, he was chilled. Each time he had to fly, he swore he'd never get on a plane again. But he always did. The landings were especially hard on him, so when it went smoothly, he wiped his brow in relief.
    As a child, he saw his grandparents' plane explode into flames just seconds after it took flight. Bits of debris hit him as he watched in horror and heard the blood-chilling screams coming from the plane. His dad had said there were no screams, but Axel still could hear them. He shuttered at the memory. He saw that Mrs. Stone was looking at him empathetically.
    "Me, either," was all she said.
    It took only a few minutes to get through the airport and out to the curb pick-up area where an unmarked St. Paul Police cruiser was waiting for them. Axel explained his plan, got Stanley's nod of approval, and Stanley told the driver his address.

Detective Morse got out of the car at his home. He would rendezvous with Axel in a couple of hours after he showered and got some clothes together.

The driver was instructed to head back to the district office.

Sergeant Mike Troy was actually at his desk when Axel and Mrs. Stone trooped into the squad room. He hardly ever sat still, so the Axel was surprised to see him.

"Hey Mike, you need some time off, don't you?"

"Depends on what you have in mind, Axel." Sergeant Troy grinned. "I could use a fishing trip up north for a week."

"Ha! No such luck, buddy." Finley told him what he had in mind.

"Sure. Let me run home and I'll be there in about an hour. Okay? Want me to pick up the kids?" Axel started to say they'd do it, but reconsidered. This would be better. Less exposure for Mrs. Stone. He gave Sally a quick call.

"Hi, sweetheart. I'm on my way home. I've got a few guests for you to take care of, if that's good with you. Are you having a good day?"

"Axel, I've been waiting for you to call. You have visitors. They just arrived." Sally sounded a little off. Her normal cheerful attitude was tight.

"Visitors? Are they still there?" "Not in the house, but they're in a car on the street. They were rude, so I wouldn't let them in the house to wait, but I don't like this Axel." Neither did Axel. *Was it Franklin and the woman? Already? They hadn't been on the same flight! Did they have one of their own, or maybe a charter?*

"Listen to me. Pack a couple necessary things and the dog. Don't let them see you put the suitcase in the car. Drive here now. Right now. Take the gun from the safe. Got that?"

"I'll be right there. I already did the rest." She disconnected, and Axel paced. *Damn! How did they get*

Whirlwind

back so fast? Or, just how many more accomplices were involved in this?

"Troy! Wait a minute." Finley held a whispered discussion with Sergeant Troy, who nodded and left.

Axel quietly picked up the phone receiver on a detective's desk a ways away from his own desk. He spoke softly. The only thing Guinevere heard him say was, "Stanley, this is Axel."

He returned to his desk and said, "Change of plans, Mrs. Stone. We've got company and they're parked at my house. My wife is on her way here and we're all going to the Saint Paul Hotel. Sergeant Troy will bring the children." Axel turned to another detective in the squad room, "Get a couple of cars over to my house immediately, someone is watching it."

Guinevere was too tired for any more of this. Axel could see the weariness etched in her face. In Axel's experience, most people couldn't deal with long stretches of stress and she had done remarkably well so far. He took her to the locker room and gave her a policewoman's uniform to change into, complete with hat. She did it without complaint and looked like she was ready for a parade when she was dressed. She looked good. When Sally arrived, he told her to dress in the same fashion. Robie, the dachshund, was jumping up on both women having the time of his life with this new game. Axel borrowed Louise's car, and an off duty officer to return it, and drove to the hotel.

Axel expected some trouble over the dog, so he went directly to the office of the manager. After promising to keep Robie quiet and not to leave him unattended, they were escorted by the manager to a suite at the rear of the second floor. It was about perfect, with a common sitting area, kitchenette, large bathroom and two bedrooms, each with two beds. It was a very accommodating space. The colors were soft and soothing and the art on the walls was not typical. Some looked like pieces from local artists.

It pleased Axel, there was no balcony or any other way into the room other than the two hallway doors. The room was next to a stairwell, but that couldn't be helped.

"I want you to order room service until I can get food to you, but only when Stanley or I are here. When I say here, I mean right next to you. Okay?"

Axel instructed Sally, who nodded in agreement. Guinevere didn't seem to hear him. "We'll be fine," she told him.

Guinevere and Sally unpacked the few things they brought and waited for Sergeant Troy to appear with the children. Mrs. Stone was pacing furiously with her hands balled into tight fists. When the knock came, Guin let out a startled gasp, and Axel had to restrain her from flying to the door and flinging it wide.

"Troy?"

"Yes, Sir, nobody else visible." Axel opened to see his sergeant carrying two small and frightened kids. Cathy had her face buried in Troy's jacket and Samuel kicked to be put down and raced into Guinevere's arms.

"Mommy! Mommy!" The force of his small body nearly knocked Guin off her feet, but she held him to her and slid to the floor. Samuel knew who she was even with this change in her appearance. Somehow it didn't surprise her. Sammy was the most observant child she had ever known. Charles often commented on it. "You'll make a good detective, someday, son." He would tell the proud boy.

"Mommy! mommy!" Sammy repeated this like a chant of desperation. "Daddy? Where is daddy?" Samuel looked into Guinevere's face then and saw her tears. He wiped them away with his hand and patted her cheek. "It's okay, Mommy, I can take care of you. Don't cry." Guinevere pulled him tighter, like she would never let go.

Whirlwind

"I know you will, baby. I know." Cathy was still clinging to the sergeant. Guinevere got up from the floor, and walked over to her and Detective Troy.

She spoke quietly to her, while gently rubbing Cathy's back at the same time.

"Hello, my little angel girl. I missed you so very much." No response from Cathy.

"Can I see you sweetheart? Will you look at me?" Cathy peeked for a second and tucked back into Troy. "Please, Cathy. I want to hold you, sweetheart." Then Cathy literally launched herself from Troy's arms to Guinevere's. It was obvious to all that Guinevere was used to this because she was braced for it.

Guin again sat on the floor. The two rocked each other and Sammy crawled up into Guin's lap as well. If Axel had any doubts about Mrs. Stone as a mother, they were completely discounted now. These children adored her. It was mutual.

"Why don't I help you get tucked in for a nap." Sally led them to the bedroom and quietly closed the door. She returned to the detectives in short order.

"Poor little tykes, they are all asleep already." Axel looked in on them and saw both kids wrapped in Guin's arms with their faces pressed to hers. Robie stood alert at the foot of the bed. He seemed to sense the need for a watch dog. It could have been a Norman Rockwell painting.

Axel's eyes filled with unexpected tears and the Rockwell changed into a Sandro Botticelli with muted pastel colors and angelic faces. He hastily wiped his eyes. Satisfied that all was well for the moment, Axel left the group and took a cab back to the station. But first, he clung to his own wife for several moments.

He met the officers who had been to his house. There had been no car parked there by the time they arrived. No surprise in that. A formal alert was put out for Prescott

Franklin and the unknown woman, although they had only an obscure description of her: tall, thin, longish dark hair, and thirty-something. Two policemen would stay at his house to keep an eye out for the pair of criminals to return. Axel thought they should stay for a day or two, but he didn't expect Franklin to return. He wondered if Franklin knew about his wife's death. Or if he even cared. Her death hadn't been reported to the press yet, but the fire had been all over the papers, complete with photos in full color. It was spectacular coverage and probably sold extra newspapers.

Finley left his office before he'd be interrogated about what was happening with the case. One stop at the grocery store, one at the pharmacy, and back to the hotel. The Saint Paul Hotel had a fine dining room, and Axel was looking forward to one of their well-known steak dinners.

This damn phone! Axel thought, as he reached yet again for the vibrating telephone.

"Finley!" He barked into it.

"Hey, it's Louise. I have some information. Connelly's widow called me. She found a file under the lining of her suitcase. Sean had dozens of photographs of Mexican antique thingies. Like statues and bowls and jewelry. Maybe they're from an archaeology site or a Mexican museum. Think we should call down there to see if anything's been reported missing?"

"This is a new twist. Sure, call away," Axel said.

"Will do. Later, Detective." Louise had been Axel's secretary his entire life in the district office, and was more than his right hand. Much more. She anticipated his thoughts and kept up almost as well as Sally did. Whatever he forgot, Louise remembered. She solved his cases as much as he did. He could depend on her quick mind, always. If there was something to this, she'd find it. Louise looked like someone's sweet cuddly granny, but her brain was forged in steel. Long, white hair braided and wound into a tight bun at the back of her head, always dressed in skirts or suits, trim and efficient, Louise was the department's jewel. He expected she would call back within the hour.

    After so many days on this case, Axel wanted to spend time with Sally. He liked to run things by her and get her ideas. Most of Axel's ideas were only partly his own. Sally saw things from another angle and it broadened his mind to things he had missed. He seriously doubted he would have been such a good detective without her advice. He often thought both Sally and Louise would make great detectives. What a team he'd have then!
    Up in the room, Mrs. Stone and her children were still sleeping the sleep of exhaustion under Robie and Sgt. Troy's watchful eyes. Stanley was perusing the papers from Mrs. Connelly. Sally was more than ready to get away for a bit.
    The restaurant in the Saint Paul Hotel was turn-of-the-century elegant to 1920s style with highly polished wood walls, floor and tables. A long glossy bar had the traditional mirror behind it and the bartender in a bow tie, white shirt, and black silk vest. He could have been any age from twenty to forty-five. The couple sat at the bar and ordered a Makers Mark whiskey and sour for Axel and a dry red wine for Sally. It was dinnertime and the place was packed wall to wall. When a table was ready, they took their drinks and followed the waitress past a wall of photographs of both famous and infamous people who had dined there since the hotel opened in 1910. Displayed were photographs of actors, governors, even his own chief of police, and probably a gangster or two.
    Axel didn't need to look at the menu; he ordered his steak medium with a baked potato and salad with French dressing. Sally took a little more time trying, as usual, to find something that wouldn't upset her blood glucose level

too badly. She finally opted for a chef's salad with grilled chicken rather than the usual cold-cuts and cheese, with diet dressing and dry toast. It sounded terrible to Axel, but she was pleased with her choice. They enjoyed the food in the companionable silence that comes from years of marriage, smiling at each other over their plates and even holding hands across the table. As they finished, Axel fished his notebook from his pocket and found a clean page. He told his wife the facts as he knew them and when he got to Lynn Stone-Franklin, Sally interrupted.

"I was at the art museum in Minneapolis a few weeks before my heart attack." Sally thought it over. "Anyway, Mrs. Franklin is some kind of expert on ancient Mexican art. She gave a series of lectures on the newest discoveries in Western Mexico. There was a guest speaker with her, a man ... what was his name? He talked about the vast wealth still hidden in shaft tombs, family tombs that no one knew about. Mrs. Franklin had slides and books. I bought one of the books. It's at home though." Sally looked pensive and Axel left her wandering in her thoughts until she was ready to share them.

"Okay, I remember now. These were archaeological sites in Western Mexico where very little digging or study has been done on private lands. Many of the large monuments were leveled some years back to grow some plant, a cactus I think, that is used to make tequila. Some archaeologists have found a town at the base of a volcano. And there were deep tombs called shaft tombs filled with these clay statues and bowls, jewelry, and even some fabric. Quite beautiful, actually." Sally sipped her coffee. "Teuchitlan. That was the name of the place. And the man was Cesar something. Very good looking," she added with a teasing smile.

Axel knew she was interested in Mexican archaeology. She followed the newest finds of Mayan and Aztec sites on the Internet and in her archaeology magazines. She had been fascinated ever since he had known her. She had an extensive collection of books and photographs of the stuff. To him, it looked like children's artwork, but what the heck did he know! She said it was part of a huge category called folk art by some. His interest dealt with modern time, not past civilizations, but he could see her fascination and he dutifully followed after her in museums all over the Midwest.

"There was to be one more lecture. This one was about stolen artifacts and how to deal with these thefts and where to return these works of art to Mexico. A man from a Mexico City museum was going to conduct the class. I heard that he even had the actual pieces to show us before they were to be returned to the Mexican government."

Axel was growing more excited. This was all coming together. He needed to talk to Louise.

The Finleys walked back to the room and Axel left Sally there. She was tired and ready for bed and he was having a second wind, anxious to return to work. The Stones were eating soup and crackers with cheese but still looked tired. Stanley was yawning. A replacement "watch dog" had just arrived from the station so the rest of the crew could get some sleep. Axel kissed his wife twice and left.

Susan M. Nelson

CHAPTER TWENTY
St. Paul, Minnesota

Louise was still at her desk when Axel came in. She was on the phone but quickly handed him a stack of notes. The top note was from the Phoenix police. They had used the warrant to enter the Franklins' condo and had removed several dozen crates of what appeared to be Mexican and Central American artifacts. Some even had museum names on the crates or jotted on the item itself. Several had the museum item number in white ink written in tiny script on the bottom. A couple of boxes were full of loose dirt that was around the art, like it had just been removed from the ground. The name on one crate jumped off the note. Teuchitlan! Louise came into his office and sat down heavily.

"I have been following leads since we spoke. Several museums and archaeological sites are reporting thefts. These are very recent, like in the past two weeks or less. None from the museum exhibits themselves, but from storage rooms. Every one of them has been dealing with a so-called expert on Mexican antiquities by the name of Cesar Montoya and his assistant who is described as a stunning dark-haired woman. Some of the museums were aware of both the Franklins and Sean Connelly as well. What is this, Axel?"

Whirlwind

"Okay, here's what I'm thinking. Sean Connelly was contacted by this Cesar Montoya and hired to invent a computer spy program about antiquities. Either they met somewhere or knew each other already, so there was some degree of trust. Connelly hired Charles Stone to develop it, since Stone was a computer game genius and has made a lot of money doing it, although we aren't positive about his involvement yet. For all I know, he was behind it. Or maybe Stone thought it was simply a game when everyone else knew it was for theft. It appears to be working very well so far, as these recent thefts demonstrate. What I can't figure out is, if the thieves are using it already, what is on the flash drive that they still need?"

Before Axel could continue, the phone on Louise's desk rang sharply. She got to her feet slowly, turned, walked back to her desk, and picked it up.

"Detective Finley's office." She listened, gasped, and said she'd relay the message. "That was the Art Institute in Minneapolis. Last night someone broke into their heavily guarded Mayan storage room. Everything is gone!"

Axel dialed the museum office with a few questions of his own.

"Were these items recently acquired?"

"Yes, last week from Cesar Montoya, who we have dealt with a number of times with no problem. All of the pieces were authenticated and stamped with Mexican approval. Our checks were made out to the Mexican Antiquity Authority, as per usual."

"Had Mr. Montoya ever seen this room?"

"No, but we also have a new employee who unloaded the crates. It was his first night on duty alone."

"His name wouldn't be Prescott Franklin, would it?"

"Close, Lynn Prescott is the name on the application. He was recommended by Mr. Montoya who said they had worked together for years."

Yeah, I'll just bet they have. Axel thought.

"Listen; put extra guards on all the Mexican, Central American, and other related cultural artifacts. That seems to be the focus of these particular thieves. Change your computer codes and passwords and give the information to only those you trust. Better yet, tell no one. The computer is how they are gaining access to your building. In fact, for now, you should bypass the computer codes completely and just go with armed guards, keys, and a licensed security company."

"Detective?"

"Yes?"

"They left one of those yellow smiley faces stuck to the table. Even I can see a fingerprint on it."

Axel looked over the stack of messages Louise had handed him a little while ago. There were messages from the National Anthropology Museum of Mexico City, the Smithsonian warehouse in Washington and another in San Francisco. Axel called them all and two names were common: Prescott Franklin and Cesar Montoya. It appeared Prescott sometimes went by his wife's name as well. These boys had been busy! Louise went to her desk again for another phone call. She stuck her head around Axel's door.

"I think you need to take this one, Axel."

"Detective Finley, this is Elizabeth Ryan. Have you been following the events at the zoo?"

"Events? Zoo?" Finley didn't have a clue. He knew that Mrs. Ryan was married to a veterinarian at the zoo, apes he thought, and that she headed up some special police squad and was reported to be quite good at her job. He thought they might have met at an event somewhere once. The memory was vague.

"Yes. One of the volunteers who works with my husband came to my attention on an unrelated case. He has reported that Cesar Montoya has tried recruiting him as a courier of some kind. This man, Enrique Santos, is from

Whirlwind

Western Mexico and his father is head of the history department at the National University of Mexico in Mexico City. I saw the name Montoya on our outstanding warrants site and thought to give you a call."

"Yeah, okay. We are working the same case, I think. If you think Santos is involved with these museum thefts, anyway. At least it is beginning to look that way." Axel filled her in on everything he knew which actually took longer than he expected it would. Maybe he had more information than he thought.

"Can I come to your office in the morning to look at that flash drive with you? I'd like to meet with Guinevere Stone as well. We have an excellent description of Montoya and I might have a lead on the mystery woman. Cesar has a sister about his age and this appears to be a family business, trading in stolen goods. Like those Egyptian families who built their homes over tombs and systematically robbed them empty. And detective, no, I don't think Santos is involved, but he may be able to help us."

"Okay, but unfortunately, no one has been apprehended as yet. Perhaps its time to involve the federal agencies in this?" Axel offered.

"I guess so, but they'll just take it and run."

"Is that so bad?"

"I suppose not, but it sure is interesting!" Elizabeth Ryan laughed dryly.

"Consider that it's still our case, then," Axel grinned into the phone. None of the Metropolitan police really liked when the Feds overran their cases, but sometimes, he supposed, it was necessary. Personally, Axel figured his tight team did a better job. Too many cooks and all that.

Susan M. Nelson

CHAPTER TWENTY-ONE
St. Paul, Minnesota

Everyone was sleeping when Axel let himself into the hotel room. Everyone, that is, except for Stanley who slipped his gun back into its holster when Axel grinned at him.

"You sleep now. I'll sit up."

"No you won't." Sally came out of the room that housed the Stone's. She yawned and stretched. "I've been sleeping for hours and you look terrible. I can handle a gun as well as you, and I'm not sleeping on my feet or weaving around like a drunk." She kissed him with a loud smack.

"She's got a point, man." Stanley yawned as well. "I'll wake up Mike to keep her company and we can both get some rest. We won't do anyone any good unless we sleep. The way I feel right this minute, a whole army of criminals could run right through this room and I might not even notice them."

Axel had to laugh, that was so absurd.

"No need to wake me. I'm here." Mike Troy quietly entered the room and nodded at the closed door. "Asleep?"

"Completely out, but restless. Robie, too. He won't leave them long enough to go pee." Sally smiled. "I think he's found a mission in life."

Whirlwind

Just then the bedroom door opened and both Guinevere Stone and Robie exited the room. "Well, I think he has to go now." Guin mentioned with a wan smile. Mike put the leash on him and took him outside even though Robie was reluctant to leave the room.

"What a good dog he is," Guinevere said to the Finleys. "I miss my own dog, Chee."

"Ah, a mystery is solved!" Axel laughed. "I've been meaning to ask who Chee was. I didn't think you had a pet."

"I didn't until recently. She sort of adopted me in Flagstaff."

When Mike returned and he, Sally, and Guinevere were settled in comfortable chairs, Axel filled them in on the events of the past several hours. Robie asked to be let back in with the children and Guinevere opened the door for him. She stood there for awhile watching them all sleep. When she shut the door and returned to the room, her cheeks were moist with tears.

"I'm so grateful for their lives but I can't help but think of Peter and Charles. Having them again brings the events right back to the forefront. I was trying to forget this family life for a new one, and now, I'm back at square one." She collapsed into a chair and brushed the tears away in a resentful manner. "I'm thinking that the marriage wasn't going to work, but I probably would have stuck it out for those kids. Charles had too many secrets and that can wreck any relationship. But those children would have more than made up for any problems in the marriage."

Axel consulted his notes. "What about Geoffrey Pelleas? Who, exactly is he?"

"I met him in Flagstaff, too, and he is a great friend already. He has my dog and gave me safety when I needed it, stability. He can be trusted. He helped me get into Charles's computer, but I hacked the files." Axel didn't believe her, but he let it go.

"Tomorrow the lab technician is going to open the files and we'll see exactly what this has all been about." Axel kissed his wife and joined Stanley, who was already snoring, loudly. Axel was so tired he didn't think even that could keep him awake.

He slept straight through the remainder of the night and was awakened by his cell phone.

"I'm sorry to bother you so early, Detective, but I've been trying to reach Rena Fairchild for hours. Days really, and I can't get her, can I? The phone at her house just keeps ringing and ringing. I called the cell I bought her, and couldn't connect. I am desperately worried."

Rena Fairchild? Who was this British accent? What … Where was he? This wasn't his room.

"Who are you?" he asked, still unfocused from his heavy sleep.

"Geoffrey Pelleas. Please, Detective, help me." Oh yeah, Axel remembered now. *Rena Fairchild-Guinevere Stone.*

"Okay, okay. She's fine. Hold on for a minute." He kicked off the blanket that he didn't remember covering himself with and noticed he was the only one in the room. He could smell coffee somewhere close. Thank God! The sitting area was full of people. It seemed everyone was up and sipping. Sally handed him a cup. The two kids were still hanging to Guinevere like she was their life-line, and Robie was following Sally. He handed his cell to Mrs. Stone.

"It's Geoffrey Pelleas, ma'am. Don't say much on the cell. In fact, get a number and call him on this phone." He pointed to the phone on the desk. She nodded. Axel wondered if that advice was coming too late.

"Hello, Geoffrey. No, I'm fine. I have the children." She smiled at their faces. "We are being thoroughly taken care of and protected. Is there a land line I can call you on?

Detective Finley doesn't want me on this one." She listened for a few seconds, said okay, and hung up.

"Geoffrey is in town." She announced to Axel. "Will I be able to see him?

Axel and Stanley held a short discussion and Stanley left quickly.

"Yes, we think it will be fine. Morse will be at the station and when you talk to Geoffrey I'll give him the station address and Morse will deliver him here. Okay?" Mrs. Stone smiled and nodded. Axel saw her visibly relax as she absorbed this. His attention went to Sally as he watched her read to the kids, who were completely enjoying the story. It was something about a cat who found a home in an unlikely place. And with mice, of all things! *Where did the woman find these stories?*

Prescott Franklin was angry. He was pacing the floor and slamming things around. He pounded one fist into the palm of his other hand and spun around quickly.

"Would you just sit?" The tall woman ordered, putting out her half-smoked cigarette in the coffee saucer that was already overflowing with ash and remains of other half-smoked cigarettes. The entire room reeked of old smoke and anger. She was only half dressed and had been thinking about sex, but her brother should be here too soon for what she had in mind.

"We can't do anything until we hear from Cesar."

"Yeah, well your brother sure takes his sweet time!" Prescott dropped into the chair beside her. "Jesus, Wyonne, where is he?"

"He'll be here." She lit another cigarette and was fiddling with a piece of shell jewelry. "I cannot figure out how this goes!" She complained and dropped it.

"Leave it then, it isn't worth much."

The door burst open and the handsome Cesar strolled casually over the threshold. He was carrying several burlap bundles and laid them carefully on the table.

"This is the last of the haul from Minneapolis. I'm going to fly back to Phoenix tonight or tomorrow and pick up the batch from the condo. Then we'll be finished with this town. None too soon, either. People are noticing the missing items and someone is linking our names with the theft. My friend at the police department has told me this."

"Are you still seeing that secretary, then?" Wyonne asked. Her tone, thought Prescott, sounded jealous. He'd noticed that about her before and wondered about it.

"So? She has been helpful in the past." The two siblings stared at each other for what seemed like several minutes. Prescott was struck by how much alike they appeared, how beautiful they were, and how cold. Especially Wyonne. She had a cruel streak that he had seen all too often. Still, he was attracted to her in a way that he never had been to Lynn, his bland, plump house-wife.

"What will you do with all this crap?" Prescott was still tense. He opened one of the new bundles to reveal yet another red clay scene of some kind of festival.

"Crap, huh?" Wyonne grinned at her brother. "Maybe he doesn't want his share anymore, Cesar." Cesar ignored her.

"We have many buyers who won't ask questions. Right now, I want that computer program. For all we know all our names are on it. Names, locations, items we've helped ourselves to, and perhaps even the buyers who I've sworn to protect and have never let down. Unless we retrieve it, our business will come to a screeching halt."

"Do you think Stone's wife has it?" Wyonne was feeling she should have shot the woman when she had the chance at the Phoenix airport. Now they didn't know where she was.

Whirlwind

"Unless those men we saw at the airport are police." Cesar looked thoughtful. "Maybe she gave it to them." Cesar threw a robe at his sister and walked to the window. She smiled, a cat-like superior smile, as she slipped her arms into the robe but left it hanging open.

"You know, I wasn't expecting any of this trouble when we started. I thought as soon as we'd eliminated Stone, after he changed his mind about our little project, it'd be smooth sailing. It should have been but for you!" He pointed his finger into Franklin's chest. Hard. "You had to take out the entire family and now we've got far too much trouble. Police don't forget the murders of children."

"I had to do it!" Prescott Franklin whined. "The brats knew who I was. They called *me* by name, not you."

"And who would have listened to them?" Cesar was really angry. Children, for God's sake! Prescott was beginning to feel like a heavy burden and Cesar was wishing his sister hadn't brought him into the family business. Hell, she could get sex anywhere and she surely wasn't in love with this man; she could barely stand him most of the time, unless he was naked and in her bed. She treated him like either her favorite treasured pet or her servant. Never like a man, though. That alone told Cesar everything he needed to know about Franklin. He, Cesar, would never let a woman treat him in such a manner.

"I'm going to the bar for a stiff drink and something to eat." He slammed out of the room and was followed by his sister, who was still in the process of slipping a silky dress over her head.

Franklin stayed behind, feeling sorry for himself. He was in over his head and he knew it. The murder of his brother-in-law hadn't bothered him in the least. The arrogant bastard had always looked down his fine nose at Prescott, but the children had been different. Their deaths haunted him still, every night and even some days. He hadn't even been able to sleep. He also knew he wanted his wife to give him some comfort like she always did. While he was with her, he hardly gave her any thought. He cheated on his marriage every chance he got, but she stayed at his side and always backed him. God! He needed someone on his side now. He went to the phone on the motel desk, picked it up and dialed her. It rang and rang but no one picked up. Where could she be? Lynn had always been at home when he'd called her before. As his eyes strayed over the room, they stopped at the bottle of clear liquid and syringe lying on the nightstand. What was that drug Wyonne injected into his muscle when she was wanting long, drawn-out sex? All he understood was that it worked and that it made him feel more like ... he wasn't sure. Maybe that was also keeping him edgy and awake?

 The police officer stood by the Franklin phone and made a note of the incoming number and time.

 The Montoyas sat at the bar and ordered steaks and drinks. They were striking, head-turning people with olive skin, dark hair, and trim, intelligent eyes. Both were incredibly sexy and moved with grace and self-awareness. But they also were truly greedy. Unlike the rest of their family, they both refused to become farmers, refused to join in the family tequila business. Cesar had tried until Wyonne convinced him this was better, more lucrative. Their father had taught them ways to earn a much easier living selling their heritage. Papa was no longer a part of this, though, and Cesar didn't understand where he had disappeared to. It had been weeks since they'd last had any contact. Cesar felt an occasional twinge when he thought of his mother, but Wyonne pushed him on, giving him little time to dwell on it. Now, through a very lucky break, they had the means to get into private museum stashes of antiquities all over the country. Most were easy pickings but they had about exhausted the wares at their fingertips. Back home in western Mexico, the family home and those of the neighbors sat on top of a vast wealth of treasure just waiting for them to excavate. Cesar practically salivated in anticipation! He didn't need to worry about the loot, either, because no one else knew he had discovered it. Not even his beloved Wyonne. His mother's beautiful face passed through his mind. It was full of sorrow and gave Cesar another of his uncomfortable twinges.

"Look at this, my brother." Wyonne slid a newspaper under his view. "**RAGING INFERNO TAKES LIFE OF ARSONIST IN ST. PAUL**" Cesar speed read the article, not sure why she thought it meant something to them. Then he caught a name, Lynn Stone-Franklin. He raised his eyes to his sister. "Do we tell him?" he asked.

"The fire was nearly a week ago. Perhaps he knows?" Wyonne didn't want to give up her newest sex toy to sorrow. Not until she had finished with him. That time would come soon. Already she was slightly bored with the routine.

"No, I am sure he does not." She finally said.

Cesar went on. "I don't care if you tell him or not. He has used up his worth anyway. Sometimes I think we should just get rid of him like the others. You are aware that I have never trusted him?"

"Not yet. Let me take care of it, brother." Wyonne had a look in her eyes that chilled even Cesar to the bone. He loved her, but she sometimes frightened him to death, just like their father had when he'd been a boy. He was a silent, strong, and disapproving master. Of all the numerous children in the Montoya clan, the patriarch had handpicked Cesar and Wyonne to follow in his footsteps. The others had legitimate jobs and businesses. Occasionally Cesar wished he did as well, but Wyonne relished this life. She had the same cruel streak as their father, and she loved to make use of it. She was thinking maybe Cesar and her father were not carrying their weight and she might just leave them in her dust! She glanced around her at all the

Susan M. Nelson

lovely young women dotting the bar, and wondered how much they would be worth …

Whirlwind

CHAPTER TWENTY-TWO
Teuchitlan, Western Mexico

About fifty miles east and south of the busy town of Teuchitlan stood a large agave and corn farm. Overlooking a vast dry valley at the foot of mountains, Rosario Elena Ramirez Montoya was planning to stand up to her husband. It would be the first time in their forty-five years together that she would do so. Married to Juan Antonio Montoya when she was barely fifteen years of age, she had always stood with him on every subject - usually the children or the farm -even though the farm was hers, her father's, her grandfather's, and his before that. They had raised six children during their marriage but only the youngest three were still with her: Diego, Roberto, and Julieta. Marta, the oldest and the most like her, had married and had moved to Mexico City, Tenochtitlan to Rosario. Cesar and Wyonne she rarely saw anymore. She shook her head in sorrow as a tear slid down her wide cheekbone. Her husband had removed those two from her care years ago and trained them himself. This was part of her concern and what she wanted to discuss with Juan Antonio.

She strolled over the ground that had forever been in her family. No one else had ever owned this place and she was proud. The house, this house, was built on top of all the houses ever built on this spot. Parts of the old ones' dwellings could still be seen in places and Rosario cherished this. Ancestors were of the utmost importance to her. Sometimes more than her immediate family. They demanded her respect and she gave it lovingly. She knew that her eldest son, Cesar, had discovered this wealth beneath the house and this was the remainder of what she wished to talk to Juan Antonio about. She had to choose her words carefully, though, so that he would really hear her. She was aware that her husband took her for granted, her oldest children as well, but it had never bothered her until now ... now that the ancestors were involved. The spirits that wound around her were restless and annoyed. Rosario was worried.

Every two or three generations had simply added to the main house, sometimes directly on top of the old one. Nothing was ever removed or destroyed completely so as not to disturb the comfort of the ancestors. But something was terribly wrong now. Her great grandparents had brought it to her attention in her dreams, and she must make amends. She gently touched the heavy, silver bracelet on her wrist and gazed at it with love, knowing it needed to go back where it had been for hundreds of years. Cesar had taken it from beneath this house and she had taken it from Cesar. Rosario was waiting for the locksmith from the town to come and install an iron door over the ground under the house. It would have an intricate locking system and she would wear the key around her neck at all times, telling no one. She was ashamed that all of this was even necessary.

Rosario Elena Ramirez was still a strikingly beautiful woman. Tall for her race, and thin, stately, and straight. Her eyes still sparkled and there was hardly a grey hair a midst her thick, black, and glossy tresses. Worn now in a braid, when it was undone it reached far beyond her waist. She had a soft look about her which her family had taken for weakness in the past. Not anymore.

The tribe of people who had lived and farmed here for centuries was not as famous as the Aztecs or the Mayans, but they had been just as creative, productive, and prolific. To their advantage, they were overlooked by the Spanish and so their numbers weren't as decimated by war or disease.

"Tarascan" was the name given to her people by the visiting scholars, historians, and archaeologists who came here yearly. Her ancestors had had no enormous metropolis like the Aztecs and Mayans, but a few smaller centers, which were mostly ceremonial places. All that was left of them were circular tamped down dirt or clay floors that only slightly indented the ground. Erosion and disuse had melted them away. Rosario knew where they were, though, and often visited these holy spots. Circular earthen mounds, flat temple altar remains and circles around circles, which from the hilltop looked like flattened pyramids, speckled the countryside that was made up of villages and farms. Lots and lots of farms. The climate here, between the mountains and the sea, was perfect for farming. Two crops were produced every growing season. Now though, except for the family gardens, agave was grown for tequila and corn for fuel. The soil was still rich from the volcanoes and the rivers that flooded their banks every spring. Only once had the volcano affected their farm and that was many generations ago. She supposed they were about due, but she was philosophical about it; it would be God's will after all.

In her wandering and thinking, Rosario found herself near the tombs of her parents and grandparents. She sat there to remember them. Unlike the current customs of the land, she still believed the dead should be buried in shaft tombs: pits at the bottom of a long shaft. So, some twenty to twenty-five feet below her lay six bodies with room for more. No, she corrected herself remembering. Other, older ancestors lie under the bones of her parents and grandparents. Eventually, hers and Juan's would lie there as well. She was uncertain about her children. Only her husband knew of these graves, all others were dead themselves.

Rosario crossed herself as she stood to leave the graves. She was a good practicing Catholic as her parents had taught her. But, Rosario also believed in the old gods as well. Most of the names of these varied gods and goddesses had long since been forgotten, even by Rosario, but not the sun god or her personal favorites, the maize goddesses. She liked them the best of all the ancestral deities. They brought food for the family, watched over the health of the family, and brought fertility to the women.

Rosario worshiped the ancestors above all others. They were involved in all family events although not to the extent they had been in the past. Often, Rosario would bring them food and flower petals after the others had all gone to their own homes. But she never forgot them, and prayed to them now, for strength. Mary, Jesus, and the Catholic God were as much in her daily life as all these others and because of this, Rosario felt blessed and honored.

The sky was hazy, a soft blue gray color much like the agave plants. The mountains looked lavender and the afternoon clouds were building. Soon, the family would gather for supper. Rosario said a quick prayer to her maize goddesses and went inside thinking now about her family.

Julieta, her baby, has told her she would like to live in the old way of staying with her parents rather than marrying and raising her own children. Even though Rosario herself had done this—she had been able to do both as her parents were killed in an accident just before she married Juan—she tried to discourage her daughter. Julieta already was eighteen and neither Rosario nor Juan showed any signs of dying anytime soon.

Ah, Julieta! Such a lovely sweet child. So like her namesake, Rosario's own mother. This farm would pass to her. In the Ramirez family, the farm had been passed to the youngest daughter in most of the generations, the one left behind, as it had always been a family of girls. Cesar would not like that. Rosario knew that already her son was plotting his ownership. She stood slowly and shook out her long skirt. It was time to prepare the evening meal.

The house had a slightly uneven stone floor, worn and discolored in spots. There were fossils embedded in a few of the stones, and Rosario felt they brought luck. She greeted them in her mind as she stepped over them. The walls were a sort of stucco, adobe, and were the color of warm sand. No glass filled the windows and there were no doors. Once, Juan had glass installed in all the windows. He didn't talk to Rosario about this before hand and she was offended. She had it removed the very next day and nothing was ever said about it, nor was it replaced. It seemed a sacrilege to Rosario to keep nature's sounds and smells out of her house. She loved the way the sunlight and moonlight crept into the deepest corners to keep her company.

Rosario Elena believed the old gods and the ancestors needed to be nourished as well as the stomachs of her family, and gave them corn meal and tokens of her faith on a daily basis. She set this food outside the house on a special ledge now. In her mind she prayed an ancient language that even she didn't fully understand. To her family and to others she spoke a mixture of Spanish and English, depending on her mood and how unsettled she was at the time. The old language, the words of the ancestors, had never been spoken to the children and it made her sad to think it would die with her. Maybe she would teach it to Julieta. Her eyes strayed to the old clock on the mantel. Julieta would be home soon from the school where she taught English classes to anyone who wished to learn. Roberto and Diego were in the fields with Juan. She could just hear them coming. Cesar and Wyonne were out of the country again. Remembering this gave Rosario new resolve to speak soon to her husband.

Susan M. Nelson

CHAPTER TWENTY-THREE
St. Paul, Minnesota

Axel, Stanley, and Troy were all present at the station the next morning. Geoffrey Pelleas was with the women and children along with three of Finley's handpicked officers. Alex felt okay about leaving them at the hotel. Two techies and several other officers, even their captain, were there for the briefing on the computer program that was on the flash drive. Elizabeth Ryan also attended. After filling everyone in on the details, Axel turned the meeting over to the techs.

"Please leave out all the computer gibberish and just tell us what's on the flash drive," Axel complained ten minutes into their explanation. Bruce Wilcox laughed. Being the technicians who worked most with Detective Finley, they were used to his sometimes gruff manner.

"Right! I keep forgetting you're computer challenged."

"Yeah, well, so go on in English then please."

"What we found is complex. First, it is a design for a sophisticated game about breaking into museums and stealing things. You go on to higher levels with more dangers and harder codes, bigger treasures and more security codes to break. Everything has a monetary value and you collect points. Somewhere along the line, Charles Stone began to make it impossible to read his notes. Rather than trying to erase his work, which he must have known was nigh onto impossible, he simply changed things. This made the game unrealistic and the information wouldn't be applicable in real settings. The end of the game is missing, too. Of course we know now that it was too late, and museums were being robbed daily. Then we found this file." Bruce clicked on his computer desktop and a series of names appeared on the pull down screen in front of the crowd. It was a list of names:

--------------------Cesar Montoya/Esteban
--------------------Juan Montoya/Juan Ramirez
--------------------Sean Connelly
--------------------Prescott Franklin/ Lynn Stone-Franklin
--------------------Herbert Brooks
--------------------Cristian Todos
--------------------Wyonne Montoya

"I know this Herbert Brooks," stated Elizabeth Ryan. "He is one of the directors of the Central American Antiquities Museum here in the Twin Cities. Cristian Todos is part of the antiquities department in Mexico City and I have talked with him. No red flags, though."

"Connelly is dead and we're actively looking for Franklin." Stanley added. "I wonder if the woman we've seen with Franklin is this Wyonne Montoya. With the way everyone involved in this case changes names, we need photographs."

"We've got the next best thing. I'm going to pick up Mrs. Stone and my wife. Stanley, you get on the horn and contact Brooks. Better yet, pick him up. I have some questions for the man and this time I will get straight answers." Axel left with a serious, "I-mean-business" strut. He was in full detective mode now.

He was getting angry. This was taking too long with no real leads. He wanted his wife's input. Sally was an unofficial expert on all things of ancient Mexico. Jeez, he was always tripping over the piles of information on the stuff that Sally left next to furniture. Documentary films about the Aztec and Mayan worlds that he'd watched with her recently struck him as barbaric. Often, when he'd finally get home after another much-too-long day, Sally was intent on some cable show about archaeology somewhere in the world. It meant nothing to Axel. He'd try to feign interest because he loved his wife, but it all happened so long ago. He found it hard to understand and to follow, and he retained very little.

His men knew he often relied on Sally's views and he'd caught both Stanley and Mike on the phone with her more than once, getting her take on things, he guessed. She was a wise and observant woman and he knew he was a very lucky man. Lately he'd been thinking of taking Sally on a trip to Mexico to see these places that fascinated her. He hesitated because of her health, but just maybe he would surprise her.

Everyone was up and about when Axel reached the room at the Saint Paul Hotel. Robie didn't bark at him, but he certainly checked him out thoroughly before he was allowed to enter. Being warmly kissed and hugged by Sally strengthened his resolve to treat her to Mexico.

He got a glimpse of his rumpled appearance as he passed in front of the full length mirror that hung on the closet door. My God, but he looked disheveled and tired … scruffy, actually. There were weary wrinkles on both himself and his suit, lots of them. *Maybe the hotel staff can help with the wrinkles,* he mused. But, he knew deep down, that only solving this case would smooth them.

"Hello, Detective Finley," smiled a shy Guinevere Stone. "Thank you so much for my children." Both children were happily playing with Robie, and climbed into her lap when they noticed Axel. He hunkered down in front of them and produced candy bars from his pocket.

"Hi kids, do you like chocolate?"

They looked to their mother who smiled and nodded.

Whirlwind

"Oh yes, sir!" Within seconds the candy was spread on faces and hands and everyone present was chuckling. Unlike a lot of dogs, Robie had no problem with chocolate and was busily lapping at fingers and faces to the delight of the children. Finley noted that Pelleas was never more than a foot away from Mrs. Stone. He was easy with the kids, too, like he'd had experience with children. Axel was momentarily surprised at how much he wanted this little family to be safe and happy. Certainly he always felt this way, but this was special to him. Getting sentimental in his dotage. He saw Sally looking at him and intuitively was aware she knew exactly what had crossed his mind. He was suddenly reminded of how much he had, and how good life was.

Axel showed Guinevere the list of names the computer techs uncovered at the station. Guinevere looked at the names and shook her head. Stanley had found photos of many of the names on the web, a fact until recently, Axel would have found hard to believe. Now, he figured anything was possible on that Internet thing.

The woman from the airport with the gun proved to be Wyonne Montoya, and Stone was able to ID Franklin. Sally, actually, was the one who was the most help. She knew both of the museum men. Most recent were Todos, who lectured often with Lynn Stone-Franklin, and Brooks, who had actual artifacts to display at the lecture location. The biggest lead was that Sally had also met Cesar Montoya. He had been with Herbert Brooks. She remembered him talking to Brooks about his sister.

"He was a sort of arrogant man who didn't always understand how priceless the artifacts were and, in his presentations, often used incorrect words to explain their meanings or how they were made. He often got the time periods mixed up as well, and sometimes presented certain styles of pottery and statuery to be far older than they actually were. Once he showed a pre-Mayan pot and claimed it to be a forgery. I'm sure it wasn't, though. Another time he had several broken pieces that he announced belonged to the same hand-made village scene, when the pieces actually represented three different scenes 100 years apart or more."

After a heavy sigh, Sally looked tired. Axel knew she was ready to go home and finally agreed to let them move from the hotel to the house. They used an SUV with darkened windows and drove into the garage before getting out. The group moved directly into the basement apartment and was accompanied by three officers. Sally let herself be seen at the windows and briefly walking her dog, but she always carried her small revolver. Life would appear to be routine at the Finleys' home to anyone who might be watching.

When Axel returned to the station after a shower and fresh clothes, Stanley and Mike were closeted in a bare interview room with Herbert Brooks. They were getting nowhere, Axel saw as he watched from the hallway. He entered unannounced and dropped several photographs down in front of the startled man.

"I demand to be told what I am doing here …" Brooks stopped blustering when his eyes fell on the pictures. His deep red complexion paled at once when he saw the spread of bodies before him. Charles Stone, Peter Stone, Sean Connelly, the two youngest Stone children, as well as the burned and grotesque, unrecognizable, charred body of And Lynn Stone-Franklin, lying on the coroner's table. No one spoke for a full three minutes.

"What has this to do with me?" The voice of Mr. Brooks was barely audible and hard to hear.

"I expect you can shed some light on this, yourself." Finley was curt. "You are involved somehow and you are not leaving here until we know how involved. You may want to contact your lawyer." A tear actually appeared in

Whirlwind

the corner of Herbert Brooks' eye. He piled the photographs and flipped them over. He laid his head down on his arms and sobbed. Stanley, Mike, and Axel were stunned. They hadn't expected this reaction. The crime team let him weep for a few minutes and then Axel pulled his head up from the table more gently than he wanted.

"This was never supposed to happen. Never! Cesar and Prescott promised me. No one was to be harmed. I didn't know what to do! They threatened my family as well. Please help me. I'll tell you everything ... just save my family." He broke down again, far sooner than Axel had expected him to cave. Okay. This was good. Axel knew the man was too weakened and terrified to lie to them at this point. He sent Mike Troy off to pick up Brooks' wife and daughter. The Saint Paul Hotel would make a bundle on this case.

"Here are my questions. Are you ready? Can I expect you to lie automatically?" Axel stood.

"No, detective, not anymore. As soon as my family is safe, I'll tell you all I know. I won't even call my lawyer, I just want all of this to stop." Stanley went for coffee and Axel for his notes, leaving Brooks alone with his thoughts and an officer.

CHAPTER TWENTY-FOUR
Teuchitlan, Western Mexico

Rosario had the meal on the table when her family wandered in. Juan smiled and they all kissed her as they filed into the aromatic kitchen. The events of the day were shared and the boys, Diego and Roberto, teased their sister in their usual manner. It made the fond parents happy. But Rosario was aware of the missing three and her heart longed to see them, even if it meant trouble between her and her husband. Her soft brown eyes would stray to the empty places at the family table. Juan gave orders for the coming morning and the children excused themselves, again kissing their mother. She placidly folded her hands in her lap and gazed at her husband across the table. She waited for him to speak out of politeness as well as a life-long respect for tradition.

"What is it, my love?" Juan put out his cigar and took one of her hands in his calloused one. "What is on your mind this night?"

"My heart is very troubled and we must make amends." She always spoke in this formal and stilted tone when she was worried or upset. She wanted to be sure her words were heard and understood when she spoke. All of her family respected this, and all of them—well, not quite—but most of them realized that something serious was about to be uttered.

Juan raised his eyebrows at her and said nothing. His thoughts were elsewhere, on this year's crop, on his missing children who would not return his calls, on the bet he'd made on last night's cockfight which he'd lost, on the treasure still to be dug out of local grounds.

"Juan Antonio," Rosario whispered his name refocusing him again on her.

"You must hear me now! Cesar is stealing from my ancestors. He is causing them to feel pain and me to feel the shame." She pulled a much read and worn newspaper from her apron pocket and laid it out on the table. She waited.

Juan moved his eyes from hers to the paper. He was stunned that she even had an idea about Cesar and Wyonne! They had been so quiet and secretive. The headlines spoke of antiquities lost and stolen from the National Museum of Mexico. The Americans were asking questions and his government was now involved. *What had Cesar done?* This was unknown to him and suddenly he felt a great fear. He had always been a hard man, in control of his family and his life. It never occurred to him that his children would stray from his ways on their own. What thing had he set in motion? The one-time deal he had worked out with his friend since childhood, Cristian Todos, seemed to have blown up into a scandal he had been unaware of. He read the article again, afraid to raise his head because he knew Rosario would see the truth in his face. When he could delay no longer, he looked at his wife. She studied him.

"Tell me," she said.

Now that Rosario knew, Juan felt defeated. He also felt a shame deep in his bones and wondered how things went so far wrong. It wasn't unusual for Juan to completely change his thought direction. It was one of the numerous reasons he proposed marriage to his lovely woman. He knew she alone could keep him on track. He should have told her about Todos long ago. He began to tell Rosario how it began as a onetime deal with Cristian Todos, who now was an important man in Mexico City. Cristian had wanted some old relics from western cultures and he had asked his friend, Juan, for help. It would earn him a promotion and more money, which he was willing to share. All Juan needed to do was provide a few never-before-seen artworks from the shaft tombs in the area. Of course, Juan knew where many of the tombs were located. Everyone did. Many of the families lived here still. Families like Rosario Ramirez's, who lived where her ancestors had lived.

So Juan had helped his friend Cristian Todos with six beautiful objects. One haunted Juan yet. It was a scene of a family burying their dead. The sculpture was deep red clay and depicted seven live people with two linen-wrapped dead souls being placed at the bottom of a tomb. It was all in one piece and without a scratch. It had earned Juan several thousand dollars, a year's crop from only one of his fields, all in the space of two to three hours. Both Cesar and Wyonne had helped him. For Juan, it was over. Obvious now to him, it was not finished. Was this the reason his children had not returned home? All of this he told to Rosario with great regret. Not regret that he was discovered, but with a true regret that he had done such a thing. He could not live with the shame he saw in the eyes of his wife and beloved companion. For her to even speak to him of this was enough of a penance! For her to know what he had done was a pain he wasn't sure he could endure.

Rosario took Juan down to the newly established iron door.

"From our own tomb?" Juan was aghast at the thoughtless and daring feat of his son and daughter.

Whirlwind

Something must surely be done to bring his children back into the fold and make them see their mistake. This was more than Juan had bargained for.

"They will probably need to go to prison," Juan said in sorrow for what he considered his mistake. Rosario nodded as tears fell from her eyes.

"You, too, my husband, and Mr. Todos." Juan went to his telephone. Prison wasn't as fearful to him as the loss of the respect of his wife and neighbors. He was a lost and defeated man.

CHAPTER TWENTY-FIVE
St. Paul, Minnesota

Guinevere woke slowly, warm and relaxed. She could hear Geoffrey's even and methodical breathing in the bed next to hers. She'd slept with both of the children at her side. She realized then that she had let Charles go and let Geoffrey take his place in her heart. She trusted him and had from the start, probably more so than Charles, at least at the end. But then, she had trusted Charles at the beginning as well. And that surely had been a mistake. God, how she hoped Geoff hadn't done something heinous. Guin did not like secrets in a relationship. She would have to be sure to say that out loud to Geoff. If, in fact, that was where they were heading. She felt a slight stirring between her thighs that moved upward, begging to be touched. Perhaps it was time to share her bed as well as her life. Maybe tonight the children should sleep in the other room.

    She quietly reached over the bodies of Cathy and Sam to pull the light chain so she could read the clock face. Oh my goodness! It was eleven o'clock. They had all slept over fourteen hours. Or at least she had. Everyone else began to move about and Geoffrey mumbled her name.

Whirlwind

"Wake up, you lovelies. Cathy, baby, let's get you to the bathroom. Come on Sam, you too." She jiggled Cathy and tickled her cheeks.

"I already went, mommy, by myself and in the dark," Samuel was proud. "I'm not a baby, you know."

"Oh, I do know that. Of course you aren't. Will you take Cathy and help her?" The tots hurried off as Cathy was holding herself and squirming mightily. Guin looked over to Geoff intending to rouse him and found his eyes on her and a smile both on his lips and in those incredible eyes. He slipped from his bed and into hers so he could hold her close.

"Good morning, love." He kissed her forehead chastely and Guin felt the dampness between her legs again. She recognized the smell of his skin and loved it. She returned the kiss only this time on his lips. It was full of longing and Geoff knew it.

"You have changed, Rena. Something is different about you this morning." Geoff pulled back slightly to look at her.

"Yes, I think I have started my life over again. The children ... you ... I feel happy. I feel like Guinevere."

"Nothing really has been resolved."

"Maybe not, but it's out of our hands and in much more capable ones. The way I feel right this minute, I could happily remain in these rooms forever." She sighed and settled into his arms.

"Mommy! Cathy won't come out of the bathroom." Sam's shrill call interrupted the couple and Guin got up, laughing. "I'm coming," she called out to him.

They found a plethora of food in the tiny kitchen, some cold and more to be heated. There was a note from Sally saying not to use a phone or come upstairs just yet. Orders from Axel. Geoffrey found eggs, toast, jelly, and orange juice, and Guin started coffee. She definitely felt like it was a new beginning. Another new life.

Herbert Brooks was returned to the interview room from his cell. Stanley and Axel were ready for him. The man was beaten, defeated, lost. Gone was the somewhat cocky museum director. He gratefully accepted the coffee Axel offered, and began to talk without prompting.

"I was at a museum conference in Mexico City about a year ago. I was part of a committee dealing with illegal antiquities." He spoke haltingly and slowly. "I met a man there, Cristian Todos, who seemed to know a lot on the subject. I said something about how it used to be so much easier to outfit a museum before all this red tape and laws, before these third-world countries wanted to keep everything. It was supposed to be a joke, but later Mr. Todos approached me with a proposition." Brooks wiped the sweat that was forming on his face and took a deep breath.

"I was aware it was illegal, but I wanted to acquire something spectacular for the Science Museum. I admit I wanted to make a name for myself rather than remain on the bottom of the totem pole, so to speak. Now, I'm sure, I will lose my job entirely. The museum will not put up with such behavior. But it all seemed so easy, and I would only do this once." He raised his eyes to the detectives who remained stoic and silent. "So, I agreed to accept three pieces at a huge expense from Mr. Todos, with no questions asked. I paid him in traveler's checks and cash that I had my wife wire to me, and was told the pieces would be delivered to me in St. Paul. They were, shortly after I returned from the trip. A man I hadn't met before, Prescott Franklin, delivered the pieces. He was with two others, a beautiful dark woman whose name I never heard, and her brother, Cesar Montoya. Montoya told me other pieces would become available in the future and expected me to buy them. I was afraid to refuse."

"Were there other deliveries made to you?" Finley was writing in his notebook.

"Yes. There were six more over the past year. They have been at my house until I could figure out a reasonable way to explain them. Mr. Montoya and Mr. Franklin made all six deliveries themselves."

"Exactly how much money changed hands over the year?"

Brooks broke out in a sweat again as he lowered his head. "Two-and-a-half million dollars." He whispered. The detectives whistled in awe.

"My wife comes from old money and I simply took it without her knowledge. I will have to tell her now, I suppose . . ."

"Yes, I suppose you will need to do that. Plus we need all the artwork you got from these people. I'll send someone to your house to pick it up as soon as you tell us where to find it."

"Please take care of my family, sir. It is the woman that I'm most afraid of! She has a mean streak and cold eyes. It was she who threatened us and I'm sure she's capable of anything."

Axel finally felt progress was being made. His cell had been vibrating for the past hour so he excused himself and left the room to answer. Mike Troy was on the other end.

"Hey Axel, the officer we left at the Franklin house just phoned in some information. An incoming call from the Hilton, room 1321. As per your orders, he didn't pick up. What do you want me to do?"

"Find out who it was although I'm sure you won't get any real names. It's something, anyway."

"Should I go over there?"

"Absolutely, but quietly."

Wyonne was actively seeking a way out from under her brother. Their father was no problem for her. She would simply ignore his wishes just as she always had. Her mother was even easier. Just don't look at her. Wyonne had grown up doing exactly what she wanted, with whom, and when. All she had to do was not look at her mother, and not go home to the questions.

These few thousands she was getting from the antiquities was nothing in her opinion. Nowhere near enough for the life she wanted and thought she deserved. Recently she'd become aware of a slavery trade in young women. A sex trade. Wyonne knew all about the sex trade in every other way, but this sounded promising and lucrative. She just needed to find an outlet, someone to take the women from her once she had them. Her country was full of luscious young girls who were stupid enough to believe whatever such an accomplished and beautiful woman would tell them. Actually, these American girls would be worth so much more ... Wyonne came up with a delightful plan she and Prescott could work together. They would leave Cesar on his own and in their dust. It never occurred to Wyonne that she could fail at something she chose to do.

The first woman to be obtained, kidnapped actually, would be that Stone person. Wyonne even had a brilliant idea of just where she could be located.

Just then, Prescott appeared. He came to her and kissed her roughly, the way she liked. He tore at her clothes and tossed her on top of the bed as he too removed his own in the same manner.

"Do you have the drugs?" he growled in his anticipation. Wyonne reached to the bedside table for the syringe and the small vial of liquid. This was the key to why she held onto this man. He was willing to use this experimental drug to enhance the size of his penis and prolong his erections. Of course, he wasn't aware that it was an experimental drug. The sex they had was beyond either of their imaginings. It was explosive and sometimes could go on all night until it became painful for them both. Prescott complained of the pain but Wyonne relished it, welcomed it even, to feel so alive! Her body tingled as she drew up the liquid. The veins in Prescott's arms and legs were so prominent that even she could easily find a place to inject the fine needle. Within seconds, the drug would begin its amazing abilities. Clothes shredded and gone, their bodies already glistening with sweat, Wyonne climbed on top of the muscular firm chest of her lover. She placed her inviting crotch over his mouth and moaned as his tongue slid between the folds and into her vagina. The warmth and softness of it caused her to come in seconds. But no worry, she would do that many times this night. He ran his hands up the length of her sides and clutched her breasts almost with iron fists as he squeezed hard until she cried out and lifted slightly off of his face. Prescott threw her over to her side and entered her from the rear, pulling her buttocks into his penis with much more force than was needed. This wasn't the way Prescott liked to take his women, but Wyonne insisted on it. Anal sex, she said, was the height of desire. His fingers again found her vagina and the little knob that he liked to suck on and both of them climaxed with screams and wild bucking movements.

    He removed the condom and entered her as he rode on top of her chest. He loved that she allowed him to do this with no protection; to feel everything he could feel inside of this woman was such a pleasure that he couldn't contain his desire and climaxed again, much too soon. Her fingernails raked down his back drawing blood as she rose to meet his every thrust. She was like a wild cat and he, the lion. Hours later, when the drug finally wore down, Prescott slept. Wyonne was still planning. Now that her physical needs had been met adequately, she was able to put desire behind her and she could concentrate.

Susan M. Nelson

CHAPTER TWENTY-SIX
St. Paul, Minnesota

Wyonne sat in a "borrowed" car about three homes down from that of the detective. Her hair was tucked up inside of a black Twins baseball cap she had found in the rear compartment. Black sweater, black jeans, black shoes … no one would see her. The cop she had surprised with a blow to his head and an injected sedative; never saw her, never even suspected anyone was there. Like a cat, she was.

There had been too much activity there over the past twenty-four hours to have been routine for one couple, too many cops coming and leaving again. Every time she had driven past hoping to catch Mrs. Finley alone she saw someone new, several plain-clothed police coming and going on regular watches. Now, late in the afternoon, all appeared quiet. No police presence all afternoon and no Detectives Finley or Morse. Not even a delivery person had stopped at the house. It would not get any easier. She laid the binoculars on the seat next to her and left the car. She wore gloves and wasn't worried she'd left anything there that could name her. Besides, she wouldn't be gone long if all went according to plan and would be back inside this car with her prize. She moved the car directly in front of the house and left the passenger side rear door slightly ajar.

Whirlwind

The front door was locked, but Wyonne had become a pro at getting into places she was locked out of. It took only seconds before she heard the click of the lock being released. Her lock pick was so small and it was amazing how often she used it. Quietly, she entered and closed the door behind her. The house was still and getting darker by the minute as the day waned. It smelled of dinner, something with beef. But she could hear nothing. Where was the wife?

As she traveled through the front of the house, she relaxed. There was no one here. At the kitchen door, though, she hesitated. What's this? Wyonne was just barely able to make it out in the dimness. The wife was moaning and on the floor. She was reaching for the telephone that was also on the floor near her side. Wyonne immediately kicked it off to the corner of the room and knelt down to the woman.

"What's wrong with you?"

The eyes of the wife were scattered and couldn't focus when she seemed to be trying to look at Wyonne. She was cold yet she was sweating. Her mumbled words made no sense. Then she pointed to a small plastic something on the floor. Wyonne picked it up but had no idea of what she was looking at. Maybe some kind of medical device? There was a vial of small plastic strips spilled over the floor and a few droplets of blood. She stood again and found a bottle of insulin and an empty syringe on the table. These she pocketed. This woman wasn't going to get in her way, she was not going to be any trouble at all. She was barely conscious. Wyonne wasn't even going to bother to tie her hands together or tape her mouth, there was no need.

It appeared she had been incorrect about finding Stone in this house. Oh well, she had to be somewhere, and either Wyonne would find her or she would settle for someone else. Younger women, or even girls, were worth more.

"What are you doing to Sally?" The voice was behind her. Wyonne chided herself for not paying more attention. Slowly she turned around and faced the questioner. It was Guinevere Stone. So, she had been correct in her assumption that she would find her here after all. Wyonne's face took on a sinister smile of satisfaction.

"Nothing. I found her like this. What's the matter with her, anyway?"

Guinevere bent down to Sally. Wyonne knocked her over the head with her tiny revolver that was just heavy enough to do the job. Of course, Wyonne knew exactly where to place the blow. She dragged her to the back door and onto the porch. The wheelbarrow she'd noticed earlier was there and made a perfect cart. Covering the body with an outdoor furniture cover, she proceeded to her car. It was now the time of day she liked best, just dark enough for people to be confused by what their eyes told them. Shadows and more shadows floated over and around her as she moved toward the vehicle.

Mike Troy watched this from the yard behind the Finleys' home. He hadn't known the Montoya woman was in the house, but he knew something was off. The policeman she'd placed in the shadows was unconscious but breathing. Now he was more worried about Sally, so he dialed his boss as he slowly followed Wyonne back to her car, staying in the deepening darkness.

"Axel, get home now!" He disconnected and crept up behind the Ford Taurus. He stuck a magnetic tracking device under the bumper just as she took off from the curb. It was dark enough that she hadn't noticed him there. This evening light worked both ways. Now, if it just held. He watched the blinking dot on the Google map on his iPhone, as she pulled away. So far, so good.

Sally was still out when Mike got to her but he knew what to do and got the glucagon kit at once. He filled the syringe and pushed up the cuff of her shorts and inserted

Whirlwind

the glucose just like Axel had shown him. Mike had spent hours practicing until Axel was sure he'd gotten it right. It wasn't that hard. Within minutes, she was stirring a little and by the time Axel flew in through the front door, she was sitting up. Axel barely listened to the story he got from Mike as he held his wife and helped her check her blood glucose level. He carried her to the bedroom and got her face washed and tucked under the quilts. He had been reading about an insulin pump delivery system and the attachment that constantly measured blood sugars, and had been meaning to talk to Sally and her endocrinologist about getting started. The machine had some alarms built in that would alert the wearer to dropping or rising sugar levels way ahead of time. Of course, Sally would have to be paying attention. Sometimes she got so wrapped up in whatever had her interest at the time that she'd forget to eat, check her blood sugar, or even know what time it was. Actually, he had to chuckle, she never knew the time or the date and he had liked that about her. These things just meant nothing to his wife. Then, when Sally was sleeping peacefully, he encountered Mike Troy, who was staring at the blinking dot on his iPhone.

Geoffrey and the kids were in the kitchen as well, with both of the kids crying for mommy and Geoff pacing the floor in agitation. Robie, who had been with the kids, had already scratched at the door of the bedroom and Axel had admitted him. He jumped on the bed with Sally and then burrowed deep under the quilt. He growled at anyone who approached the bed, including Axel.

"How could this happen? Where are the guys that were supposed to be out front?" Axel demanded. Mike held up a finger.

"It's stopped moving. It isn't far away and she's stopped already."

"Who? What's stopped moving?" Axel asked.

"The Montoya woman has Mrs. Stone. She knocked her out and drove off with her. I stuck a magnetic GPS transmitter on her car, though. She's not moving at the moment. She also just left Sally on the floor and did nothing to help her." That alone disturbed Mike more than the missing Stone woman. She was one cold bitch!

"Well, let's go get her then!" Geoffrey exclaimed as he rushed toward the front door.

"Hang on there! You and those kids are going nowhere. Maybe back to the St. Paul Hotel or the station, but not after Guinevere and Wyonne Montoya! No way, no how." Axel grabbed Geoff's arm and handed the baby girl over to him.

"Take care of these kids, will you?" he pleaded. Geoffrey must have seen there was no sense in continuing this as he did what he was told. Axel was on the phone again getting a couple of squad cars over to his house. Mike was on the phone to the station as well, getting an exact address for the stopping point of the Ford Taurus.

Wyonne could hear the Stone woman stirring in the trunk of the stolen car already. The sounds were just audible but could attract attention. She smacked the trunk as she passed it.

"Shut up!" she ordered. She had parked a good distance from other vehicles in the lot, but still was unsure of the loudness. Rather than go to the room for Prescott, she dialed him on her cell.

"Meet me at the end of the lot," was all she said. Five minutes later, he was walking toward her, still buttoning his shirt.

"What's up?"

"We, you and I, are starting a new business. She's in the trunk."

"Who is?"

"Your friend, Guinevere Stone. She will be our first sell."

"Wyonne, have you gone nuts? What the hell are you talking about? We can't just sell somebody!"

"Yes, we can. You cannot be that ignorant of what goes on in the world! The white slavery trade. We'll make millions. It has become big business even here in the United States. Girls go missing all the time. They get shipped off to the Far East or Africa or Central America, places where American girls are considered to be exotic." She had stars in her cruel eyes. "I have a house on the outskirts of St. Paul where we can stash her until we have a few more before I make any contacts. We might as well have several for the client to choose from, eh?" A cruel smile spread across her face. Again with the cruel smile. He was beginning to dread that expression. It always meant trouble, usually for him. He still was unclear as to her intentions, but had learned it was safer to go along assuming he'd figure it all out eventually. He didn't want to earn her scorn. That was often painful in the physical sense. Maybe it was time to cut and run. This was all getting to be too much for Prescott.

Ever since he'd killed those little kids. He wasn't sleeping any more, too many bloody nightmares. But, he knew she'd never let him just leave her. He had a plan though, and maybe, just maybe, now was the time for implementing it. It might be dangerous, but so was everything else where Wyonne was concerned.

"The slave trade? But that goes on in Europe, Asia ... places like that, doesn't it? And, aren't most of those girls willing prostitutes? I don't understand how we sell them. Wyonne..." But he shut up when he saw the look she was shooting at him.

"Perhaps you should just leave the details to me, then. I know what I'm doing. Obviously, you have no clue." The scorn he didn't want to hear was dripping from her words that hung in the air in front of him.

Wyonne got back into the car, turned the key and gave him only a second to follow her inside or she'd drive off without him. He got in. Twenty minutes of totally silent driving later, she pulled into a gravel farm lane. It was rough and covered in deep ruts and long weeds, proof it hadn't been in use of late. The old, weathered white house sat a quarter of a mile from the road and was hidden by a small wood, thick with underbrush and dense trees. It was completely hidden from view. He could see that even in the total darkness. The house had been a typical Minnesota farmhouse at one time. A sprawling place, with several rooms added on as time passed and families grew. It was listing off the foundation and that gave it a menacing appearance. *Unsafe,* Prescott thought. *This whole thing is unsafe.* Two stories with boarded over windows upstairs. And downstairs ... those windows looked like deep black holes into some kind of hell. Shivers traveled up Prescott's spine and sweat began to form. He did not want to enter that door.

Wyonne pulled into a barn and turned off the ignition. The place was still full of square bales of hay, the old fashioned rectangular ones. A tattered and frayed rope was attached to the rafters and a pile of loose hay lay beneath where children had swung and jumped at one time. Prescott had smoked his first cigarette in a barn just like this one when he was ten years of age. He'd been paddled severely by his uncle who caught him nearly burning down the place, he remembered grimly. He'd hated the man. Still did, and he'd been dead for over ten years.

The house was on the top of a low rise. There were several piles of scattered lumber, insulation, and old furniture partially hidden in the grass. Wyonne kicked off her heels and went to the side door barefoot. The side had a small porch that was sagging but appeared to be the main entrance to the dark house. She fished a key from her pocket and opened the door. An odor of stale, closed-up old house wafted from the doorway. Mold, dead mice, and other smells immediately brought bad and evil images to Prescott's mind, again reminding him of the uncle. They entered a large square kitchen, or at least it had been that once. There were huge holes in the bare wooden floor and large chunks of planks were partly ripped up. It looked like someone was either in the process of remodeling or tearing the place down. He couldn't tell which, though.

"Is this place yours?" He asked Wyonne, not believing it for a minute.

"Not for long. Let's bring her in."

Prescott followed her back to the Taurus and watched while she raised the trunk. As the light came on he could see a disheveled Guinevere with blood all down the side of her head. She was dazed and blinking in the sudden harsh light. She tried to speak but Wyonne slapped her hard across her face, stunning her completely. Prescott felt some sympathy. He knew what a slap from Wyonne felt like.

"Bring her." She turned on her heel and went back to the house leaving him, as usual, to do the work.

"Come on. It's better if you just come."

Guinevere pulled as far from him as she was able, totally aware this was the person who'd killed her family. Suddenly she was worried about Cathy and Sam. Had these people discovered two of the children were still alive? She didn't dare ask, too risky. But she worried just the same. Her eyes were full of hatred as she focused on her brother-in-law.

"Suit yourself." He told her as he roughly pulled her from the trunk, scraping the skin from her legs as he did so. She winced but did not cry out. Her wrists were still bound together and behind her back. It was an easy thing for Prescott to flip her over his shoulder and carry her. He made sure to run his hands up under her shorts to feel her bare buttocks. He'd been eyeing that lovely rear for months now. It felt as firm and tight as he had expected it would. He wondered if he'd get a chance to do more than feel.

"Bring her up here." Wyonne's voice came from above him and he saw the stairway to the second level just outside the kitchen. It was a long, narrow stair like in most houses of this era: straight up most of the way then a level spot of three feet or so, a turn and three more steps to the top. Wyonne had turned on several dim bulbs that lent little light to the empty house. It looked too much like an old Hollywood movie set for a haunted house film done in black and white. Those films still could still give Prescott the willies. Shadows and dust, cobwebs and cold, dead air were everywhere. It gave him the creeps. There was a longish hallway with several doors leading into what he assumed were bedrooms. Wyonne stood at the end of the hall holding open a door. Inside was a small metal bed frame with a thin, very dirty mattress. Nothing else. Wyonne pointed to it and he dropped his bundle of woman there. Guinevere glared at Prescott with such loathing that it intrigued Wyonne.

"What's between the two of you?" she asked. Prescott shrugged.

"Nothing. She was always too good for me."

"Oh course she is!" Wyonne gave him that smile once again and it chilled him thoroughly. Yep, it was time for his plan. Before she followed through on any plan he was positive she had made for him.

Wyonne rummaged around in her bag and found a vial of pills and a bottle of water. She took three of the small white tablets and looked at Guin.

"Hold her head back."

Prescott did as ordered. Wyonne shoved the pills down deep and then poured in the water. Guin had no choice but to swallow before she choked. She received another slap just because Wyonne could do it so easily. So,

Whirlwind

Guin thought, *I'll get beaten up whether I do as I'm told or not. Might as well be a problem then.* But she had no time to think further. The tablets dissolved almost immediately and she felt her mind getting foggy and her vision darken. It began around the edges and . . .

"Okay. She's out." Wyonne looked at her watch. "We've got about six hours before she'll wake up, but cuff her to the bed anyway." She tossed the handcuffs to Prescott. Again he did as told. He also unbuttoned Guinevere's blouse and shoved her bra up over her breasts.

"Go ahead." Wyonne gestured. "We might as well get a good look at the merchandise. See how much she's really worth, eh?" She folded her arms over her own chest and watched as Prescott roughly undressed the woman. It gave Wyonne great pleasure watching his cock harden in his tight restricting jeans. She wondered briefly if it was as painful as she thought it would be. She almost told him to go ahead and release his pent up frustration on this unconscious woman, but her selfish nature took over. Slowly, while she watched Prescott fondling and exploring Guinevere, Wyonne stripped her own body of her clothes. Prescott watched in silence wondering where this was going.

"Come here," she was nearly growling, her throat was so husky. He'd never come in contact with anyone with a stronger sexual appetite. It both aroused him and terrified him simultaneously. He followed her into another room. Wyonne crawled up on the mattress like a sleek tawny jungle cat, her long shiny hair swaying with her movements. She lay on her back and spread her legs.

"Do me. Do me now!" She ordered as she reached for Prescott's jeans snap and opened the zipper releasing his cock. It burst from his pants in anticipation and eagerness like a caged animal suddenly released from its small prison. My God this man was too easy!

"Just like this? Here? Now?" He was unsure of what was expected.

"Do me now! She repeated spreading her legs so far open that there was nothing to imagine. She was glistening and wet and he wanted to, but she was making him nervous, like a boy with a prostitute for the first time.

"Would you rather do that dead thing in the other room?" she snapped at him. His answer would have been yes, but he was afraid. So, he dropped his pants and shoved into Wyonne. As they rocked together with her screaming and raking his back which still had not healed, he momentary considered wrapping his hands around her neck and just squeezing her life away.

This was just too delicious. Wyonne thought as she climaxed and climaxed again. The thoughts of Guinevere in the next room were exciting, almost like she was able to hear this and speculate on her own fate. Perhaps, Wyonne thought, she should leave her conscious for the next time. Let her listen to them, let her be frightened to death. Wyonne knew herself very well; she felt strong when others were afraid, especially afraid of her. Wyonne thought she might just enjoy this new line of work.

"She's on the move again," Troy announced to Axel, who was behind the wheel. Damn, he'd spent too much time with Sally. But there'd been no other choice.

"I'll at least get some backup." Mike was on his cell to the station while he watched the monitor. Axel drove, intent on bringing an end to this madness. He wanted the woman who'd left his wife to die on her own kitchen floor, alone and unconscious. He wanted her behind bars. Now.

Cesar was hunting everywhere he could think of for his partners in crime. He was ready to leave for Scottsdale and where the hell were they? Wyonne had been too secretive lately and, if he'd stopped to really think about it, he would understand that she was becoming bored. Tired of him and the artifacts which held little interest for her in the first place, and tired of Prescott Franklin and his whining and lack of imagination in lovemaking. She was constantly telling him about it and he hated to hear those details from her. Hard to tune them out, though. That was never a good thing. Even as children, a bored Wyonne was a dangerous and devious Wyonne. It was always trouble for someone. As school children, if there was something amiss, the nuns always looked to Wyonne first. Usually they needed not look further. No punishment fazed her. In fact, Cesar remembered a satisfied expression on his sister's face when she received her punishment.

On his second trip back to the room at the hotel, Cesar was met by four policemen with guns drawn. They'd been waiting for him. He didn't understand how he'd been found out, but there they were nonetheless. It never occurred to him that his own father would have had anything to do with it, but he had. So had everyone else he'd been involved with except for his sister and her worthless lover. Everyone still alive in this mess had folded so easily, even him. What did that mean? Todos and Brooks were already in custody, as was his father. So where was Wyonne?

When he pictured his mother's face in all its sorrow and disappointment, Cesar ignored his initial response to either fight or flee. He never even reached for his gun. Cesar simply gave up. He held up his arms and turned to face the wall before he was instructed to do so. He would have given up his sister and Franklin if he'd known where they were. Maybe prison was a penance he could handle for this. He was discovering that he had no stomach for this crime anyway. Perhaps after prison he could settle down to farming again, something he had enjoyed in the first place before Wyonne and his father had led him so far from the home he loved. He wanted desperately to tell his mother how sorry he was. He wanted to beg for her forgiveness and that of the ancestors. It amazed Cesar how much relief he felt at that moment. He would have put an end to this endeavor long ago if he'd known. A funny thing, life. As he turned to face the police, they were startled to see the look of peace and well-being that was on this young man's face.

    The police had gathered up everything from the room, including the bundles of antiquities. He was then taken to the station where he was placed into a holding cell alone. He was to wait for a Detective Finley, he was told. It was okay. He was ready. Cesar Montoya sighed heavily, mostly out of relief, and settled in to wait for the detective. He felt like praying, but he'd long since forgotten any appropriate words.

    On the patio of the beautiful sprawling adobe house in Teuchitlan, Western Mexico, Rosario rocked in the quiet evening light. Her hands were folded peacefully in her lap. She looked out over her agave fields. All was well this night. She could feel her grandmother's hand resting on her shoulder as she slowly rocked.

Whirlwind

CHAPTER TWENTY-SEVEN
St. Paul, Minnesota

Guinevere was waking up.

She realized she was tied to the bed, before she could even remember the events of earlier. She was cold and her head ached severely. She remained as still and quiet as possible and just listened. After several more minutes she determined that she must be alone, and slowly opened her eyes. There was light coming into the room from the hallway but it was a dim murky light that didn't reveal much. Only that the room had no window and that she was naked. As far as she could tell, the entire house was empty—quiet anyway. Guinevere twisted her body around to try and see beyond the room with little luck. The mattress smelled bad and she was afraid she might add to that by vomiting. She tried to slip from the cuffs, tried until her wrist bled, but to no avail. Until someone came, she was stuck here. With her face turned away from the mattress, she took several deep cleansing breaths to try and clear the drug from her brain. She would need her wits about her if she were to survive this jailor. She thought she might have heard a car driving away from this place, but that might have been hours ago. It was hard to think in this fog that had become lodged in her mind. She had been in and out of a stupor and wasn't able to discern much of what was happening to her. She resumed her struggling.

It was midnight. The upscale night club called Jump Start, in the heart of downtown Minneapolis, had just getting started with its live music and lively drinks, social bartenders, and friendly patrons. The place was famous for some concocted drink they had invented. Supposedly one shot propelled you into a mood to party. You were rejuvenated, ready for anything. This was Wyonne's idea of a good time. Dancing and drinking and the promise of sex.

It was a large club with lots of dark corners for private intimate acts of whatever. The tables sat up high and looked like glossy elongated bar stools. There were no chairs as everyone was expected to talk, drink, or dance. Prism light balls hung from the ceiling and turned slowly, sending shattered splashes of glittering light over the faces of the patrons. The live rock bands were backed up by multi colored strobe lights that flashed and alternated colors in time with the beat. The music was loud and strong and incendiary with a beat that got under your skin and joined with your heartbeat. Bodies tended to pick up on the feeling and moved in time with the bass beat without really noticing they were doing it. The atmosphere was one of excitement and anticipation. The whole club appeared to be new and expensive and looked a little European. Retro-London, Prescott thought.

This kind of lighting made everyone look good, Prescott realized as he gazed at the women. At this moment, Wyonne and Prescott were photographers from a new college co-ed magazine, scouting out fresh faces to fill the pages. Young, beautiful girls who wanted nothing more than to be models would believe anything. Prescott had no less than three cameras around his neck and was composing and shooting photos continually. He could be suave when he wanted to. And Wyonne was a pro. She found that

Whirlwind

people will believe anything a beautiful woman tells them. In fact, this plan wouldn't be working so well if she hadn't been so striking. People flocked to her.

The plan was simple. Interview interested girls to discover who was a college student from out of the area, decide which ones they would easily be able to unload, promise a free photo shoot, drug them, and get them to the car, and off they go. Easy.

"So, which ones do we want?" Prescott inquired after several interviews that all followed the same pattern.

Wyonne watched the crowd. She was definitely looking for someone or something specific. Prescott wasn't sure. The women she seemed to be watching, though, were all of a type, clean cut and all-American, pink, apple-pie cheeks and fresh and wholesome in appearance. The proverbial girl next door. Not too much makeup or flash, nothing trashy or sexually inviting. There were dozens of them, all happy and carefree and easy pickings. No one could easily tell Wyonne "no," she was so exotic and exciting, and Prescott figured that the girls all would want to be just like her.

"I don't really care as long as we stick to the plan. Hair color is no problem. They need to be trim and under about twenty, though, for the best money."

"How do you know this? What do you know about the modern slave trade anyway?" Prescott dared ask with a sneer.

"The man we will be dealing with was very specific, Prescott." She explained as to a child. "The clients want young, healthy women, not girls or boys, but college-age women like any of these. They have to look new and unused, fresh-faced, and innocent. I want them to be from out of the area so we have a couple of days before they are reported as missing."

"I always thought they needed to be a lot younger."

Susan M. Nelson

"Sometimes. But this guy wants college girls. I don't know why and I don't care. I did not ask him for his reasoning."

"How did you find this man? One can't simply look in the yellow pages for 'Slave Traders,' can they? Who else do you know? Wyonne, you never tell me anything."

She brushed his questions aside as she usually did. He resented it and was beginning to resent her as well. He wasn't the child she treated him like. Damn it, he was at least her equal. So, not only was he afraid of her, but he didn't like her much anymore. She was just too cruel. Too mean to him. Prescott wanted his Lynn badly.

"Well, what are you intending to do with them then?" Prescott didn't feel like he was even necessary for this and was on edge, not knowing much about the details of her plan, nothing really.

"Darling, do you not trust me?"

"I just need more information." *God!* He knew that he sounded like he was whining.

"Oh yes. These girls will probably go to Russia, Israel or maybe somewhere in the Ukraine or Hong Kong before being sold or rented, whatever term you feel comfortable with. The Eastern parts of Asia are a large market place for humans. Particularly American fresh faces. We could have sold those Stone children for a fortune." She gave Prescott her disdainful look. "More, even, than these college girls."

Prescott had the grace to blush at this reference to his one lapse in judgment. He looked out over the crowd again.

"Who will take them off of our hands?"

"You do not need the names. An enterprising group from Russia will pick them up and fly them overseas in their private plane. The girls will be held somewhere until the transaction takes place, and then they disappear."

"And the money?"

"We get our money before the girls leave our possession. Whatever price the next trader gets is up to him and out of our control. It is quite easy, you see. I have done all the research already to save you the work my love."

"It certainly sounds trouble-free, once we get them out of here. They won't be expecting it. Not here in the Midwest."

Wyonne gave him her dazzling smile this time, although she was thinking *at last the fool gets it.*

"Listen. Before we decide on the girls, I want to pick up my car. There's something in it I need." Prescott had wanted to bring this up for hours, but only now decided it was absolutely necessary. Wyonne was tossing the "darling" and "my love" around much too freely and he was sure she was up to something that would do him harm. Like murder.

"Sure, let's do it now. It's only about ten minutes from here." Wyonne smiled at the queue of girls and waved to them. She glanced once more at them and selected two, dismissing the others.

"We will be back here in a day or two for more interviews if you are still interested." She told them as they wandered away with obvious disappointment in their responses.

"We'll be right back with some information for you," she called gaily to the chosen. "Don't go anywhere."

Wyonne had had several of the special shots at the bar and was revved up and excited. She was a queen, a goddess, unstoppable. Her blood pounded in her ears and she loved it. She drove and she drove fast.

But they were in for a real surprise at the hotel. In fact, they drove past it and kept on going. The parking ramp was full of police cars with flashing lights and groups of cops standing around talking together.

"What the hell is all of that?" Prescott sounded worried.

"It's most likely nothing to do with us."

"So why did you drive past then?"

Wyonne drove around the block and approached the rear of the hotel, entering the parking lot. Prescott's Infiniti was at the far end, parked there so no one would open their doors into his beloved car. Wyonne didn't understand this attachment. A car was just something one used to get to places, nothing more. There was no police activity here, just at the front of the hotel. She was very relieved but acted nonchalant about it and parked next to the Infiniti. It was even darker in this spot, which they had selected purposely for that very reason when they arrived. It had been a good spot for loading and unloading illegal antiquities from trunks.

"We'll meet back at Jump Start, okay?" Wyonne did not wait for a reply but spun from the lot. First, though, she intended to switch this current vehicle for another. Just in case.

Prescott unlocked the door and slid into his car. He loved the new car smell that still lingered there. The bottles of Sangria were still there, under the seat, as was the plastic tube of liquid anti-freeze. He held both of them in his hands for a moment contemplating what he was intending to do. The wine had a strong taste and would hide the sweet anti-freeze. He doubted that Wyonne would taste it. This was her favorite wine and he figured she'd down the bottle without a second thought. He wondered how long it would take to kill her. Or, would she just throw up? Either way, he'd have time to get away and get to his wife. They'd take the first flight out of town and stay away for a while. He again reached under the seat and pulled a small plastic zip lock baggie from the darkness. He had crushed all the tablets he could find in their hotel room and added a few other little poisons to the mix. Wyonne hadn't noticed that her personal pharmacy was lacking and he thought he might need to add the works to the wine. She was a strong woman, after all. He'd give it to her as soon as they were back at the farmhouse. With any luck at all, he'd do her in before she did him. He never doubted that was her plan. Not for a moment.

Prescott headed back to the Jump Start.

Axel Finley and Stanley Morse sat hunkered down several vehicles past the Infiniti. They'd been watching the car and waiting for Franklin, but now they had the possibility of getting both him and the Montoya woman. They'd heard the name Jump Start and knew of the club and where it was located. But they did not know where to find Guinevere Stone. They silently waited until Franklin pulled away before turning on the ignition and following.

"We should have some kind of an idea of what we're doing?" Stanley asked.

"Great idea. You got one?"

"Nope."

"Okay then. Call Troy and have him meet us with a half dozen uniforms. Tell him just to hold tight and remain out of sight until we have a brainstorm. Maybe they should be in a utility van or a UPS type truck." He grinned at his friend.

"Right-o. I'm positive we'll get one of those idea things. I can almost feel one comin' on right now," Morse said with a grin, hoping to relieve some of the tension they were feeling.

"Tell me, Marissa, where did you say you were from again?" Wyonne asked the question although she remembered perfectly well where she was from, and everything else about her.

"Nebraska, ma'am. My dad went to the U and, well you know how dads are! He wanted me to go to the same school. So, there I am! I can hardly wait to surprise him with the first magazine with me on the cover!" She was nearly bubbling over in her starry-eyed willingness.

Wyonne placed another shot before the girl, one she had doctored up some.

"Please call me Wyonne. Can you pose tonight? We want a few shots with the lights of Minneapolis in the background." She sat poised with pen over paper as though she were jotting down her thoughts about the girl.

"Night shots? Will I have clothes on?" She looked worried for the first time. "I don't think I can pose nude or anything like that. You know, pornographic stuff."

"Of course you'll have your clothes on. This is a classy magazine." Wyonne acted offended.

"Okay then! Yes! Right now if you like."

"And that girl" Wyonne stretched out her index finger at a perky red head waiting anxiously several tables away from them. "She's your only roommate and is from Florida, correct?"

"Yes, Connie."

"Do either of you have any scars on your bodies or blemishes or abnormalities that I should know about?"

"No, both of us are about perfect." She replied with no small amount of pride. "We are both up for Homecoming Queen this year. I'm positive that I'm going to get it, though."

"Oh my." Wyonne said absentmindedly as she was dwelling on those perfect bodies.

"Tell her to join us for one more drink and we'll be on our way. We need just the two of you for the night shots. Your blonde hair and her red will photograph terrifically in the lights."

Marissa trotted-skipped to her friend with the great news. God-damn but this was fun.

"Well, that was easy." Prescott whispered. "Now what?"

"Get them two of whatever sweet crap they're drinking and put this into the glasses." She handed him two tablets that were crumbling already, so he guessed it was the same drug he watched her give to Guinevere.

"It's not the same, idiot." She read his mind. "This will just make them helpless but not unconscious. Easier to get to the cars. You take the blond and I'll bring the red head."

Now Prescott had another reason to resent her. She'd been calling him an idiot for days. He didn't reply, though, as he was going to get his revenge . . . later. Very soon. Tonight.

Axel watched with Stanley as the four came out of the night club fifteen minutes after they had entered. The two girls seemed slightly drunk and needed to be physically supported by Franklin and Montoya. When they separated into the two cars, he punched up Troy on his cell and told him to follow Franklin. They'd take the woman. He was sure they were going to the same location, he just didn't know if that's where they'd find the missing Guinevere.

"What do you suppose they're up to now?" Stanley thought out loud.

"God only knows," was Axel's terse reply.

"Axel, the GPS is still attached to her car and is transmitting." Troy was still on the phone. "Should the uniforms just track her from farther behind so we can all meet up?"

"Absolutely. Good thinking buddy. That GPS gadget was brilliant. Maybe you'll get that fishing trip yet." Troy chuckled.

There was little moon that night and following was somewhat difficult when they crossed the Mendota Bridge where there were fewer street lights and less city traffic. Axel had to hold back more than a little. Troy was keeping him informed with the GPS, though.

"Up ahead there, by those dense trees. See them?" Troy asked.

"Yep."

"Slow down. Both cars turned in just past there, around the corner from Lone Oak Road. I don't know what that cross street is, but there's a farm lane, no longer in use, just there."

"Have the guys kill the lights and park sporadically up the road and meet us on the road side of the trees. There aren't many houses out here, are there?" Axel was surprised by that information, this close to downtown St. Paul and with the airport just across the bridge. He knew that Fort Snelling was there somewhere also. Close but yet so far, he thought. Someone chose this spot well.

Axel loved this smell of woods; damp, green and musty leaves that he was crushing beneath his feet sent even more of the scent to his nose. It was a smell from childhood, of playacting and building tree forts in the woods near his home. His brother and their friends built a new one each and every summer and those memories were such good ones. This night hunt brought them all back and he wished he were here for a different reason entirely. Idly he wondered if Sally might like a camping trip.

The six of them spread out to surround the old faded and dilapidated house, where feeble light shone through several cracks in the boards covering the upstairs windows. He knew Troy and his men where covering the exits from a distance. Troy would be poised to follow if anyone left. They still didn't know if Guinevere was there. Stanley wondered if maybe they had yet to bring her to this place. Either that or she was already dead. It was far too quiet here. They again waited for word from Axel.

The young women had been too drugged to give any resistance in the cars. Even now, their eyes were only half open and when they tried to talk, only small sounds made it through their lips. They rode slumped in the passenger seats with their heads bobbing up and down with the movement of the drive.

Whirlwind

"Try not to hurt your lovely head on the door, sweetheart." Wyonne admonished.

But when it was time to leave the relative safety of the vehicles, both girls resisted and pushed as far into them as was possible. Prescott simply grabbed an arm and tugged until they were sprawled on the gravel driveway. Then he moved the cars to the barn once again, out of sight. Not that anyone was watching. He figured no one knew where they were, or what they were doing. No sane person would be out here at this hour. Of course it was Prescott who half carried the coeds into the house and up the stairs. God forbid that Wyonne should break a nail.

"Put them in here." Wyonne gestured to a larger room at the front of the second story, facing the driveway, such as it was. Franklin was worried about the underside of his car, his Infiniti, and was just barely paying attention to Wyonne's barked out orders. God how he loved that word, Infiniti! But rather than go to check it again, he did as he was told.

Both girls were silent, but their eyes spoke volumes. They still hadn't fully realized what was happening to them. Stupid, vapid bitches, but they knew something wasn't right with their world. These mattresses were not as soiled as Guinevere's. There were pillows and rough army surplus blankets as well. Prescott tossed these over the girls.

"Check them out if you want." Wyonne offered generously. But Prescott had lost his desire and his interest in this cruel game. Wyonne's sexual appetite was getting the best of both of them. His penis was sore and he could hardly stand the fabric of his expensive shirt over his raw back. He pictured it rather like the backs of the religious zealots who whipped themselves with leather cord that had pieces of metal and glass tied into them, until they were raw and bloody. For Christ, or something. He never was sure. Religious beliefs gave him the creeps.

"No, you're enough for me," he lied. "Reminds me, I've got something in the car for you. I'll just get it."

Wyonne loved his gifts. They were always small but interesting and most led to sex play. She cuffed the girls to a double bed and left them in the dark while she went to check on Guinevere. She noticed the bloody wrists even in the dim light. Had she awakened already? Wyonne glanced at her wrist watch. Impossible. They still have nearly three hours according to the snaky pharmacist she'd enticed. Of course, why should she believe him? But Guinevere's breathing was shallow and steady as was her pulse. She was out.

But she wasn't. Not entirely. She had been fighting sleep for what seemed like many hours now. When she heard the arrival and the voices she forced herself to remain still, forced her rapid heartbeat and breathing to slow and even out. And she listened, trying hard not to gasp at the smell of the mattress or the spiders that she could occasionally feel on her limbs. The criminal pair had brought someone with them. She hoped it wasn't her family but she was unable to detect more.

"Wyonne? Where are you, baby?" Prescott whispered from the hallway.

"Here, with your girlfriend." She answered him in her snotty short tone.

Prescott grimaced at her voice but was resolved to carry on with his plan. He joined her, determined to do whatever it took. Hell, he would even drink some of this tainted wine if he had to.

"Here, it's your favorite love making beverage, darling." *Uh oh, he'd better cool it with the endearments.* After all, that's what had given him pause with Wyonne.

"Ah, so it is. Are you trying to tell me something, Prescott?" She reached for his crotch and kissed his mouth. "Do you want a repeat of the last little adventure then?"

Whirlwind

She gestured with her head at the room just outside of this one.

"Not exactly. I thought maybe we could have a drink first and then do it without the drugs. You know, just the real us, like it used to be."

Wyonne was slightly disappointed in this. She had really been anticipating the feel of the other woman listening to them in the throes of passion. That thought had been a surprising turn on. She fingered the vial of insulin and the full syringe in her oversized pocket.

"Whatever you want, Prescott." She removed the syringe cap and approached him. "Ready?"

"Wyonne, not this time. Just straight sex, okay?" He was complaining. Wyonne could not believe it! After all she'd done for him!

"No, it's not okay!" She snapped at him and rammed the syringe into the muscle of his arm. She pushed the plunger all the way home before he reacted.

"Damn you Wyonne! Not right now! I've got something to do first. I'll get it done and get right back to you. We'll drink the bottles to celebrate and make love then. Anyway you want it! Good enough?' He rubbed his arm where the mark of the syringe lingered in his skin. Damn that hurt!

"Listen, I'm back here in less than one hour."

"Sure. I'll wait and even hold the wine until you return. The drug will still be working. In fact, you'll be so ready for me by then that ..." She tried on a sweet smile but it just didn't work with her eyes and even she knew it. Wyonne was fairly sure he didn't have an hour left. Maybe not even twenty minutes. In fact, she had pulled the cork from the first of the two bottles before he was out of the house and had swallowed one third of the bottle before she heard his car door slammed in anger. She smiled again and finished the wine. It was delicious. Wyonne decided she would make her call now.

"What!" The voice she knew as Steffen Kouropoulos answered roughly. Cesar had introduced him to her as "The Russian" as if were his name but Wyonne had done more research than her brother had. "Do you know what time it is?"

"Yes I do, but are you not anxious for my call?" Wyonne used her sultriest voice.

"Wyonne! So good to hear from you. What do you have for me?"

"There are two of them tonight. Exactly what you asked for plus a bonus, a free sample."

"Ah, yes. That sounds very good. I will come to you?"

"Yes. But not until I call again." She disconnected. She was feeling slightly ill suddenly and completely unexpectedly. She never was ill, never had been. Sick to her stomach. She wasn't able to remember the last time she ate. She always felt the wine faster if she hadn't eaten in awhile. Sure, that was all it was. No food and a full bottle of wine. No problems, then. All she needed was something to eat. Would any of her favorite restaurants deliver out here at this hour?

Whirlwind

CHAPTER TWENTY-EIGHT
St. Paul, Minnesota

Prescott Franklin wanted his wife. He hadn't listened to any news or read any newspapers in months and had no idea that she was dead. Nor had the Montoyas told him. Now he needed to be held and caressed and told that everything was going to be fine, that she forgave him and even understood. Of course he'd never be able to explain about her brother and his family, but maybe he could live with that. He'd make something up to extricate himself from this mess just like he'd always done. After all, it had been the Montoyas who had killed her family, not him. He had been devastated by what they had done. He, Prescott, would never be able to harm anyone who was dear to his wife. It wasn't his fault and he was sure she would be able to see that. He had always told his parents that his friends did it and they'd believed him. Not accepting any responsibility had always served him well. He was trying to picture his lovely home with his accomplished wife waiting for him and a warm meal on the table, but it all kept slipping away from him. In fact, everything was going by the wayside in his mind. Prescott couldn't seem to hold onto any thought for more than a second, not long enough to form a solid and cognitive idea.

Mike Troy was following the Infiniti as per instructions, but he was becoming concerned. The driver was acting erratically, switching lanes too often when there was no need. His speed was irregular as well, sometimes so slow he was barely moving. Next the vehicle would speed up to eighty or more, hugging the median or the shoulder. Starting and stopping, he was forcing the flow of traffic, scarce as it was, to maneuver their cars to get away from him. Horns were blaring and each time, the Infiniti's brake light shone bright red. Troy could see a construction zone coming up on the right side of the highway. Large signs blocking passage. He remembered that the Mendota Bridge was undergoing some refits. Should he pull the car over? Was Franklin drunk? Would he take note of the barricade?

Sweating so much he could hardly see the road in front of him, Prescott thought it was raining and he'd left the sun roof open. He kept fiddling with the controls but the rain wouldn't stop. His hands were very wet and it was difficult to grasp the steering wheel. The hands felt like they were not connected to him in any way, and kept hitting his lap. He was now unable to feel his feet on the gas pedal or the brake. In fact, he was sure there were no feet at all. His lips tingled and then went numb like they had been shot full of Novocain. He tried to rub them but wasn't able to tell if his fingers made any contact with his lips. He kept wiping the rain from his eyes so he could see the road, but it didn't help. Then, suddenly and without warning, his vision blurred to the point of him needing to rub his eyes. He was sure there was a kaleidoscope in front of his vision and everything looked fractured. What the hell? He was shaking badly, trembling and cold. Very cold. No, he was burning up! Sweat, not rain! But what was wrong with him... This didn't feel right at all. Next, his conscious mind started to slip away. It was still working, but his thoughts made no sense. Prescott kept seeing Wyonne's computer game of spider solitaire in front of his vision and he didn't

Whirlwind

know how to play. The blinking and moving construction arrow signs caused Prescott to see everything in that manner, moving and blinking. It was impossible, so he'd close his eyes for seconds at a time. Somewhere inside of his brain he knew that Wyonne was responsible for this, he just didn't know how. Was she here with him now? When his hands dropped from the wheel once again, he fell unconscious, lost all sense of himself and plowed through the wooden road barricades and the heavy metal fence like there was nothing there. But he did this without noticing. The insulin was rapidly destroying his brain by then, and, if he lived, would most likely remain in a vegetative state. Prescott drove his beloved Infiniti straight off the right side of the Mendota Bridge and fell over a hundred feet into the Mississippi River.

    Mike Troy stopped at the barricades and phoned Axel. He was trembling and having some trouble with the tiny buttons on his cell. He knew what he'd just seen, but what had he just seen? He traversed by foot over the wreckage of the barricades to the edge of the bridge and looked down. There wasn't a sign of any kind and the river was moving along as usual. Some boys in a boat were yelling and gesturing. What the hell! Had Franklin just killed himself? Was he alone in his car? He called in the dive recovery team.

    Wyonne took another bottle of wine, an old sandwich that she had stuffed into her bag that morning at the hotel, and a chocolate bar into the room with Guinevere. She was walking a little strangely she realized, unsteady, clumsy. Wyonne was never clumsy. She thought of herself as the height of glamour and grace. Her body and clothes reflected it. But then she actually stumbled. Really stumbled and fell to her knees. What? She looked at the bottle but she hadn't spilled too much. Nor had she had much from that second bottle so she knew she wasn't drunk. Odd. Of course she hadn't eaten in hours. Yes, that must be it. She walked more slowly and cautiously into the small, close room, leaning heavily against the wall and sort of sliding along it. Wyonne just couldn't stop herself; she was fascinated with that woman. This time Guinevere's eyes were open.

"Well, well, what have we here? Are you comfortable? I'll bet you're hungry my love. Sorry, all I have is this stale sandwich and I need it. If you're a good girl, though, perhaps I might share this wine." She showed her the bottle before she tipped it to her lips.

"Now, let's get to business. Do you have the computer program from your husband's computer?"

"No, the police do."

"Wrong answer!" She delivered a harsh slap to Guinevere's already bruised face cutting her swollen lip with the edge of her large diamond and sapphire ring. She swallowed more of the wine.

"Damn! You got blood on my ring. My brother bought me this. It's worth more than you will be." At least that was what Wyonne had intended to say. It came out a sort of gurgle but she didn't even notice that. Guin looked at her oddly and saw that she wasn't standing straight anymore but looked a little hunched over. Guin was startled at how beautiful this cold and cruel woman was, stunning with an evil sort of beauty.

"That may be the wrong answer for you, and you can slap me all you want but it will not change that fact."

"Did you see what was on the flash drive?" Wyonne had raised her hand already to slap if she didn't like the response. This time she was articulate. Guinevere figured correctly that the slap would come no matter what the answer. Wyonne stumbled again and awkwardly fell hard against the bed.

"No. I have no idea what's on it. Some computer game, I think."

Whirlwind

Wyonne pulled herself back up and paced the length of the bed with her sharp eyes never leaving Guin's face.

"You're lying."

"So hit me then." But Wyonne was staring at the bottle. She sniffed it. Something wasn't right. Normally she could drink three or four of these bottles by herself without feeling this woozy. No, more than woozy, over the edge. If she could throw up maybe she'd feel better. But vomiting had never been easy for her. Even as a child she had to force herself to do it, to convince her mother she was too ill to go to school, to face the nuns in all their piety. But she had to admit she was ill, and getting worse by the minute.

"I won't hit you again if you help me." Her voice no longer sounded like her own. She was whining from a great distance away.

"Smell this." She shoved the lip of the bottle under Guin's nose.

"Sweet. It smells sweet. Maybe too sweet even for Sangria."

"Taste it!" But her fingers couldn't hold the bottle and it slipped to the mattress and spilled out the contents. Sticky, too sticky, too thick.

"What's in it?" Guin asked her tormenter. Wyonne's eyes widened in shock. That hadn't occurred to her.

"Do you think there is something in it?" She was gasping now.

"Yes I do. Can you taste anything beyond the wine flavor?"

"No. Yes. I don't know!" Wyonne was about to panic, something she had never done in all her life.

"I have to get to the hospital! Call 911, take me, help me." But she had forgotten that the woman was naked and cuffed to the bed by her doing. And her words were garbled all together and came out as a howl, long and soulful ... full of fear. The animal sound of it filled the house with its anguish and tore out into the silky night. But no one there was capable of taking her anywhere. Only Prescott would have done it and he was … he was … but … but … where was he? Had she already killed him? No …

Wyonne's body was betraying her will and shutting down. First her kidneys, then her liver slowly stopped doing the jobs that kept her alive. Her heart and lungs quit at about the same time, her lungs filling up with body fluids while her heart slowed to a minimal rhythm. Bubbles of pink liquid escaped from between her lips as she struggled for enough air. But there wasn't room in her lungs for air. Her eyes looked wildly around her for help, knowing it was too late for that. Her brain remained active long enough to realize that Prescott had poisoned her with her favorite drink. The bastard had outsmarted her and she'd had no idea! Her limp form slipped down the wall and she landed on her butt with her head lolling to the side, eyes open, rich thick black hair trailing down the rough stucco wall. She was no longer breathing but her eyes were staring at Guinevere. Empty eyes.

It took several minutes for Guinevere to realize her predicament. Her jailor was dead and she had no way of releasing the handcuffs. This was not good. The dead woman most likely had the key on her, but how could she get it? Maybe Prescott would come back. If she could just wait a little longer. Guin twisted and twitched her body trying to move the mattress off the frame. She tried reaching with her bare feet but it was just too far. She rested a moment before renewing her efforts.

Frustrated, Guinevere screamed. Howled, actually. Long and full of fear.

Axel ended his call and turned off his cell. Troy had informed him of the fatality. He was quite sure that it had been Franklin behind the wheel although Troy made it a point to mention that he never actually saw him.

Whirlwind

"It's likely that only the Montoya woman is in this house since we have the rest of this group in custody. We saw her and Franklin leave the club with the two college girls, so they have to be here too. Hopefully Mrs. Stone is here and still alive. But, they didn't want her to remain alive so that's anyone's guess." He wiped his brow.

"Let's approach slowly and see if we draw any fire. Stanley I'll let you go in the front and I'll take the main door. At least I think that's what it is. With these old places it's hard to tell."

"Yeah, foot traffic has flattened the grass on that side, Axel. Take it slow."

"Listen! Is that an animal in there?" Axel held up his hand and they all heard it. The scream of a wounded animal filled the night air for several seconds.

"Let's go in," said Axel. They all clicked off the safeties on their weapons.

All five of the remaining policeman approached from all sides until they were up against the rough chipped outside of the farmhouse. No signs of life from windows, no sounds from the house. Axel tried the door and it opened easily as it wasn't quite latched. Someone had most likely slammed it and it popped back open because the lock had been set. Whoever took off in the Infiniti in such a hurry, he guessed. He entered the darkened room. Somewhere overhead he could hear scrapping sounds and loud grunting. It sounded like a human was working very hard at something up there. A dim bare light bulb hung over the steps going to the second level, swaying gently and creaking with each movement, flickering as though it were almost spent and could quit at any moment. The thick dust on the wooden steps had been disturbed by many feet. Then he heard it, soft barely audible crying.

Stanley gestured to two of the officers to clear the first floor. Then he pointed to the stairs and gestured that he and

Susan M. Nelson

Axel should go up. Axel nodded. Slowly, so slowly, they crept upwards.

Whirlwind

CHAPTER TWENTY-NINE
St. Paul, Minnesota

Geoffrey and the two little ones had said they'd stay with Sally, even though there were two officers with her. She wasn't recovering as quickly as usual, even after the glucagon injection. She had actually needed to vomit and that only happened with the extremely low sugars, the nearly bottomed out ones. She had no strength at this moment. The entire group was on edge including Sammy. Cathy was happily oblivious and was reading a story to Sally and her brother.

"And then the little pig let the wolf blow his house apart because he really wanted to do it." She stated firmly.

"No! That's not how it goes. Do you want me to read it?" Samuel asked disgustedly while Sally smiled at them with Robie wrapped up in her arms.

"Okay then!" Cathy shoved the book away.

"You do it!" She said in equal disdain. She always liked the stories that mommy made up better than the ones from books and mommy would have told it just like Cathy did.

The phone jangled. Geoff dashed for it and had it to his ear before the second ring. All eyes in the room were on his face.

"Guin, Guin . . . Oh, hello Sergeant Troy. What? Can you say that once more?" He listened for several minutes.

"Tell Axel that Sally is doing well now. No worries here. We're quite well supervised." He hung up then, not wanting to relay any messages to the kids yet.

"Geoffrey? Samuel was at his elbow. "Was that about mommy?"

"Yes, little lad, it was. Come and sit by me." He took the boy's hand and sat next to Sally pulling Sammy into his lap.

"Mike Troy watched one of the criminals drive off of the Mendota Bridge about one half hour ago. We don't know exactly who was in the car or how many. Detective Finley, Stanley Morse, and several others are at some old farmhouse and are about to enter. They don't know who is in there if anyone at all is. He called because Axel asked him to find out about you, Sally. That's it." His shoulders slumped and he gently rested his chin on Sammy's soft hair. He made eye contact with Sally who looked as worried as he was.

"It's okay, Geoffrey, don't worry. New mommy always comes home. She told me that she would." Cathy said solemnly in all her three-year-old wisdom and innocence. God how he hoped she was right! Samuel picked up The Tale of the Three Little Pigs once again and began to read. When he got to the part about the wolf huffing and puffing, he told it exactly like Cathy had.

Guin hesitated. What was that? What had she heard? There was someone on the steps. She opened her mouth to call out but reconsidered immediately. If it was Prescott, he'd kill her. Hadn't that been his plan all along? She shuddered both from the chilly, sticky goop on her body and from the fear that it would be her brother-in-law coming for her. She tightly closed her eyes. Whoever was out there was getting closer.

"Mrs. Stone?" The voice was soft and kind and familiar. Her eyes flew open and stared into those of Detective Finley. Oh, thank God! Another man she couldn't quite see was bending over the prone woman on the floor and fishing around in her pockets. Somewhere outside of her tiny cell, Guin could hear other voices and was suddenly conscious of her nakedness but she was so completely relieved that the thought of her naked body left her mind as soon as it had entered.

"Here it is." Axel reached for the key that was being offered and quickly had the cuffs off Guinevere. He helped her to sit up on the edge of the bed she was shackled to. Stanley picked up Guin's clothes and a blanket that was in a pile in the corner of the room. He handed them to Axel who caringly helped Guinevere get dressed. Then he gingerly wrapped the blanket around Guin's shoulders. She had never been handled so gently and with such consideration. Morse had left the room to see how the others were doing.

"My children?" Guinevere asked as tears of relief formed. "Are they here, too? Is Geoffrey? Sally?" It all was coming back to her now. The Finley house, Sally on the floor, the dark haired woman bending over her, then … Had the children been with her?

"Everyone is fine. Wyonne Montoya didn't know the kids were alive so she never looked for them. It was you she was after. They're all together with my wife. I believe that Samuel has taken over and is reading them all a story." Axel smiled at her tender expression when he mentioned the boy.

"How are you? Anything I should know about your condition other than you are nearly blue from the cold?"

She shook her head.

"There are two other women in another room who are in slightly better condition than you. What happened here? Do you know anything about them?"

"I can't tell you much, detective. I think it was just the woman at your house. I think she knocked me out with something. I don't know what she did to Sally, I just heard Sally fall and went to check on her. I came to in the trunk of a car. They cuffed me to the bed and gave me some drug. When I woke up I heard someone leaving and then she came in." Guin looked at the dead Wyonne, the beautiful but evil Wyonne Montoya. She felt nothing but hate. This was the person, along with Prescott, who took her family from her. She was glad the woman was dead.

"She was on her way to getting drunk although the bottle was almost full. Then she seemed to think there was something wrong with the wine. She asked me to smell and taste it, but I just played along with her and told her that I thought it was a little off. It must have actually been, too, because she just died. Right there." Guin looked at her again.

"Prescott Franklin is somewhere in the Mississippi River, so he's gone too. The rest are in jail. It's over now, Mrs. Stone, all finished." Axel helped her to stand and then just picked her up when he saw how weak she was. He carried the slight woman out of the room, down the stairs, and all the way to the porch of the house where he set her down delicately on the steps. The other two girls soon joined them there. They were able to walk with help, since the drug hadn't entirely worn off. They were just now beginning to realize what had happened to them the night before.

"So, they weren't going to take our photographs for a new magazine?" Connie asked. Stanley shrugged.

"There is no magazine about college co-eds? Well, what were they going to do with us then?" she demanded. Someone here must know what's going on.

Whirlwind

Axel handed her a newspaper article that had been found among Wyonne's belongings in her bag: "White Slavery on the Upswing Around the World." There was a small notebook as well but he kept that to himself. It was a list of names with phone numbers, body types, ages, race and sex. There were notes about Cesar, Juan, and several antiquities with either sketches or actual photographs.

He wanted to startle the girls into being more careful in the future although he doubted they would ever realize just how close they had come. He found that young innocent people never do. Like his nephew who declared he was too young to get AIDS. It worked, temporarily anyway, as both of the young women were struck dumb by the headline alone.

"Slavery? I don't understand … what slaves?" the redhead asked.

"Us, you idiot, we were to be the slaves." The other seemed more alert and caught on immediately.

"And me?" Guinevere had seen it, too. "Was that to be my fate also?"

"I don't think you would have lived long enough to be sold. Montoya was ruthless. As soon as she found out that we had her brother in custody because of the flash drive we got from you, well, you would most likely have been her revenge."

Stanley was back with one of the police cars and Troy had just pulled up as well. A tech team followed behind Troy and was unloading the evidence collecting gear. The policemen would stay behind so the detectives were free to leave with the women.

"Now let's get you all to the hospital. We'll take your statements in the morning." The paramedics had not arrived yet. Axel told Stanley to take Mrs. Stone and the two girls to the hospital. Axel was anxious to get to his wife.

"That ... is not going to happen!" Guinevere stated emphatically. "Detective Finley, you are taking me to see my children. You are going to do that right now."

"Of course, Mrs. Stone." Axel knew better than to argue. The woman knew her mind and was not likely to change it.

The Finley residence was brightly lit even though the sun was up. Everyone had been too busy thinking and hoping to pay attention to the time of day. Guinevere was able to walk with help into the house but she had badly strained her leg tendons trying to reach Wyonne for the key. Her wrists were torn up badly but she refused to go to the hospital until she saw her family. Axel was afraid maybe she had been raped but didn't say so. He stood with his arms around Sally and Robie while the children attacked Guinevere's legs and just held on. Then Cathy released her mommy and turned to Geoffrey.

"See, I told you! New mommy always comes home."

Geoffrey was so relieved that he was crying openly. He hadn't been able to imagine his life without this woman and it had been all he could think about. Guinevere walked into his embrace and kissed away his tears. The children giggled at these funny adults. Samuel looked unsure, though, and Guin figured he was wondering about Charles and Peter. She would try her best to explain it all to them.

"Mommy?" Sammy waited for her to look at him before he went on. "Is my daddy dead? Did Uncle Scotty really make him dead? Is Peter dead, too? I didn't see them at the hospital, did I? Can we just go home now?"

Oh, this was going to be hard!

"Do you want the truth baby? The real truth even if it hurts you very much?"

"Yes."

"Okay. Uncle Scotty and his girlfriend killed your daddy and Peter. They tried to kill you and Cathy also but a

Whirlwind

very nice man from the ambulance saved you and the doctors fixed you both right up."

"But the doctors couldn't fix up daddy and Peter?" Samuel wanted to be sure.

"No, honey, they couldn't. But they tried really, really hard." Both children thought about this for a minute. Samuel was old enough to understand but it was beyond Cathy's understanding, her experience, and Guin really didn't want her to get it. Not yet, anyway.

"Well, let's go home then." Samuel took both her hand and that of Geoffrey.

"We can't do that sweethearts. Our house burned down. It's no longer there." She figured they didn't need to learn that their Auntie Lynn had set the fire or that she had died in their home. That was too much information after everything else that she was sure hadn't been absorbed yet.

"Okay," Samuel looked at Sally. "But we can stay here with you, right?"

"Yes, dear. For as long as you like."

"But do we have to stay in the dark basement?" Cathy was getting in on the game of twenty questions now.

"No. There are lots of rooms upstairs and you can pick out one to share. Okay? I'll help you." Sally followed the children as they raced up the stairs. Sam stopped there and turned back.

"Geoffrey ... will you stay here with us?"

"You can be sure of it."

"Mrs. Stone, I'm taking you to the hospital now, so tell your children you need bandaging up." Axel's firm tone told her he wouldn't back down on this so she obeyed.

"I'm coming, too." Geoffrey was on his way down the stairs.

"Please, Geoff. Stay with the little ones." Guin gently pleaded.

"But I ..."

"Please Geoffrey. Stay here. You already told them you'd stay." He looked closely into her face and saw something he didn't understand but he acquiesced and walked them to the door.

"See you soon, love." He kissed her goodbye.

She knew Axel wanted a rape kit run and she was afraid of the results. It would be so much harder to hear that she had been raped by her brother-in-law if she had Geoffrey at her side. So much harder to look at his fallen face. She knew he would not blame her, but it gave her a very unsettled feeling. It might change the way she felt about herself for awhile.

Axel was with her the whole way. He was so kind and she trusted both him and his friend Stanley completely. They had gone so far out on a limb for her; she doubted most detectives would assume her innocence so readily. And how many others would have opened their home to her like Axel had?

Guinevere had several cracked ribs but she had no memory of being hurt there. The cuts and abrasions on her wrist were wrapped in gauze and she was given antibiotic cream to rub in the open wounds. She needed half a dozen sutures at the base of her skull where the butt of the revolver had struck her head in the Finley's kitchen, and that was it. The physical exam revealed there had been no rape, no penetration of any kind. It was odd but she felt lucky. The drugs were nearly out of her system by then and her thinking was back to normal. She found that, more than anything, she wanted to return to Arizona with her family.

"Would you like to stop anywhere before we go home, Mrs. Stone?" Axel asked kindly when he saw her exhaustion. Maybe she needed something he could not provide.

"Please, Detective, my name is Guinevere." She smiled then. "And I just want to go back to my family."

Whirlwind

CHAPTER THIRTY
St. Paul, Minnesota

Geoffrey and Guinevere were making plans to go back to Arizona now that all danger seemed to be over. Axel and Stanley finally came to the conclusion that the three original intruders were Franklin, the Montoya woman, and her brother. Cesar confirmed this. He made it a point to mention that the children were not to be harmed, but Franklin just panicked when the oldest, Peter, recognized him and called him by name. Cesar even had tears in his eyes when he talked about Franklin losing control and rapidly killing all three. Axel saw no harm in telling the man that two of the young ones had survived. He could see the relief in Cesar's face.

As all the criminals had confessed and were already in jail or dead there would be no trial, although both Guinevere and Geoffrey would have to come back at a later date to go over their statements again. There always were more questions. Even Mike Troy was having trouble absorbing all the details and the reasoning behind the actions. Not often had they come across anyone quite like Wyonne Montoya. After listening to Cesar talk about his sister, they felt lucky she was gone from this world. She easily could have become the worst kind of criminal, one with absolutely no conscience, regrets, or mercy.

Axel and Sally took the little happy family to the airport the following day, and waved them off after promises of future visits and phone calls. Sally seemed a little low after she and Axel left Guinevere, Geoffrey, and the children at the TSA checkpoint. Axel had anticipated this and had an idea up his sleeve.

"We need to make one more stop, my love, are you up for it?" She nodded absentmindedly and they walked hand-in-hand, as was their fashion, to the car. They drove in the direction of home but pulled into the driveway of a house they'd never visited before. Sally looked at her husband with raised eyebrows but said nothing.

"Welcome, welcome!" They were greeted by a lively woman of about sixty with pink cheeks and a generous smile in patched jeans and a man's loose flannel shirt. "You are just in time. They've eaten and are in the back yard. Come with me."

"Axel?" Sally was beginning to understand that this was for her. In the backyard they found a litter of eight small long-haired dachshunds rolling and chewing on each other. Some were red, others black and tan like her Robie. There was a brindle coated one and even a sort of strawberry female who was definitely the boss and the fight instigator. Some were splashing in their water dish, some eating blades of grass. One was trying to pull a zinnia from the flower bed but couldn't quite manage to get it up all the way, and gave up and lay down in its shade. Two were fast asleep on their backs with their bellies exposed, lying head to foot right up close to each other until little miss strawberry jumped on top of them and took off, expecting to be chased. The two sleepers were too confused for a second to do anything. The adults watched in glee as the eight-week-old puppies frolicked for several minutes, but when the strawberry female noticed there were people present, she followed by the rest came dashing and rolling over each other to get to them.

Sally laughed in delight and sat down on the ground so the puppies could crawl into her lap. She picked up and examined each of them in turn. No matter who she was holding, though, it was the strawberry female who kept coming back demanding to be picked up again and again. Sally set her down and she made a mad dash over to the water dish, low to the ground, and splashed through it, then came full tilt back to Sally where the dripping puppy literally climbed up her body from her momentum.

"I think this one has chosen us." Sally picked her up and stood. "Yep. This one." The puppy was settling in her arms and licking her chin quite content to be held.

"Poor Robie." Axel shook his head in mock concern as he lifted the red bundle into his own arms to inspect her. She nipped the tip of his nose and then flopped over to her back as if apologizing to him. She batted at her muzzle and wagged her tail and looked so cute even Axel was pleased with her. Then she tried to crawl into his shirt pocket. One third of the way down with her rear end and tail hanging out, she held still.

"A bossy female to upset Robie's calm, ordered existence."

"Robie will love it." Sally pulled the little dachshund from the pocket.

"What will you call her?" the puppy lady asked.

Sally looked at her new baby again. The small furry thing was gazing all around her like she was queen of all she saw and very pleased about it.

"Karne. I've always thought I'd name a child that, but since we never had any, I might as well use it now."

"Ah, a Celtic name for a German dog! Why not?" The puppy lady laughed a deep satisfying chuckle. She was pleased with these people and wouldn't worry for a moment about this pup's new home.

While they were out, Axel made a stop at the coroner's office for a preliminary autopsy report. The coroner had reluctantly agreed to working on these two bodies before all others in his care. The report was silently handed over but the doctor also patted Axel's shoulders as he passed, letting Axel know that he really hadn't minded the rush.

"Thank you very much." Axel told the man.

"It was very interesting, very odd."

Axel opened the report and read. Wyonne Montoya had some alcohol in her bloodstream but she also was pumped full of anti-freeze. The typical brand used during Minnesota winters to keep radiators from freezing. She had nearly a cup of the stuff in her system. But there were various other toxins: rat poison, garden pesticides, and cleaning granules that had been dissolved along with various kinds of prescription drugs. Wow. Someone surely wanted to be positive that she died. Prescott Franklin was the obvious choice. He probably hadn't known for sure what it would take to really kill her and didn't want to take any chances that she would get even. However ...

The autopsy report on Franklin was proof positive that she had gotten even. This explained the missing bottle of Sally's insulin. The entire contents of that bottle had been injected into Franklin's body, his arm. The biopsy stated that it was the site of the injection. Why would he have let her do this? Farther on he read that there were illegal drugs present also, drugs related to sexual stimulants but they were not sold in this country. They were however, sold in Mexico. From the scar tissue on and in his body, he had been using these for months. If the drop into the Mississippi hadn't killed him, the insulin would have. The contents of that little bottle lasted Sally over a month. These had been very strange killers. Funny that they should have killed each other. Fitting, somehow. Poetic justice and

Whirlwind

all of that. Axel believed in poetic justice although he knew that rarely did one ever get to see it.

Susan M. Nelson

CHAPTER THIRTY-ONE
Somewhere over the Rockies

Cynthia, the flight attendant, watched the family sleep. They all were so exhausted and she wondered what had happened to this woman that she remembered from a few months ago. Cynthia tucked the soft blankets up under their chins and dimmed the lights. The baby was so sweet all snuggled up in her mom's embrace and the little boy was also half on her lap and half on that of his father. This time the woman was flying to Arizona rather than Oregon and she wondered about that, too.

Winston and Albert were at the airport with Chee. Since they weren't allowed to bring the dog inside, Winston stood just outside the doors waiting. As soon as Chee spotted Guinevere though, she pulled out of his grasp and was through the automatic doors and jumping on Guin before he knew what happened. Of course, the children were thrilled. Already they had been worried about what Robie was going to do without them.

"'Lo there!" Albert was waving an email printed copy under Geoffrey's nose. "You better read this right now, mate!" The two friends introduced themselves and the dog to the children while Geoffrey read the message out loud to Guin.

Whirlwind

"Geoffrey. Come to London as soon as you can for the children. I'm getting married and leaving for Brazil in two weeks and cannot bring them along. They've always wanted to live with you anyway. In fact, they never even unpacked. Let me know. Yours truly, Phillipa."

"Short and to the point as usual, is Phillipa." Geoffrey said in disgust as he tucked the note in his pocket.

"Does she expect you to come right this minute?" Guin was smiling knowing how thrilled he must be.

"Oh yes. With Phillipa it's always was right this minute. There never was room in her life for any other time."

"Well then?"

"Do you fancy a visit to London?" He winked at her.

"The kids too?"

"Absolutely, all of us."

"Can we just go home first and rest a little? Maybe take a shower get some new clean clothes and tell the children about yours? Oh yes, we have no passports."

So, in the end it was decided for expedience sake, and before Phillipa could be allowed to change her mind, that Geoffrey would go to get his children while Guinevere and hers remained in Phoenix with Chee and photo albums of Geoffrey's three children. Guinevere thought it would be a good way to introduce this new extended family. Geoffrey snapped several shots of Guin, Sam—who now was too old for "Sammy," he informed them—and Cathy with Chee.

Guinevere drove Geoff to the international departures drop-off area at the airport. He got out of the SUV, retrieved his carryon bag from the back seat, and set it on the curb. He got back in the passenger seat, turned toward Guin, took her head in his hands, smiled, and kissed her ever so gently. He whispered, "I love you."

Before Guin could reply, he said, "See you Thursday, next," and was walking away with his bag rolling behind him.

Susan M. Nelson

Guin quickly hit the button to roll down the passenger side window. She yelled as loudly as she could, "I love you!" then broke into a giddy laughter.

Geoff turned and looked over his shoulder and smiled. He then melted into the terminal surroundings.

Guinevere decided she, the children, and Chee would go to Flagstaff to visit with Maggie, Joey, Sherry, and John. She knew they would want to know how she was. Though she was still sore but healing, she felt a strong and almost urgent need to thank them and let them see she was ok.

Flagstaff, Arizona

Maggie wasn't at home, and Joey was nowhere to be found. Guin settled down in her small home and was so happy to be there. Chee had already shown the children all around the place and they now were exploring the creek bed under Guin's watchful fond gaze. She sat at the rickety table on one of the equally unsteady chairs, sipping tea. Joey's head popped from the bushes.

"Hello Joey, come out and meet my children," Guinevere called to the boy.

"But you said you didn't have any!" he accused her.

"It's a long story, honey. I'll tell you some day. But for now, I do have them and they'd like to meet you."

"Well, that dog used to be my uncle's," he announced to Sam and Cathy.

"Not anymore." Sam told him as he rested his hand on Chee's neck.

"Okay then, what shall we play? My mom will be home soon and she cooks really good snacks for me in the afternoon, when she gets home from her new job at the restaurant. You can have some, too. She works in a real restaurant with my new daddy. At least he will be my

Whirlwind

daddy when they get married. I get to be in the wedding, too! So do you." Joey gave Guin one of his cheeky grins.

"You get to be the best maid, or something."

And that was that.

Teuchitlan, Western Mexico

It was three o'clock in the morning and Rosario Elena Ramirez Montoya could not sleep. Both her beloved Juan and eldest son Cesar, were in prison and would remain there for many years, fifteen for her son and ten for Juan. Not so long in an entire lifetime, perhaps, but long enough for Rosario. Still, there was a certain amount of peace in knowing that they were atoning for their crimes. And they would soon be sent here to Mexico to serve their sentences as per her government's request. At least she would be able to see them on occasion. Her daughter, Wyonne, she gave no thought to whatsoever. Rosario had long ago given up any ideas that the girl was normal and she was very relieved when Wyonne left the house. While she had lit candles for Juan and Cesar, there were none for Wyonne. Nor could Rosario say any prayers for the girl. But she had apologized to the ancestors for that. Rosario explained that she had tried. She could not come up with any more tears; her daughter had used up her allotment years before.

Rosario got up from her bed and wrapped her robe tightly around her as she descended to the tomb of her ancestors below the house. She took the key from around her neck and unlocked the cast iron door. It was very heavy but she struggled until it opened. She then walked down several hand carved dirt steps, that no one else knew existed, to a secret door that was carved into the dirt hillside and was invisible unless you knew where to press. The door had been plastered over with common dirt and blended in so perfectly. She entered a long dark chamber. A candle and box of matches sat on a tiny shelf just inside the door. She lit one and proceeded farther down into the cool and musty dryness of the tomb. This was a secondary entrance that she would one-day show to Julia, but no one else. Only the Ramirez women who owned this farm could ever know of this place. This was the real tomb of her ancestors, the private hidden place where her relatives rested peacefully and undisturbed forever. A stone block was there for her to rest on. As she sat there praying to the ancestors for a good, well-lived life, she also apologized to them for coming so late.

    When she finished her prayers, she left some cornmeal and sweet cakes on the block. She dusted off several of the ancient fired clay statues of various family events and religious holidays. Rosario loved these relics and had cared for them all her life just as her mother had done and her mother before. Many generations of Ramirez women had done this and many more would. It was the tradition and a work of love. They were so beautiful, some even with paint still on the clay, some with real feathers still attached to the headdresses, some with blood remaining on the tips. She took special care to gently clean the statues of her maize goddesses and rearranged them slightly. The last thing she did was to remove the heavy ornate silver bracelet from her thin wrist and place it on the wrapped bones of her grandmother. She thanked her for lending it and promised it would never leave the tomb again. Then she climbed back to her house and into her bed where she finally slept. All would be well. The goddesses had said so.

Phoenix, Arizona

    Guin woke slowly as the first of the morning light started to come through the east window of the loft bedroom. She felt an emptiness ... the source of which she

Whirlwind

could not put her finger on. Charles and Peter were gone and their absence was painful. But it was something else ... Her thoughts focused on Geoffrey. And there it was! He was not with her. He had been there for her during most of the tumultuous last couple of months. Even though he wasn't always physically there, she realized she had felt his presence. She loved him for it. He had been the center of calm in her whirlwind.

Guinevere was holding on to her coffee mug, then she smiled completely from the inside out. She realized—it was "Thursday, next."

Susan M. Nelson

Whirlwind

Dear Reader,

Thank you again for your interest in *Whirlwind*

RocketDog Books welcomes your comments regarding Susan's writing or corrections if you see something that is amiss. Please contact me via email at steven@rocketdogbooks.com or on the Facebook page RocketDog Books.

Steven

Susan M. Nelson

Made in the USA
San Bernardino, CA
30 November 2013